"Seems Dolly fee
Beatrice murmu

Levi grinned at her. "I kind of like knowing that."

"Me, too."

He held her gaze, searching for and finding a sense of belonging even if it was only because they shared a concern for this orphaned child.

He broke the eye contact first, knowing his thoughts had gone to dangerous territory. Beatrice was a city girl with secrets. She was here only to do a job, then she would leave. And he did not intend to open his heart to more pain.

But his eyes wanted to return to hers, to explore further, perhaps even to let her glimpse something in his own heart. Instead of listening to the demands of his heart, he focused his attention on her hand, resting on little Dolly's knee.

Without giving himself time to change his mind, he placed his hand on Dolly's other knee. So much for not listening to his heart.

The three of them sat together. No one speaking. No one moving.

He could get used to this feeling of contentment.

Linda Ford lives on a ranch in Alberta, Canada, near enough to the Rocky Mountains that she can enjoy them on a daily basis. She and her husband raised fourteen children—four homemade, ten adopted. She currently shares her home and life with her husband, a grown son, a live-in paraplegic client and a continual (and welcome) stream of kids, kids-in-law, grandkids, and assorted friends and relatives.

Books by Linda Ford

Love Inspired Historical

Montana Cowboys

The Cowboy's Ready-Made Family
The Cowboy's Baby Bond
The Cowboy's City Girl

Christmas in Eden Valley

A Daddy for Christmas
A Baby for Christmas
A Home for Christmas

Journey West

Wagon Train Reunion

Montana Marriages

Big Sky Cowboy
Big Sky Daddy
Big Sky Homecoming

Cowboys of Eden Valley

The Cowboy's Surprise Bride
The Cowboy's Unexpected Family
The Cowboy's Convenient Proposal
Claiming the Cowboy's Heart
Winning Over the Wrangler
Falling for the Rancher Father

Visit the Author Profile page at Harlequin.com for more titles.

LINDA FORD

The Cowboy's City Girl

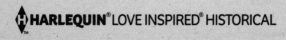

HARLEQUIN® LOVE INSPIRED® HISTORICAL

Recycling programs
for this product may
not exist in your area.

LOVE INSPIRED BOOKS

ISBN-13: 978-0-373-28358-3

The Cowboy's City Girl

www.Harlequin.com

Printed in U.S.A.

I praise You because I am fearfully and wonderfully made; Your works are wonderful,
I know that full well.
—*Psalms* 139:14

To my grandson, Christopher, on your graduation.
I am proud of the young man you have become.
This Irish blessing is my hope and prayer for you:
May the dreams you hold the dearest
be those which come true and the
kindness you spread keep returning to you.

Chapter One

Summer 1899
Near Granite Creek, Montana

Beatrice Doyle squealed as the buggy lurched to one side and ground to a halt. What had happened? She pulled her hat forward to protect her face from the slashing rain, looked down on both sides of the buggy and groaned. One wheel had fallen off the narrow track that would allow her to cross the tossing water of the river and get safely to her destination.

Clouds darkened the afternoon. Flashes of lightning crisscrossed the sky. Thunder followed in a constant roll and crash. She sat, staring straight ahead, the reins slack in her hand with no notion of how to get out of this predicament. Until two weeks ago she had lived a sheltered, protected life and had certainly never driven a buggy. She'd lived in the city, the only child of her parents, and she'd thought her life would continue on the same pleasant note. How could she have been so wrong?

Now here she was in Montana, a far cry from Chicago. Thankfully Uncle Elwood and Aunt Opal had welcomed her into their home. Beatrice had come west with the intention of learning skills that would enable her to become independent, and she was learning them at an incredibly brisk pace.

When the influenza epidemic hit the town, Uncle Elwood's responsibilities as the preacher had included ministering to the sick. Aunt Opal had helped and taken Beatrice with her.

"Though I've a long ways to go before I can hope to run a house or take care of children," she muttered to the raging sky. Learning to do anything else of practical use seemed even more impossible.

When Uncle Elwood received news that Mrs. Harding was injured and needed help, Beatrice had begged to be allowed to take on the challenge.

"But I don't have time to take you there and you don't know how to drive the buggy," he'd protested.

"You can show me. Besides, how many times have you said Old Sissy, your mare, knows what to do?"

Her uncle began to relent at that point and had finally given in to her arguments as to why this was a good idea.

"Well, Old Sissy," Beatrice yelled. "What are you going to do?"

The horse stood with her head down. Seems she found the rain every bit as miserable as did Beatrice, whose clothes were clinging to her. With no help from that direction, Beatrice gathered her wet skirts about her and climbed down to look at the wheel. She determinedly ignored the ankle-deep water soaking through her impractical shoes and further wetting her skirts as she studied her problem.

If she pushed while Old Sissy pulled, they just might get the buggy back to level ground. Beatrice leaned her weight into the wheel and yelled at the horse to go.

Beatrice's foot slipped and she barely managed to catch herself before she fell downward in the water. As it was she stepped off the rocky road bed and into cold, dark water that licked at her knees and left her no closer to achieving her goal.

Lightning streaked across the sky, momentarily blinding her. A bone-shaking crash of thunder followed almost directly on its heels and the air filled with a sulfur smell.

She had no desire to spend the rest of the afternoon in the middle of a river with rain pouring down on her head. "I have to get out of here." She grunted and again leaned into the wheel.

A hand caught her shoulder and jerked her back. "Lady, leave it be."

She struggled against the grasp of the water and the weight of her sodden clothing to turn and face the owner of the voice. She grabbed at the wheel to keep her balance and blinked at the man before her. She recognized the tall, dark and handsome cowboy, whom she'd seen previously in town. Her first thought on that occasion was that he seemed so sure of himself and where he belonged in the world.

Not that she didn't know exactly what her role in life was. Her father had made it abundantly clear, making her glad to leave home and head west. "With no son, it's your duty to help the family by marrying well," he'd said.

"You're Levi Harding." His father, Big Sam, ran the biggest ranch in this part of Montana. "I'm on my way to your place. I understand your mother needs help."

He blinked, another flash of lightning bringing his features into sharp detail. The thunder followed almost immediately.

"Lady, did no one tell you about the dangers of lightning and water?" Rain dripped from the brim of his sodden cowboy hat, providing a damp curtain in front of his face, but not so much she couldn't see the frown on his lips.

"Of course they did." But she couldn't think what she'd been told.

"You're a perfect lightning rod."

"You mean…?" Her voice trailed off. She couldn't take in the danger to herself.

He swept her off her feet and plowed his way through the water to solid ground. She should protest his boldness, but instead she clung to his shoulders and wished the rain would quit.

He set her on her feet. "Stay here." Levi turned back to the river, reached the horse and grabbed its reins, pulling and calling. A bright flash of lightning made Old Sissy rear in fear and revealed the sharp features of the man, his arms upraised like some kind of modern-day Moses.

Beatrice's heart lurched. How bold and strong he was. How many times had she wished for such a man to save her from her father's plans? Reality squelched her eagerness. Yes, it might be looked upon as a romantic rescue except for a few small details. Like the pouring rain, her soaked clothes and the cold that had reached the marrow of her bones. And the hard, unyielding lump in her heart that warned her to never again trust a man to be what she wanted and needed.

Shiver after shiver raced through her and her teeth rattled.

Within a few moments, the buggy stood on solid ground again.

He held out his hand to assist her to the seat. When she was as comfortable as her dampened state allowed, he tied his horse to the back and climbed up beside her. "I'll get you safely to the ranch."

"Thank you." This was not quite what she had in mind when she'd fled Chicago with Father's words echoing in her ears and her mind set on making her own way in life.

"You'll not receive another nickel until you obey me," he'd said without an ounce of sympathy, and Mother had stood resolutely at his side.

She had no doubt he meant every word. All her life she'd known she was a disappointment to her parents for being born a girl instead of a boy. But not until recently did she realize the depth of their disappointment.

It had begun when she fell in love with Henry St. James, a handsome, blond man who worked as a clerk in her father's office. Because of his lowly station in her father's business, Henry had insisted on meeting her in secret, but she fully expected he would eventually confront her father with a declaration of his love for her.

How wrong she'd been. When her father discovered Henry's interest in her, he had paid him to vanish. Henry hadn't even cared enough to object or offer her an explanation. She began to suspect his interest all along had only been the hopes of financial improvement.

After that Father had presented three suitable young men to her. "Any of these men can become my son and heir."

She'd wept in secret to think her father was selling her like something in the stockyards.

She refused to marry any of them. "I will marry for love," she had declared. Though she had no intention of ever marrying. How could she ever trust another man? Henry had vowed to defend her. Look how that had gone.

Father had said she was simply being immature and selfish. But she had refused to be coerced, which caused her father to buy her a one-way ticket to Granite Creek, Montana, with the warning that she could return home when she came to her senses.

The misery of being cold and wet matched the misery of her spirit.

She lifted her head, ignoring the water dripping from her hat brim to her nose. She was not going back home to be married off by her father. She would use every opportunity to learn the necessary skills she would need in order to get a job so she could take care of herself. Mrs. Harding's need was an answer to Beatrice's prayer for a chance to prove herself.

Never mind that Levi had rescued her and she'd felt safe in his arms. She would never again allow herself to trust in a man's good intentions. No. She'd learned her lesson on what value she held.

Levi had said nothing since they began the journey together. What sort of man was he? One who sat straight and focused on the trail ahead. Out of the corner of her eye she studied his profile. Strong, bold, angular. She'd seen him once before in town. Tall and dark. Aunt Opal said his mother had been a full-blooded Lakota Indian. The woman she was going to help was his stepmother.

A half-breed. She didn't know what to think. She'd seen the way her father treated the natives they'd encountered in Chicago with ruthless disdain. Yet the way Levi sat so straight and almost regal, she couldn't imagine her father doing the same to him.

Besides, he'd been willing to rescue a silly maiden standing in the river even at risk to his own safety.

She turned to him. "Thank you for rescuing me."

His smile was fleeting but had lasted long enough for her to appreciate the way his features softened.

"No problem. I could hardly stand by and hope you wouldn't get hurt."

"I suppose not." Though she'd met men who cared little about her personal needs and lots about lining their own pockets.

The buggy hit a rough spot and she jostled, tipping toward the side.

She was off balance and might have fallen off except Levi grabbed her arm and pulled her back upright. That was twice he'd saved her life. She didn't know what to make of it.

Just happenstance. As he said, he could hardly stand by and watch her get hurt.

It was no cause for her to think it meant anything. She knew better.

Levi had wanted to get one of his new sisters-in-law to help his stepmother. Or even his brother Johnny's new sister-in-law, Celia, but Maisie had refused, saying since she'd been helping care for the sick, she might be contagious and didn't want the rest of the family exposed to the illness that had ravaged the town of Granite Creek and the surrounding area.

Preacher Gage had said he would send someone to help her.

Levi had been tracking the latest trail of the men creating havoc at the ranch when the rain erased any signs he might have followed. Near as he could tell, there were three riders, but who they were or why they seemed to take delight in making mischief around the ranch, he could not say. So far nothing had been seriously damaged nor was anything missing, but everything they did had the potential to be more serious. Gates had been left open, but he discovered it in time so the horses did not escape. A pile of oats had been left where the milk cow could get into it and founder, and again, only his vigilance had prevented it. The woodpile had been upset so he'd stacked it again before the rain came. The list went on and on. It frustrated him to no end that he hadn't been able to catch the culprits and put a stop to it. Especially with Pa and the hired hands away.

Levi had been left in charge and he meant to fulfill the responsibility.

But losing the trail just as he reached the river had proven to be fortuitous. He saw in the water a young woman he didn't recognize attempting to get her buggy unstuck while lightning flashed about her. His thoughts had turned to Helen. His heart had slammed into his ribs so hard he had grunted.

Thankfully, he had not witnessed Helen drowning, but he'd imagined it many times. It was not something he wished to see repeated with this woman, though she was more likely to be struck with lightning than to drown.

Before he could even give the thought consideration, he'd gone into the water and carried her to safety. As soon as he lifted her into his arms, he recognized her as the city girl, Miss Doyle, visiting her aunt Opal and uncle Elwood Gage. What was the preacher thinking to send her to help Maisie? From what he'd heard, she was more used to having servants than being one.

No doubt, the preacher had his reasons. For instance, the fact that so many were ill with the influenza and more were falling sick all the time. Levi would just have to make the best of it and be grateful for whatever help she offered.

A suspicion edged into his thoughts. Perhaps no one else was willing to work in a house where a half-breed lived. Did Miss Doyle know about his heritage? Or had Preacher Gage neglected to mention it? Maisie often reassured him that he was just as white as native, yet he knew many didn't see it that way.

Like Helen. He and she had been friends for a couple of years. He'd fancied himself in love with her. At sixteen he had begun to pressure her to promise to marry him when they both turned seventeen. Her reply had shocked him clear through.

"We can be friends," she'd said. "But Levi, I could never marry you. Do you know what people would say? Why, there would be homes where I wouldn't be invited because I'd married a half-breed."

"How is that different than being my friend?"

"People don't have to know we're friends. We can enjoy each other's company out here far from town."

He had stalked away. He did not want a secret friendship any more than he wanted to be looked upon with shame and regret.

Helen had drowned two weeks later, swimming alone. He couldn't help thinking if he'd been there he might have been able to pull her to safety when she banged her head on a rock. Her loss had been devastating, but little did anyone know he'd felt the loss well before she drowned.

A year ago, at eighteen, he'd met Fern Dafoe and had been attracted to her. He reasoned she would accept him because she was a half-breed like himself. But his interest in her had been short-lived. She had wanted him to join her father and her brothers in their nomadic way of life, a life that brought them perilously close to getting arrested on more than one occasion. After he'd told her that he didn't want to leave the ranch and he didn't want to join up with her wild family, she'd been angry and accused him of being too white.

Too white for Fern. Too native for Helen.

At that point, he'd made up his mind. He would never again open himself up to loss and rejection. Some might say he had grown too guarded, but he knew his heart could not withstand more. Perhaps losing his ma when he was only five had made him extra cautious.

Miss Doyle's voice brought him back to the present. "Mr. Harding, how far do we have to travel to get to your ranch?"

"We're almost there. I prefer you call me Levi. Mr. Harding is my pa, though mostly he's known as Big Sam."

"So he's a big man?"

"In every way imaginable."

She tipped her head as if trying to fathom what he meant. "Big in size and big in heart?"

"Yup. And big in personality."

"Oh." She considered his reply for a moment. Her voice was soft as she asked her next question. "Will he frighten me?"

Levi laughed. "Only if you let him. But he's not home right now. He and a bunch of cowhands have gone up the mountains where some cows are trapped by a landslide. They have to dig them out."

"You did not go with them?"

"Someone had to remain at home to take care of things. Good thing I stayed behind. I can't imagine what would have become of Ma if she'd been alone." His voice hardened. If something happened to Ma he would have himself to blame.

"I thought she was your stepmother."

He smiled. "I barely remember my own ma. Maisie is the only ma I've known. I should tell you why she needs help. I don't know why she thought it was necessary to carry a sharp hoe into the loft of the barn just because she wanted to clean up the mouse droppings." Couldn't she have asked Levi to help? But she hadn't. "She said she could smell mice every time she entered the barn. She fell from the ladder, landed on the hoe and laid open a deep cut on the back of her thigh." He closed his eyes but that did nothing to erase the picture of blood soaking her skirts. "If she doesn't rest her leg, she'll end up crippled, or maybe worse."

Miss Doyle made a sympathetic sound and then sat up straighter, though he would have thought she was already poker straight. "I'm here to help." She peered into the rain. "I see no houses. Do you have neighbors, Mr. Harding?"

"Levi, remember?"

"Yes, Levi. And please call me Beatrice."

"Thank you, Beatrice." Her name suited her. Regal and distant.

Though how distant had they been a few minutes ago as he carried her from the river? Should he explain it meant nothing? He was being neither bold nor inappropriate, only intent on saving her life. He decided the less he said about it, the sooner they would both forget it. "To answer your question. We don't have many neighbors. My brother Tanner married this spring. He and his wife, Susanne, and the four children they adopted live a few miles to the west. My other brother, Johnny, married more recently and he and his wife, Willow, live three miles north. She brought a baby boy and two sisters to the marriage. Other than that our neighbors are no closer than town."

"Willow? What an unusual name."

"An unusual gal. She wasn't at all bothered that my brother is part native. Nor was Susanne, the girl who married my oldest brother." Levi looked at her with silent challenge. "My mother, Seena, was a full-blooded Lakota Indian. She was injured fleeing the Battle of the Little Bighorn. My pa found her, saved her life and then they fell in love and married."

She met his eyes. The rain softened sufficiently for him to see that her eyes were golden-brown, as warm as freshly baked bread. Then she ducked her head enough to hide behind the brim of her hat.

"You say that like you expect me to get off the seat and walk the rest of the way."

He couldn't decide if he should laugh at her suggestion or stop the buggy and let her off. "I'll take you back to town if you wish."

"I knew the situation before I came this way. I have no intention of turning back."

She knew he was a half-breed and still she came? Her response both surprised him and pleased him. "You're sure?"

She nodded. "I intend to do the job I came to do."

He pulled up before the house. "We're here."

She squinted into the curtain of rain. "Where's here?"

She wouldn't be able to see much of the place in this downpour. "The Sundown Ranch." Pride filled his voice. They reached the house. He swung down and went around the horse to reach up and help her.

"Come on in. It's simple but I think you'll find we're very comfortable."

"Indeed." Not another word, leaving him to wonder if she'd find the place to her liking or not. Hadn't he heard that her father was one of the richest men in Chicago? She'd surely think the ranch house small. But she had agreed to come here of her own free will. That must mean something.

"Come and meet my ma." He drew her inside, but his heart slammed against his ribs as a result of what he saw. "Ma—" Maisie balanced a steaming cup of tea as she tried to make her way to the table while hobbling on one leg. "What are you doing?" He sprang forward, took the cup, set it aside then half carried her to the nearest chair. "You are supposed to be resting with your leg up. Have you started the wound bleeding again?"

"Levi, stop fussing and introduce me to this young lady who looks ready to turn tail and flee."

He looked back at Beatrice. She looked miserable and cold. Leaving Maisie safely settled on her chair, he beckoned her forward.

But she didn't move, glancing at the puddle forming at her feet. "I'm dripping wet."

"It's only water. It will dry. Come to the stove and get warm."

He caught a look of uncertainty in her eyes. She shook from head to toe and started to wobble.

He sprang forward just in time to catch her before she fell to the floor in a faint. Snagging a chair with his foot, he dragged it close to the stove, lowered her to the seat and considered his predicament. He should be out chasing the scoundrels responsible for causing problems around the place. The pouring rain provided perfect cover for them, but the woman who had come to help Maisie was of no use. He couldn't leave her alone—or expect her to take care of Maisie's needs.

He was stuck inside with two incapacitated women. What was he going to do?

Chapter Two

Beatrice closed her eyes against the darkness clouding her mind. Her wet clothes were too tight. The cold had seeped into her brain.

The warmth from the stove and the firmness of the hard chair eased her faintness but she dare not open her eyes yet, afraid the room would spin and make it impossible to stay upright.

Levi hovered nearby. He'd saved her from disaster yet again. How long before he decided she was a bad risk and sent her back to town? How could she prove she could do the job if he had to continually rescue her?

Sucking in the deepest breath her constricting clothing allowed, she willed away the dizziness and opened her eyes. She would do what she'd come to do. "I'm fine."

"Perhaps if you changed into dry clothes." Mrs. Harding's voice revealed no criticism, a fact that gave Beatrice a bit of courage.

"Yes, of course. My bags…" She could hardly expect Levi to go out in the rain that still pounded down.

"I'll get them."

"Oh, no. I couldn't ask you to do that. It's still raining."

"You didn't ask me. Besides, I could hardly get any wetter."

Indeed, puddles followed his every step. He was as wet as she, and surely as miserable, yet he was willing to venture back out into the inclement weather. It wasn't like he had to. He wasn't one of Father's servants, who were expected to run and fetch no matter the conditions.

Before she could answer or object he was out the door. She stared after him. If she wasn't so miserable she might wonder if he was always so accommodating or was he anxious to be done with her?

She'd faced so many strange and frightening things since she'd left home. Only one thing had sustained her—her trust in God. She'd clung to His promises on the trip west and as Aunt Opal showed her how frontier life was lived. *God is my strength and power: He maketh my way perfect.* A fragile calm filled her. God would provide everything she needed.

Her gaze went to Mrs. Harding.

"Are you sure you're okay?" the woman asked.

Beatrice nodded. She should get to her feet and introduce herself but she feared having another weak spell. "I'm Beatrice Doyle. The preacher's wife is my aunt. They've sent me out to help you."

"Pleased to meet you, my dear. And you shall call me Maisie. May I call you Beatrice?"

"Of course." Beatrice's insides steadied at Maisie's kindness.

"I am blessed you have come."

Levi returned at that moment.

"Put her things in Tanner's old room," Maisie said. She turned to Beatrice. "Go with him and please make yourself at home. Change into something dry then come back and tell me about yourself."

Levi waited at the doorway to the next room for her to rise and follow him. He watched her as if expecting he would have to drop her bags and catch her again.

She held herself very upright and, doing her best to ignore her very uncomfortable clothes, she followed him into a sitting room, where there was a cluster of comfortable chairs, bookshelves full of books and a round stove for cold winter days. "What a warm, inviting room," she murmured. She could imagine the family gathered round the stove on winter evenings.

"It's nothing special. Tends to get a little crowded when the whole family is here and as you can see, there's no place to go but here or the kitchen."

She couldn't tell if he meant to complain or if he was happy about having such a large family to crowd the house. "I would think sharing the room with family would be joyous."

He paused before a door, a smile curving his mouth. "It is."

She could not get over the way his features softened when he smiled. Like a happy feeling from inside him rushed to get out.

And then he opened one of the four doors along the wall, carried her things inside, then stepped out and indicated she should enter. He fled across the sitting room before she could even thank him.

The room was bright and pleasant, which made her realize the rain had softened to a mist. She parted the curtains and looked out the window. Trees stood shrouded in moisture with a trail through them. She was rather disappointed she couldn't see the barn and whatever other buildings there would be. In fact, it was the first time in her life she'd been unable to see any sign of human habitation from her dwelling place and it both frightened her and filled her with a sense of awe.

Closing the curtains, she inspected the rest of the room. A little table stood beside the bed and upon it were a lamp and a Bible. Her courage grew by leaps and bounds. At least she'd come to a place where the Bible was important enough to be put by the bedside in their guest room, giving her hope they loved and honored God as much as she did. Another thing her parents and she had disagreed on.

"I do hope you are not going to be fanatical like my sister," her mother had said with enough disdain to fill volumes. "She chose to marry a penniless preacher when she could have married a wealthy man."

Since spending time with Aunt Opal, Beatrice decided being like her was a compliment. Aunt Opal was kind and gentle and loving.

She changed into a dry frock—one less fashionable but infinitely more comfortable—and hurried out to the kitchen. She drew to a halt when she saw Levi, in dry clothes, sitting at the table with his mother. She'd heard the outer door open and close and assumed he'd left.

Maisie reached out a hand. "We're having tea. Come and join us. Tell me about yourself. Levi, pour our guest a cup of tea. My dear, sit down so we can talk."

"But I'm not a guest. I've come to help you."

"First things first," Maisie said. "Levi, get her a cup."

Beatrice crossed to the table feeling Levi's gaze on her every move. Did he think he might have to spring up and catch her again? No more weakness, she told herself. She had to prove she could do this job. If she did it well enough, Maisie would be able to recommend her for another job. But her legs quivered at Levi's attention. Why did she allow him to make her nervous?

Beatrice sat in the chair indicated and reluctantly allowed Levi to pour her tea. "Thank you." She dare not look at him for fear she would see doubt in his eyes as to her suitability to do her job. So far she had done nothing but make more work for him.

"Now tell us about yourself. Where are you from?" Maisie asked.

"Chicago," Beatrice answered.

"What does your father do?"

"He's a businessman with many interests. Perhaps you've heard of Bernard and Wardell Doyle?" Bernard was her father, Wardell her uncle. "They own a railway, a manufacturing plant and several other businesses, though Father says his greatest asset is his name." All the more reason Beatrice being a girl had been a disappointment.

"No, I'm sorry," Maisie said. "I was raised in Philadelphia but haven't been back east in a number of years. Do you have siblings?"

"I'm an only child."

"Me, too." Maisie laughed softly and gave Levi an

adoring look. "Some might see that as a blessing, isn't that right, Levi?"

"I've never thought of it much." His grin was so mischievous that Beatrice almost stared. The man had a beautiful smile that left her breathless. "Except when Tanner and Johnny tied me to a stake and said they were going to torture me."

"Tanner and Johnny are Levi's older brothers," Maisie said. "Tanner is twenty-one, Johnny twenty. My, how time flies."

Beatrice waited for Maisie to supply Levi's age. But she seemed to have forgotten the subject.

"How old are you, my dear?"

"Eighteen. How old is Levi—?" She blurted out the question then stammered to a halt. "I'm sorry. That was very rude of me."

"Not at all." Maisie smiled at Levi. "He's nineteen."

Beatrice concentrated on her tea while she gathered her manners.

Maisie continued. "Did Levi tell you about my injury?"

"He said you cut your leg."

"I fear it's rather a bad cut on the back of my leg." Maisie told of her accident. "My wound needs dressing, but I can't reach it so I will need you to do it for me."

Beatrice had seen more illness in the past two weeks then she would have seen in four lifetimes back in Chicago. But she hadn't tended a wound. "I'll do my best." She meant to sound strong and confident, but knew her voice revealed too much uncertainty.

Levi's expression hardened into sharp lines. No doubt he wondered what sort of help her uncle had sent.

She could and would do the job. He'd see. So would his stepmother.

"Ma is to rest with her leg up, so you'll be in charge of the kitchen, the meals, the laundry—everything she'd normally do."

"I understand. My aunt explained my duties." And had done her best to teach her in a few short hours how to do them. Beatrice had been shocked at how much a person had to know in order to run a house.

"I can't emphasize too strongly that she is not to be moving about," Levi continued. "Her leg must be allowed to heal." His dark gaze held hers in an invisible iron grip. She couldn't free herself from his look. Did he think she was incapable of doing the job? He must never learn how close to the truth such doubts were. She'd prove to him and to her father, and even to herself, that she could handle the things her choice of life required.

"I believe you've made yourself clear," she said with far more assurance than she felt.

Levi looked ready to say more, perhaps warn her further of the cost of failure on her part. He didn't know the half of what failure would mean, not only to Maisie, but also to Beatrice.

Maisie interrupted their conversation.

"Levi, would you bring in one of the easy chairs from the other room and a footstool? I believe I'll rest better if I can sit in the kitchen and talk to Beatrice as she works."

Levi hustled to do so, arranging a chair and stool by the table and getting Maisie comfortable in it.

"Thank you, my boy." Maisie patted Levi's cheek.

"Now you run along and leave us to take care of things."

"Do you have everything you need?" He directed his question to Beatrice.

"I'm sure I can manage." Not for all the grass in Montana would she admit she might have ventured in out of her depth.

"Then I will take care of the horses and the buggy." He hurried from the house.

Beatrice gave a nervous glance about the room. No doubt there were things she needed to do, but she had no idea where to even start. Aunt Opal had always given her instructions about what to do next.

"My dear, don't look so nervous."

Beatrice took in one deep breath and then another. "I hope I can do what's expected of me. I confess I'm not very experienced. I might make a mistake." The word stuck in her mind. According to her parents she was a mistake.

"You can learn whatever you set your mind to and I don't believe it's a mistake you are here."

"How do you know that?"

"I'm an old lady. I've learned a few things. And I will tell you this. I don't think God makes mistakes. I prayed for a nice young woman to come help me. I had no idea how God would answer my prayer, yet here you are. An answer to my prayer."

Beatrice released a shaky breath. "I also prayed." She could not say she asked God to help her find a way of being independent. How would she explain that after telling them her father was a wealthy businessman?

"Then we'll let God do what He has planned. I'm willing to teach you if you're willing to learn."

Encouraged by those words, Beatrice looked around the kitchen. "What do you need me to do at the moment?"

"It's time to prepare supper."

She swallowed back her rising panic. If only Aunt Opal was here to tell her what to do. *I can do this. I must do it. I have to be able to support myself if I'm to avoid my father's plans.* Hoping she portrayed more confidence than she felt, she got to her feet and hurried to the cupboard.

"Levi brought in potatoes and chops before the rain started."

A few simple words and Beatrice felt like she'd stepped off the deep end of a wharf. *I can do this,* she repeated.

A few minutes later she was ready to change her mind. She knew to scrub the potatoes and put them to boil, but when she looked at the basin holding the chops she had to push back a desire to gag. What was one to do with them? Fry them? She could do that. Aunt Opal had taught her that much.

Hoping Maisie might make a suggestion, Beatrice turned toward the table.

Maisie's head was against the back of the chair, her eyes closed, her mouth open. She'd fallen asleep.

That left Beatrice to manage on her own.

She would not give either Levi or his stepmother reason to suggest she return to town.

Levi took the horses to the barn, where he groomed and fed them, all the while wondering if everything was all right in the house. Beatrice hadn't looked any sturdier after she'd changed her clothes. If he was to describe her to his brothers, he'd say she was beautiful but fragile, and something about the way her eyes flashed gold and the way she tilted her head gave him cause to wonder if she was as strong as she obviously wanted him to believe. So far, he'd seen no evidence of strength. She'd already fainted once. Was it something she did often?

He paused in his task and glanced in the direction of the house, his nerves twitching with apprehension. If she fainted again, he could see Maisie ignoring the need to rest her leg and rushing to look after Beatrice.

He better go to the house and make sure that didn't happen.

He hurriedly finished taking care of the horses and left the barn.

A horse and swaying rider crossed the yard in the general direction of the barn.

He groaned. His cousin Charlie often hit the bottle too hard and the way he tipped half off his horse informed Levi that this was one of those days. He made it to Charlie's side in time to prevent him from crashing to the ground. He staggered under the weight of his cousin but thankfully stayed upright.

"Hi," Charlie slurred.

"Charlie, it's men like you who give us half-breeds a bad reputation. Stay away from the liquor and get a job." He took the bottle from Charlie and poured its contents out on the ground.

His cousin tried to grab the bottle before the alcohol watered the grass but he could barely stand. "It's mine. Give it back."

Levi tossed the empty bottle into the bushes. "You've had enough." Way too many times, he and his family had tried to help Charlie. Pa had even hired him on several occasions. But Charlie ended up wandering away, leaving a job undone and searching instead for something he thought he'd find in a bottle.

Charlie lurched to one side, then caught Levi's arm to steady himself.

Levi glanced toward the house. The rain had stopped, allowing anyone who happened to glance out the kitchen window a full view. If Beatrice saw them would she not think the same as so many people did? *Drunk half-breed.*

His jaw muscles tightened. He couldn't help what she saw or what she thought. He wasn't like Charlie but not many would choose to believe that.

Charlie was kin, but even if he hadn't been, Levi would not have left him in his present state. He led him and the horse to the barn and turned the horse loose to tend to later. He took Charlie to the water trough and ducked his head underwater twice. It wasn't like he could get much wetter. He must have ridden throughout the storm that had now passed over. "Maybe that will sober you up."

Charlie sputtered his protests.

"Let's go to the bunkhouse." None of the cowboys was around to protest Charlie's presence. They made it to the meager quarters and Levi found a change of clothes for his cousin, who was beginning to sober up. Maybe Levi could persuade the man to sign on again. Pa wouldn't object and Levi could keep him busy with odd jobs.

Levi took a good hard look at Charlie. "I guess you'll do."

Charlie grinned somewhat crookedly. "For what?"

"For coming to the house for supper."

Charlie's grin widened. "Aunt Maisie is always happy to see me."

Levi grunted. "She doesn't care for you showing up drunk."

"I's okay now." Charlie held out his arms and walked across the bunkhouse.

Levi had to admit he did an admirable job of walking a straight line considering he couldn't stay upright less than an hour ago. "Let's go, then." He judged that Beatrice had had plenty of time to prepare a meal and his growling stomach informed him it was time to eat.

They strode toward the house, avoiding the puddles in the yard. Hot water filled the basin on the outside stand, so they washed up then stepped inside.

Charlie ground to a halt as he saw Maisie resting in her chair. Seeing her there relieved a degree of Levi's worry.

"What happened to you?" Charlie asked.

Maisie reached out welcoming hands to Charlie as she explained her accident. Levi followed and they both kissed her on the cheek.

"This lovely young lady has come to help me so I can rest my leg. Beatrice, this is Levi's cousin, Charlie."

Charlie turned to meet Beatrice. His mouth dropped open.

Levi thought it must take a great deal of effort but Charlie managed to close his mouth and swallow loudly. "Pleased to meet you." He didn't offer a hand, perhaps wondering if she would object to him touching her.

Levi allowed himself a little self-satisfaction. Not only had he touched her, but he'd also held her in his arms. He could have told Charlie she was as light as a newborn colt but smelled like a whole field of wild roses. Of course, both times she'd not been in a position to object to being held by him. Something he must bear in mind before he got too cocky about it.

"You're the prettiest girl Levi ever brought here," Charlie blurted out.

Levi pressed the heel of his hand to his forehead. "Charlie, you're going to make her think I have a habit of bringing girls to the ranch."

Charlie struggled to find something to say.

Levi held his breath as he wondered what his cousin would drop into the conversation to further embarrass Levi.

Finally, Charlie got his words out. "Only Helen. No one else."

Helen. The only reminder of how others viewed him that he needed. "Sit down, Charlie."

Beatrice scurried past him to set another place at the table.

"Yes, please sit down," Maisie said.

Beatrice placed the serving dishes on the table and sat across from Levi and Charlie. Maisie sat at one end of the table. The other end remained empty. No one ever sat in Big Sam's place when he was absent.

"Levi, would you ask the blessing?" Maisie said. She reached for Levi's hand on one side and Beatrice's on her other.

With his head tipped, Levi watched Beatrice. Would she take Charlie's hand?

Beatrice stared at Charlie. Neither she nor Charlie reached for the other. He wasn't sure who to be annoyed with.

Maisie squeezed his hand, bringing his attention back to the need to fill his empty stomach. He closed his eyes and prayed. "Lord, we thank You for Your provision of the food upon this table. Amen." For no one else's ears, he added, *Help this woman take care of Maisie so her leg can heal.* He did not add, *Help me remember she's white and a rich city girl—and I'm a half-breed and a rancher.*

"And thank you to Beatrice for preparing the food," Maisie added as she passed the meat to Levi.

He forked off a chop. Looked at both sides of it and gingerly put it on his plate. It was almost black but he was hungry enough to eat almost anything.

Charlie poked at three chops before he selected one.

Beatrice murmured, "No thanks," and passed the platter to Maisie.

Maisie took a piece of meat without comment.

The rest of the food was passed around.

Charlie grunted as he spooned out some peas. "Still got water on them." He edged the vegetables from the bowl.

Conversation died as everyone tackled the food. Levi tried to cut through his potato. It was as hard as a marble in the center. The lumpy, gluey gravy did not make it go down easier.

Maisie bravely ate the food on her plate, though he wondered how she could get it down.

Charlie rearranged his.

Levi put a piece of burnt meat in his mouth, choked a little and washed the food down with a glass of water. His eyes watered.

"I'm sorry." Beatrice pushed her chair back and bolted outside.

Chapter Three

Shock burned through Levi's veins as he stared at the door through which Beatrice had disappeared. He'd said nothing about the ruined meal. "She mustn't have followed your directions," he said by way of apology to Maisie.

"She did the best she could. The poor girl has never been faced with this kind of work before."

Charlie grabbed the two remaining pieces of burnt meat. "Better'n starving," he said and downed them with the aid of several glasses of water.

Maisie chased the remaining food around on her plate. "Try and picture yourself fitting into her world. I expect you'd feel clumsy and ill-at-ease."

Levi jerked to his feet and scraped his plate into the slop bucket. "At least the pigs will enjoy the food." He faced Maisie. "I'm sorry to foist this woman on you. Charlie, where's your sister? I'll get her to help Maisie."

Before Charlie could answer, Maisie pushed herself upright, then lowered her foot to the floor.

He sprang forward. "What are you doing?"

"I can't say what I need to say while looking and feeling like an invalid." She grimaced.

When he started to protest, she held up her hand. "Levi, I want you to give Beatrice a chance. She needs to be here."

"What? Why?"

Maisie gave him a look that he'd years ago learned to respect. "God has brought her here for a reason and I, for one, am grateful for her company. Don't let knowing she's from high society prejudice you."

"Me? Prejudiced? Haven't you got that backward?"

"I don't think so. I know you are a fine young man, worthy of any young woman. Do you know it?"

"Of course I do. But what difference does it make in this situation? The only thing I want from Beatrice is for her to help you."

Maisie nodded, her look gently reprimanding. "I wouldn't want to see you denying the call of your heart."

What on earth was she talking about? "The call of my heart? What's that?" He half mocked, but his affection and respect for Maisie kept him from voicing his true feeling on the subject. It would be his head that he followed, not his heart.

"I hope and pray that someday you will hear it and be brave enough to listen to it." Before he could protest, she hurried on. "Now go apologize to that young lady and persuade her to join us again." She lifted her leg back to the stool and leaned back, sure her orders would be obeyed.

"You better do it," Charlie said. "You know Aunt Maisie always gets her way."

"Thank you, Charlie," Maisie said, seemingly happy to be described that way.

Levi strode to the door, jerked it open and stepped outside. He closed his eyes and tried to gather his thoughts and calm his mind. He'd said nothing about the meal. Why should he apologize? He opened his eyes, expecting to see her in a weeping heap nearby. Instead, she stood before the rose bush Maisie cherished and lovingly wrapped every fall to protect it through the winter. When he was done here, he would cut some of the fresh flowers and take them inside for Maisie to enjoy.

Beatrice touched the dusky pink petals of one of the blossoms then bent over to inhale the sweet scent. Hearing him approach, she slowly lifted her head, her eyes wary.

He forgot everything that had been said inside. He forgot his annoyance over being ordered to apologize. He even forgot about being a half-breed, though there lingered a warning note that he would regret his lapse. But all those things disappeared in the way his heart reached out to her in a desire to erase the uncertainty in her eyes. His mouth was suddenly dry and he had to admit it wasn't from the taste of burned chops. He'd admitted she was beautiful but seeing her shyly at the rose bush emphasized her beauty in a way that left him tongue-tied.

She smiled but no light came to her eyes. "I haven't gotten off to a very good start, have I?"

Still speechless, he could only wait for her to continue.

"I'm not used to running a house on my own but

I hope you'll give me another chance. This job is important to me."

He found his voice. "Why? From what you said I understand you came from a rich family. Can't you simply go back home if this fails?"

Darkness clouded her eyes.

He glanced overhead but the clouds were not dark enough to bring those shadows to her eyes. They came from inside and again he had an urge to pull her close and protect her. It was only because he'd already rescued her twice and now it felt like his job.

She answered his question. "My reasons would be of no interest to you."

He could argue the point, but she likely wouldn't believe him and he had no desire to invite a snub. "Come on in and finish supper."

She laughed, a sound of derision. "I think it is quite inedible."

"There's always bread and jam."

"Very well." She took two steps toward him and stopped, the scent of roses wafting toward him. "Does that mean you're going to give me another chance?"

His head told him to say no. She wasn't qualified for the job. Even worse, he felt his resolve to never again look with any interest at a woman faltering. Especially a white woman. Even more dangerous to the security of his heart, a rich city woman. But the word *no* would not leave his mouth. Instead he replied, "I surely am." Besides, if there had been a better person to send out to help Maisie, wouldn't Preacher Gage have sent her?

They reached the house. He grabbed the doorknob

and opened the door for her, again breathing in the scent of roses as she passed him.

"I'm sorry for rushing away like that. Please forgive me." She addressed the words to Maisie.

"You're forgiven. Now let's finish our meal."

Maisie's plate was empty, as was Charlie's. Not wanting Beatrice to eat alone, Levi bravely took the smallest potato he could find, drowned it in butter and ate it in two mouthfuls.

"We have a little custom," Maisie said. "We go around the table and tell about our day."

Levi wanted to beg off for this once, but he thought it might be interesting to see how Beatrice would describe her day.

"Levi, with your pa and older brothers away, that leaves you as the oldest. Tell us about your day."

"I found Beatrice crossing the river, on her way to help you, then found Charlie needing someone to shake him up and that's about it." He left out all the details that mattered, such as the jolt of fear when he saw Beatrice in the water with lightning flashing about her and the painful reminder of Helen's death, which brought with it the memory of her rejection. The way his arms tightened around Beatrice as he carried her to dry land and then catching her as she fainted and feeling it was good and right to be there to protect her. Nope. He wasn't going to admit any of those things. Not even to himself.

Maisie chuckled. "Short and sweet and to the point. Charlie, tell us about your day."

Charlie sat up straighter. "I wasn't drunk. I don't care what Levi says. I still had half a bottle to go."

Silence greeted his words. No doubt anyone with two eyes could see that Charlie had had more than enough to drink, despite his half-full bottle. Levi could hardly blame Beatrice for refusing to hold Charlie's hand as he asked the blessing. But was it because of his drinking or because of his mixed blood? Was she of the belief that half-breeds weren't fit company for a white woman? Especially a high-society woman. A Doyle, which seemed to mean something to her, but meant nothing in Levi's world. Not that he cared what her opinion might be except to object to it on general principles.

Except it mattered far more than he wanted it to.

"Charlie, where have you been and what have you been doing since we last saw you?" Maisie asked.

"Been around." He hung his head. "Tried to find work but no one wants to hire a half-breed."

Levi refrained from pointing out the bottle was as much a hindrance for Charlie as his heritage.

"Not everyone feels that way," Maisie soothed. She turned to Beatrice. "Tell us about your day, my dear."

Beatrice chuckled, drawing Levi's gaze to her, filling his mind with surprise and his heart with relief. He'd expected her to compete with Charlie for the worst day. "My day has been full of so many surprises I cannot begin to name them all. Being allowed the chance to do this job is an answer to prayer. Then I was rescued from the river by Levi. I am blessed beyond measure." Her smile faded. "I apologize for the ruined meal. I found preparing it more difficult than I imagined." She reached for Maisie's hand. "And I thank you for being patient with me."

Maisie looked pleased. "You're welcome."

When Maisie didn't continue, Levi reminded her, "It's your turn to tell about your day."

"My blessings are self-evident. I was afraid I'd be lonely with Big Sam away, but here I sit with three young people at the table. How blessed I am."

"You're glad to see me?" Charlie asked, his tone indicating both doubt and longing.

"I'm always glad to see you. I hope you plan to stay a while."

He grinned and pushed his longish hair off his face. "Maybe I will."

If his cousin stayed it would keep him out of trouble. For some reason—perhaps their shared heritage—Levi always felt protective of Charlie. He looked at Beatrice to see if he could guess her feelings about Charlie being invited to stay. Their gazes collided. Her look went on and on. Challenging him. He wanted to say, *Look after Maisie, make meals as best you can and leave my heart alone.*

His heart? His heart had nothing to do with Beatrice. That thought was Maisie's fault. It was she who had said he should listen to the call of his heart.

There would be no such call and even if there was, he would not hearken to it.

Beatrice didn't realize how tense Levi made her until he and Charlie left the house again and a long sigh emptied her lungs.

"I'm a city girl, too." Maisie's voice brought Beatrice back to the here and now. "A teacher. I planned to teach in a girls' school but when I saw an ad Big Sam had placed seeking someone to instruct his three boys, I changed my mind. The idea intrigued me. And I applied for the job. Big Sam demanded character references. He must have liked what my teacher and pastor said, as he said I got the job. My father wasn't happy. He said it was a whim and I'd regret it."

"Did you… Do you?" It amazed Beatrice to think of Maisie as a city girl.

"Not once. I fell in love with the boys immediately. They were wild and untamed. Big Sam had taken them with him everywhere after Seena died. I had my hands full teaching them manners and how to read and write. By Christmas, Big Sam and I were in love. How I love that man still." She looked into the distance. "I hope he comes home soon. I miss him." She gave a regretful chuckle. "He is not going to be happy to see what I've done to myself."

"I'll make sure you rest so you can heal as quickly as possible." Beatrice prepared the water to wash the dishes.

"If you help me move closer I can dry," Maisie said.

Beatrice would have refused but she heard the lonely tone of Maisie's words. She pushed the chair and stool closer, then handed Maisie each dish as she washed it.

"Levi is very protective of me," Maisie said. "So don't mind him if he's…" She waved her hands to indicate she wasn't sure how to describe him.

Beatrice nodded as if she understood, but kept her attention on washing dishes, certain her cheeks were pinker than leaning over the hot water would make them. And she supplied her own words. *Darkly hand-*

*some. Protective—even of a young woman he'd barely
met. Has strong arms that make a girl feel safe.*

Enough. She'd learned her lesson about trusting
men. She had only one goal in mind—a life of independence that allowed her to follow her own plans and
be freed of her father's.

Thankfully, Maisie didn't pursue the subject and
they were soon done with the dishes.

Beatrice took the dry plates and returned them to
the proper shelf. She stood back to admire the clean
dishes. "Why did no one tell me how satisfying it is
to see dishes washed and stacked in the cupboard?"

Maisie laughed. "Most people don't find it quite so
satisfying after doing it three or four times a day, three
hundred and sixty-five days a year."

Beatrice faced the older woman. "Do you find it
satisfying?"

"Immensely so, but then I'm doing it for those I love
and that makes all the difference."

Love made all the difference. What a wonderful
idea. Beatrice sighed almost inaudibly.

With the last of the dishes done and the kitchen
clean so far as Beatrice could tell, she could think of
no reason to stand about continuing this conversation,
though she wished she could. It was nice to hear Maisie
talk about love and marriage in such positive tones.
Marriage, according to her parents, was more of a business deal than romance.

As if reading Beatrice's mind, Maisie caught her
hand. "I wish you and everyone could know the kind
of love I've found. Don't settle for anything less."

She wasn't interested in marriage of any sort but

wouldn't tell Maisie that. "What do I do with the scraps and wash water?"

"Dump the water on my flowers by the house. They thrive on it." She chuckled. "Though they've had plenty of water today. The scraps…" Maisie looked doubtful, as if uncertain Beatrice could deal with the task.

"Tell me and I'll do it."

"Very well. Take the bucket of scraps out to the pigpen and dump them over the fence into the trough. Watch for puddles on the path. "

"Where will I find the pigpen?"

Maisie gave her instruction.

Beatrice emptied out the basin of water then carried the heavy, slimy bucket from the house, being careful not to let it brush against her skirts as she passed the barn. She smelled the pigs before she reached the pen and gasped. Nothing had prepared her for so many strange and, sometimes, unpleasant odors. She reached the fence and counted two big pigs and half a dozen small ones that rushed toward her squealing and grunting and running into each other, pushing one another out of the way and climbing over each other.

She laughed.

"Amusing, aren't they? Now you can see why bad-mannered people are often called pigs."

She jerked about to stare at Levi. "I didn't see you."

He shrugged, a glint of mischief in his eyes. "I was over there." He pointed. "If you'd taken two steps to the right you would have tromped on me but you were too intent on your task." His gaze shifted to the bucket on the ground beside her.

The pigs squealed loudly.

"They're getting impatient." Levi picked up the bucket and dumped the contents over the fence into a wooden trough.

Beatrice stared, fascinated as the pigs buried their snouts in the trough, not caring if they stepped on each other. She shook her head. "Pigs are...well, pigs."

Laughter rumbled from Levi, drawing her gaze to him. How his eyes danced, and his face crinkled in a friendly sort of way. Just because she called a pig a pig?

She turned back to the animals. "They're noisy, rude and loud. And they stink."

More rumbling laughter. "Johnny says he thanks God he wasn't born a pig."

That brought a burst of laughter from Beatrice. Her eyes connected with his and something sweet filled the air. She couldn't remember a time she had shared real, honest amusement with a man. It caused her insides to bounce up and down...not an unpleasant sensation. She reminded herself not to stare, but despite her ad-monition she could not break the look between them.

He shifted his gaze first, letting it go toward the house. "Have you done Maisie's dressing yet?"

Her thoughts jarred back to the reason she was here. Changing the dressing was not a task she looked for-ward to. She had not a clue how to tackle the job. "No, I just finished cleaning the kitchen." She turned to re-trace her steps.

Levi fell into step with her. They reached the barn. She welcomed the chance to shift her thoughts to some-thing else. "I thought there would be horses and cows in the pens."

"The horses are out with the men at the moment

except for those we need for getting around and Pa's breeding stock." He pointed toward the animals in the pasture. "He has big plans for expanding our bloodlines into something that will make the Sundown Ranch horses more desirable than the average horse. We seldom keep cows in the pens. They are out grazing. Except for the milk cow. Do you want to see her?"

"Is she friendly?"

He grinned. "She won't say hello if that's what you mean, but she also won't be rude like the pigs who act like pigs."

He was teasing her and she didn't mind. "It's good to know she has her species figured out."

They were at the barn door. He edged it wider open and she stepped inside.

"I hope you don't find the smell obnoxious," Levi said.

She sniffed as she turned her head from side to side. "There's a warm, earthy scent, a musty odor and a kind of mushroomlike smell. None of it overwhelming or unpleasant. It's rather a reassuring odor."

He stared at her. "Reassuring? You make the smell seem vital."

"Vital? Yes. That's exactly how it feels."

He shook his head. "I don't know what to make of you."

She wasn't sure what he meant, nor was she sure she wanted to know. If it was good she would be flustered, if bad, she'd be wounded. No, better not to know. "So where is this milk cow?"

He swept his arm toward the alleyway and she preceded him the direction indicated. Old Sissy munched on her feed. There were wooden pens on either side, some with boards that looked as if they had been chewed. She glanced upward at the sound of something scurrying overhead.

"Mice," he explained. "The cause of Maisie's accident." His expression hardened like black rock.

"Wouldn't cats take care of that problem?"

"Cats are hard to find and harder to keep. We had a mama cat but she was half-wild and packed up her kittens and moved on."

An amusing mental picture flashed through her mind of a cat carrying a valise out of which three little kittens peeked and she laughed softly, wishing immediately that she had kept her amusement hidden.

"What makes you laugh?" Levi asked.

She glanced at him to see if he was annoyed but he appeared more curious than anything and she explained. "After all, you did say she'd packed up."

He grinned. "She carried them one by one to a new place."

"Carried them. How?"

"By the scruff of the neck."

"I remember a time the groom was angry with the boy who helped with the horses and grabbed him by the scruff of the neck and shook him. It didn't look pleasant." She shuddered to think of baby kittens being carried that way.

"It's the way cats do it, and the kittens don't seem to mind. Now, do you want to see the milk cow?"

"Yes, of course." Though she'd momentarily forgotten their reason for coming to the barn.

He moved along the alley and stopped where a gate

had been pushed open. A tawny-colored cow stood patiently with Charlie squatting at her side squirting milk into the bucket at his knees.

Beatrice knew where milk came from…in a picture-book sort of way. But she'd never seen it foaming up in a pail. For some strange reason it brought a sting of tears.

Charlie gave Levi a pained look. "I ain't no chore boy."

Levi leaned back on the side of the pen and gave his cousin a steady look. "Nothing wrong with good honest work."

"This is squaw work."

Levi's laugh lacked mirth. "Not here. Big Sam says it's man's work."

"Don't see him doing it, though." Charlie stood. "I'm done here."

Levi straightened. "Not until you've stripped her. I don't want her going dry. We need the milk. Finish the job."

Beatrice looked from one to the other as the words that made no sense hung about in her brain looking for something to connect to. Charlie looked ready to explode. Levi's expression was hard. What would he do if Charlie disobeyed his order?

Looking rebellious, Charlie sat on the little stool again and returned to milking until no more hit the pail. "Happy now?" He pushed past Beatrice.

"Take it to the cookhouse and take care of it."

Muttering under his breath, Charlie stomped from the barn.

Levi took off his cowboy hat and dragged his fingers through his hair. "Sometimes I wonder if he's worth the effort."

A shiver raced down Beatrice's spine. Did he think the same of her? Not worth the effort? She drew herself up to her tallest and faced Levi. "Is anyone who can't do the things you do considered not worth the effort?"

His dark eyes were bottomless, revealing nothing, though the way he crossed his arms over his chest made her think he was prepared to defend his view. "It isn't that he can't do the chores I've assigned him. It's that he doesn't care to make the effort. He believes chores are beneath him. For that reason I find him difficult to deal with." His gaze bored into hers. "I believe in an honest day's work for an honest day's pay."

She floundered to think what that meant to her. She didn't expect to be paid, didn't want to be. "Maybe he's doing the best he can."

He unwound from his position at the fence. "If I thought that I would be happy. But Charlie is capable of doing almost anything he puts his mind to. Come along, I'll show you the cookhouse." He paused at the doorway, retrieving the slop bucket where he'd left it. "That is, if you're interested."

"Yes, I am. I want to see everything." She might have told him she found it fascinating to see life at its roots, but he seemed cross so she kept the words to herself and accompanied him across the yard to a low building. They stepped inside and she stopped to take it in. To one side, there was a long wooden table with backless wooden benches on either side. Hooks on the wall next to the door held a variety of items—bits of leather, furry leggings and two soiled hats. To the other side was an enormous black stove, a long wooden counter and pots, pans, crocks and kitchen utensils of every size and kind. Apart from that, the room was bare of any sort of decoration. The windows lacked curtains. The only bright color in the whole place was the red rim of some of the granite pots.

"What do you think?" Levi asked.

She closed her eyes and drenched her senses, then she opened her eyes and told him her impressions. "The room is sparse." She pointed out the lack of color. "But the air is alive with spices and warmth. I smell apple pie, gingersnaps, chocolate pudding. I smell mashed potatoes in a huge bowl, fried chicken and tomato sauce rich with basil and oregano. It's like walking into an open market with a hundred things cooking at the same time."

His laughter rumbled. "Soupy would be pleased you can't smell dirty boots and manly sweat."

She opened her eyes and grinned. "There might be a touch of that, as well." Why was it she felt trapped by his gaze when he smiled like that? As if the rest of the world had slipped away and left them standing there alone? And when had she ever had such fanciful thoughts? Certainly not with Henry, whom she'd loved, and never with the young men her father presented as suitable.

Levi turned his attention to the room. "Charlie has left the milk." Every trace of humor had disappeared from his voice and a cold chill crossed Beatrice's shoulders.

"I'll have to do it. You don't need to wait if you don't

want." He started a fire in the stove and filled a kettle with water from the pump at the sink.

The bucket of milk stood on the wide counter. Levi pulled out a jug and draped a white cloth over it.

Curious as to what he meant to do, she said, "I'll wait and watch if you don't mind."

His eyebrows arched as if uncertain what to think of her answer. "I don't mind." He poured the milk through the cloth until the jug was full, then covered it with another cloth that he dampened in cold water. "Normally Soupy would use most of the milk. We use a little at the house. But with him and the cowboys away, we don't need it all. The rest will go to the pigs." He rinsed the straining cloth then filled a basin with boiling water and rinsed it again.

He took the milk bucket to the door and set it down. "Maybe Charlie will stir himself to take this to the pigs." He looked around for his cousin. "He'll be trying to find a bottle about now."

Beatrice couldn't decide if Levi sounded condescending or worried, so she made no comment.

He hung the straining cloth to dry, took the jug of milk and the empty slop bucket and escorted her back to the house.

"I was getting concerned when you were gone so long but I see I shouldn't have been," Maisie said. "You were with Levi."

"I'm sorry to make you worry." She'd be more conscious of Maisie in the future.

"I'll hang about while Beatrice changes your dressing, in case she needs anything," Levi said.

Beatrice's insides stiffened. The last thing she

needed or wanted was to have Levi watching while she tackled a job she didn't know how to do. Her spine grew rigid. Her hands curled into fists. She would do this and whatever else she must learn in order to make her own way in life.

Levi struggled to sort out his thoughts. What was there about Beatrice that kept him off balance? He wanted to see her as a city girl. Unfit for ranch life. And she was. But she was more. Or was she less? He wished he could decide.

He'd expected her to grimace when she stepped into the barn. Instead, she'd been intrigued by the odors and even managed to make them seem pleasant. Yes, she'd been put off by the smell of pigs, but he didn't know anyone who wasn't. And wouldn't Soupy have been amazed at her assessment of the cookhouse? A hundred cook fires at the same time. It gave him a mental picture that made his mouth water.

He shook his head, hoping to clear his thoughts. All that mattered to him was that Beatrice took care of Maisie and that Charlie stayed out of trouble.

How did he manage to get both Charlie and Beatrice here at the same time? He couldn't possibly be in two places at once.

"Ma, can I help you to your room?" She was able to hop about, but he preferred she didn't cross to her bedroom on her own.

Maisie looked from Beatrice to Levi. "It's too early for Beatrice to retire. What will she do if I go to bed now?"

"I'll take her for a walk down to the river if she

likes." He'd said the words without thinking and now that they were out, they couldn't be pulled back.

"I'd like that," Beatrice said.

Maisie nodded. "Then I'll prepare for bed and Beatrice can tend to my dressing."

Before she could struggle to her feet, Levi jumped forward and helped her upright. He'd pick her up and carry her, but Maisie would fight him so he settled for holding her firmly as they left the kitchen and crossed the living room. He threw back the covers, eased her to the bed and lifted her injured leg, then stepped back, loathe to leave her to Beatrice's inexperienced hands.

Beatrice eased forward.

Ma must have sensed her uneasiness. Though she could hardly miss the way Beatrice wrung her hands and the way she chewed her bottom lip.

Ma spoke softly to her. "Don't look so frightened."

Beatrice nodded but didn't relax.

Maisie smiled. "Why don't you tell me the sort of things you did to amuse yourself as a child?"

She got a faraway look in her eyes. "I read lots. Did needlework. I'm quite good at it, actually." Her smile was faintly apologetic.

"Didn't you play?"

She shifted her gaze toward the window. "I was taught a young lady should properly conduct herself with decorum."

Levi had no idea what that meant, but Beatrice made it sound as if she was not allowed to enjoy normal childhood play.

Maisie put into words Levi's thoughts. "Maybe here you can learn life is meant to be enjoyed."

Beatrice smiled and the tension slipped from her eyes. "I've already seen glimpses of that."

Levi wanted to ask for specifics. Was he part of what she had enjoyed?

But she stepped forward. "Now let me tend your dressing." The look she gave Levi dismissed him from the room.

His neck burned. He had no intention of seeing his stepmother with her petticoats pulled up to reveal her legs. "I'll be in the other room if you need anything." He closed the door behind him as he left the room, but stayed in the front room, his head turned toward the bedroom in case Maisie called for his assistance.

He heard Maisie's calm voice, but he could not make out her words. He thought he heard Beatrice although he couldn't be certain and took a step toward the door. Then he stopped. No need to press his ear to the door. If Maisie needed him, she'd let him know.

His thoughts wandered as he waited, searching for a place to put Beatrice in his mind. She was a city girl but anxious to be on her own. What did that mean? From a rich family but expressing pleasure at the simple things of ranch life. Light and easy in his arms. But a classy white lady.

She simply did not fit into any of his classifications. And that left him unsettled, wondering if she had the same problem trying to see where he fit.

It was obvious he was a half-breed.

She had no such problem.

Maisie's oft-spoken words echoed in his head. "Boys, there will always be those who say things about you. Hearing them say it doesn't make it true. You don't have to believe what they say about you."

He tried not to believe what others said. But Helen had taught him one thing he would never forget. What others believed about him did make a difference. In the way they treated him, whether or not they were willing to associate with him or even be seen with him.

The doorknob rattled and Beatrice stepped out carrying a basin of water and some soiled rags.

He sprang forward. How had his thoughts gotten so far off track? Was he trying to convince himself that Beatrice was like Helen? The idea condemned him. If he wanted to be judged on his own merits—not his heritage—shouldn't he be willing to offer her the same consideration? "How does her leg look?"

The water in the basin sloshed and he took it from Beatrice's trembling hands. "Are you okay?"

"She did very well," Maisie called. "Now take her out for some fresh air."

Fresh air? He'd detected no odor. "Your leg is infected?" He set the basin on the closest hard surface, pushing a stack of books out of the way to make room for it, and hurried to her side.

"Levi, will you stop fussing. No, my leg isn't infected. But remember it's Beatrice's first time at dealing with a wound. It's been a little challenging for her." Maisie lifted her head to look at Beatrice. "You did very well."

"I was so afraid of hurting you." Beatrice's voice quavered.

"You were very gentle. Thank you." Maisie squeezed Levi's hands. "Take her out for a walk. Get her to relax."

"Yes, Ma." It never entered Levi's mind to refuse until he had cleaned out the washbasin and set the soiled rags to soak in cold water.

Why had he offered to take her for walk, told Maisie he would do so, as well? It wasn't as if they had any intention of becoming friends. She was a city girl. He was country to the core and proud of it.

But she had taken care of Maisie and that was all that mattered.

He had agreed to escort her on a walk and when he said something he generally meant to keep his word.

She stared at the cupboard, though he could see nothing to hold her interest.

"Are you ready?" he asked her.

She started and drew in a sharp breath. "For what?"

"A walk?" Had she not heard Maisie's suggestion? Had she forgotten his offer? His eyes narrowed as he studied her.

Or was it his company she objected to?

But she followed him out the door and fell in step at his side as they followed the trail through the trees to the river. For several minutes before they stepped into a clearing they heard the murmur of moving water. Water flashed silver and blue, highlighted with gold from the lowering sun. The rain had freshened the air.

Levi held out his arm to signal her to stop. He could have saved himself the effort. She hadn't moved since they reached the edge of the trees.

He pointed to the right, to the huddle of ducklings following in the mother duck's wake. "Oh," she gasped involuntarily.

The duck turned, raced the babies into the shelter of some reeds and flew away.

"I'm sorry," she murmured. She looked past him. Her eyes widened.

"Levi, look."

At the sharp note in her voice, he turned slowly, thinking how foolish he was to bring her out here without a gun to defend her.

He saw no wild animal. No wild man. "What is it?"

"Look in the shadows of that rock." She pointed.

He squinted to bring the object into focus. He blinked and stared, speechless.

"It's a child," Beatrice whispered.

"I see that, but what is it doing out here all alone?"

Chapter Four

Beatrice blinked, wondering if her eyes deceived her. But no, there was a child huddled against a boulder. She could see clearly enough to make out a little girl. "Is she lost?" She turned to Levi as she asked the question and saw how bottomless his dark eyes had grown. His black shirt made his features more angular.

"I don't see anyone else around."

They eased closer as they spoke.

Levi's hand caught Beatrice's elbow. "Go slow. We don't want to frighten her."

They were close enough to see the child's almost white-blond hair had once been braided, but now hung in tangles about her tear-streaked face. Her purple dress was blotched with mud. Her bony knees stuck out from under the skirt in matching V's. A half-grown kitten was clutched to her chest.

The kitten meowed plaintively.

"Honey, are you lost?" Beatrice asked gently. "If so, we can help you."

The child's eyes widened. She sprang to her feet.

Levi reached out to stop her but the child fled into the trees.

The dark shadows swallowed her up.

"Come on, we have to make sure she's okay." Levi grabbed Beatrice's hand and they chased after the little girl.

"There she is." He ran faster, tugging Beatrice after him.

She flung out her arm to protect her face against the flailing branches.

Then he stopped, her hand still gripped firmly in his.

She might have pulled free but the woods were dark and filled with all sorts of terrors.

"I can't tell which way she went. You go that way and I'll go this. We'll meet at the far side of these bushes." He dropped her hand and was gone before she could protest.

For a moment she stood immobile. The evening air had a damp coolness to it and the light from the west gave the air a golden glow. She couldn't hear Levi. Behind her came the murmur of the river. Courage returned. She couldn't get lost if she could hear the river. All she had to do was follow the sound and find the trail that would take her to the house.

That poor child had no such assurance of safety. Careful of where she stepped, she eased through the branches that would allow her to skirt the thick bushes. She stopped after a few feet to listen.

At first all she heard was her own rapid breathing, then her breathing returned to normal and she heard a faint "meow." The kitten. Unless the cat had escaped that meant the child was nearby.

Afraid she might frighten the little girl away, Beatrice stood very still and studied her surroundings. There in the shadows. The child tried to hide.

"I won't hurt you." She didn't move, feeling the little one's fear as clearly as if it was her own. She knew how overwhelming it was to find oneself in a strange place, with no parents to help and protect. "I just want to help you." She waited, letting the child take her measure of Beatrice. "Would you like me to help you find your parents?"

The child didn't move but her eyes seemed to consume less of her face.

Beatrice held out her hand. "Do you want to come to me?"

The little girl looked at her kitten as if consulting it. She shook her head.

"Oh, little dolly, I know what's it's like to feel all alone and frightened. Let me help you."

The frightened little girl took a step forward, then stopped, shuddered and took another.

Beatrice didn't move until she could reach one of the little hands and she caught it and pulled the child close. Her tiny hand clung to Beatrice's fingers.

Beatrice knelt to face the little girl. She was so fair, with contrasting dark brown eyes. A true beauty. "What's your name?"

"Dolly," the child whispered.

"As in Dorothy?"

A nod yes.

Beatrice thanked God for letting her use an endearment that made the child trust her. "How old are you?"

"Five," she whispered again.

"Where are your parents?"

Dolly rocked her head back and forth.

"When did you last see them?"

"I don't know," she again whispered. Then her eyes widened and she would have escaped if Beatrice didn't have a good hold on her.

She followed the child's frightened gaze and saw Levi a few feet away. "Stay there. She's afraid." She turned back to Dolly. "This is Levi Harding. He can help us find your parents. Will you let him do that?"

Dolly nodded.

Levi edged closer, cautiously, making sure he didn't alarm the child. He knelt by Beatrice's side. "Were you lost last night?"

Dolly shuddered and clutched the kitten tighter. "I was scared," she whispered.

Levi waited for her to calm. "Were you with your mama and papa?"

An affirmative nod.

"Were you with anyone else?"

A shake of her head to indicate no.

"Were you in a wagon?"

Again, yes.

Levi rose to his full height. "Then I will find them for you." He indicated Beatrice should stand and when she did so, he whispered close to her ear, his breath fanning her hair. "They must be frantic with worry. I'll do my best to follow her tracks back and if that fails, I'll search the trails. The child can't have wandered too far."

Beatrice nodded. "I'll stay here with her."

He glanced past her. "You could take her to the house."

She considered it. "I get the feeling she would be uncomfortable with that. I'll wait." The woods were growing darker by the moment. "I'll wait by the river right at the foot of the path. If you haven't returned by the time the sun drops below the horizon, I'll go to the house." That would give her enough time to get back before darkness descended. She turned to Dolly. "Did you hear? Does that meet with your approval?"

Dolly nodded.

"Pray I find them quickly." He squeezed her shoulder and slipped into the shadows.

"I will," she called, not knowing if he heard her or not. She was alone with a child in the darkening woods. Fear edged her thoughts but she clung to the courage his touch had given. She took Dolly's hand. "Let's go." She followed the sound of running water back to the river and returned to where the path led to the house. "Let's sit here to wait." She sat on a fallen tree and pulled Dolly up beside her.

The little girl had the pungent odor of having wet her pants. Should Beatrice suggest she wash in the river?

"This is Smokey." The whisper introduced Beatrice to the kitten. "Do you want to hold her?"

"I'd love to." She took the kitten and let it sprawl in her lap. "It's so soft." She'd never had a pet. Never been allowed one. It took her about thirty seconds to realize she might have missed a source of comfort.

There was something soothing about stroking the kitten, who purred loudly.

"She's my friend," Dolly whispered.

"Honey, why are you whispering? It's okay if you talk out loud."

"Mama told me I had to be quiet 'cause Papa was sick. He needed me to be quiet so he could get better."

"I see." Only she didn't. How long had the father been ill that the child thought she must continue to whisper? Hopefully Levi would return with some answers.

"It's getting cold," Dolly whispered.

"It is, isn't it?" She'd hoped Levi would return with the parents but the reunion would have to take place at the ranch. "Let's go to the house."

Dolly shrank back. "Maybe I'm bad."

Beatrice wondered if she had heard the agonized whisper correctly. "What makes you think you're bad?"

But Dolly didn't answer as tears pooled in her eyes and she gathered Smokey into her arms.

Beatrice waited but when it became obvious she wasn't going to get any answers, she rose, took Dolly's hand and turned them toward the trail.

Dolly stood rooted to the spot.

"It's okay. It's a very nice place."

"Is it your place?"

She wished the child would stop whispering. "No, I'm just helping, but they are very nice people. Levi has helped me several times." It was hard to believe she'd been there less than a day and found herself perilously close to trusting him. *Remember Henry,* she reminded herself. *Remember what your father was prepared to do. Never give a man any right or opportunity to again hurt you.*

Dolly let out a long sigh. "Okay."

Hand in hand, they walked the trail back to the house. Dolly drew to a stop in the clearing.

"It's okay, little Dolly."

Dolly nodded and allowed Beatrice to lead her inside and there they ground to a halt. Beatrice was every bit as uncertain of what to do next as Dolly.

"Would you like a bath so you'll be nice and clean when your mama and papa get here?"

The child had very expressive eyes that at the moment revealed a whole bunch of emotions—fear, hope, sadness and embarrassment. "I had an accident."

"That happens sometimes." When Levi returned with the parents they would have clean clothes. In the meantime, a bath, a good hair brushing and scrubbing of the current outfit seemed in order.

She listened for any sound from Maisie's room but heard nothing. Perhaps she'd slept through the noise of them entering the kitchen. She didn't have to worry about Dolly, who was so quiet it made Beatrice wonder what had happened to her.

Moving as softly as possible, she put water on to heat and found a big laundry tub. As the water heated, she thought of what to feed the child. Like Levi said, there was always bread and jam and fresh milk.

Dolly ate neatly but with enough vigor that Beatrice knew she was extremely hungry and wondered how long the child had been lost and alone.

Her heart went out to the child. As an adult, being

alone and lost in her new world was frightening enough. She couldn't imagine what it felt like as a child.

By the time Dolly had eaten enough that she refused any more, the water was ready and Dolly allowed Beatrice to help her out of her soiled clothes and into the tub of water. Beatrice scrubbed her from top to bottom.

Dolly giggled as Beatrice cleaned between her toes. "That tickles," she whispered.

"It does, does it? You mean this?" She tickled the little girl's feet, enjoying the muted giggles as Dolly pressed her hands to her mouth as if to drown out the sound.

"There, you are all clean." She lifted the child from the water and dried her off. With no clothes to wear, she wrapped her in a dry towel. "Now let's get your hair pretty for when your mama and papa come."

Again a look of fear and sadness and guilt crossed through Dolly's eyes.

Beatrice turned Dolly to face her. "Why does doing your hair make you afraid?"

"Not my hair," she whispered.

"Then what?"

"He'll never find them."

Beatrice understood that she meant she didn't think Levi would find her parents. "Why do you say that?" She brushed Dolly's hair as they talked. Long, baby-fine and so fair.

"'Cause they's gone."

Gone? Had they abandoned the child? She rebraided the hair and hung the long braids in loops on either side of Dolly's head. The child was beautiful. Why would anyone want to abandon her? "Where are they gone?"

Tears filled her eyes but Dolly blinked them away and didn't answer.

Smokey, who had watched the entire proceedings from beside the stove, where she enjoyed a dish of milk, had turned to grooming herself. Dolly scooped her up and held her close. "Smoky is all I got now."

A shiver crossed Beatrice's shoulders at the finality of Dolly's words. *Lord God, the One who sees and knows, please guide Levi to this child's parents that they might be reunited.*

The minutes ticked away. Several times Beatrice went to look out the window but there was no sign of Levi returning. Darkness descended. She found a lamp and lit it. She washed the little garments in the bathwater and hung them behind the stove to dry, then carried the water out to Maisie's plants, though with the rain of earlier and the dishwater later, it seemed they might have had enough to drink. Instead, she poured the water around the pink rosebush and paused to smell the evening scent of the flowers before she returned inside.

Poor little Dolly's head fell to her chest and she jerked awake just in time to avoid falling off the chair.

"Do you want to go to sleep in my bed?"

Again, that look of fear.

"Maybe in this nice big armchair." She indicated the one Maisie had Levi bring from the other room.

"You're going to stay here?"

"Until Levi gets back."

"Okay." Wrapped in a big towel, Dolly curled up in the chair and fell asleep.

Giving up any attempt to be calm about Levi's absence, she stood at the window watching and praying.

Levi rode up to the barn. It was late. Likely past midnight.

He'd found Dolly's parents. He only wished he could have found them alive.

He unsaddled Buck but before he tended to feeding him, he examined every corner of the barn. The troublemakers would have had plenty of time to do their mischief with Levi gone long past dark. He discovered nothing amiss. Charlie's horse stood in the stall where Levi had left him. His cousin must be sleeping in the bunkhouse. Perhaps his presence had been a deterrent to those responsible for so many things in the last few days. He'd have a good look around outside before he went to the house.

His throat tightened at the news he had to relay to Dolly. The poor child. She'd likely been with her parents when they passed on. What an awful thing for such a young one to deal with.

He lit a lantern and circled the ranch buildings. The gates were all up, the breeding stock content in the pen. He could find nothing to cause him concern so returned to the barn and finished taking care of Buck before he made his weary way to the house.

A lamp still glowed in the kitchen window. Had Beatrice stayed up or had she left the lamp burning to welcome him home?

He paused at the door, hating to take this information to the child. A surge of gratitude filled him knowing Beatrice would be there when he did.

As quietly as possible he opened the door and slipped in. At the sight before him, he paused and smiled. Dolly curled up like an overgrown kitten in the chair Maisie had previously occupied, her little kitten beside her.

Beatrice sat at the table, her head cradled in her arms on the well-worn wooden tabletop. All three of them—woman, child, cat—were sound asleep.

A sense of rightness stirred his senses. A feeling that this was the way his life should be. Coming home to a pretty young woman and a contented child.

His jaw muscles clenched. Helen had ruined that possibility for him with her judgmental ways. Not that she was entirely to blame. It's just that he had allowed himself to think she saw him differently.

But for just one moment he let himself think of a wife and family. Then with a quiet sigh he pushed his thoughts back to where they belonged and tiptoed to the table. He touched Beatrice's shoulder.

She jerked awake, looking confused, and then recognition dawned. "You're back." She smiled.

Her smile was not one of welcome for him. At least that's what Levi told himself as he tamped down a matching response. "Shh." He indicated the sleeping child. "Come outside. I'll tell you everything."

Together they tiptoed to the door. He snagged a jacket from the nearby hook and draped it over her shoulders as they stepped outside. The night was cool and damp and filled with the scent of roses. Or was that Beatrice's unique scent? It must have been because he couldn't remember ever being so aware of the roses filling the air with their perfume before.

She turned to him, her features barely visible in the dark. He shifted so the glow from the window allowed him to see her face.

"Did you find them?" Her question jolted him back to reality.

He sought to find the right words. But how else could he say it but just say it? "I found the wagon a few miles away." He drew in a deep breath. "A man and a woman were dead inside."

She gasped. Her eyes widened.

Fearing she would faint again, he caught her shoulders and steadied her.

"She's an orphan? How awful. She tried to tell me." The truth of the situation flooded her eyes with horror. "She was with them? How long have they been gone?"

He told her everything he knew. "It looks like they died of the influenza. The sheriff agreed. I took the wagon to town, where he arranged for a quick burial. He examined the contents of the wagon. Dolly is Dorothy Knott. The sheriff discovered information that she has an aunt Martha in Ohio and will send a telegram in the morning. The aunt will take care of Dolly once she can make arrangements."

Beatrice shuddered. "The poor child. I keep thinking of her watching her parents die, being so alone and not knowing what to do. Oh, Levi, it's too awful to think about."

At her agonized wail, he gripped her arms and she squeezed his. They held each other. He found comfort in her arms and hoped she found the same in his. Two people who barely knew each other united in their concern for an orphaned child.

"What's to become of her in the meantime?" Beatrice's voice was muffled.

"The sheriff suggested someone in town could care for her until her aunt arrives, but it didn't take him long to realize everyone was dealing with either illness or death. He asked if she could stay here for now."

"You said yes?"

He inhaled the scent of roses, letting the smell soothe his senses. "I said it wasn't up to me."

She drew back and looked into his face. "Who is it up to?" Her eyes searched his for the answer.

He didn't say anything but she must have read the answer in his face.

"Me? Why is it up to me?"

"You'll be the one responsible for her. You already have Maisie to care for and the house to run."

She stepped back. "And you don't think I can manage Dolly, as well?"

The thought had crossed his mind. She admittedly lacked experience. "Are you familiar with caring for a child so young?"

Her shoulders rose and fell as if she drew in a deep breath. "I have not looked after any children. Just as I have not run a household or cared for a wound such as Maisie's, but I don't intend to let my lack of experience be a deterrent. I will gladly look after Dolly until her aunt comes or sends for her or whatever she decides to do."

"You're sure?"

She presented him with a tilted chin. "Do you doubt I can do it?"

He grinned. "I would not be so foolish as to even

suggest it. In fact, I hoped you'd agree, but you won't have to do it alone. I will help you in every way I can."

"That's good to know." Her shoulders sank. "Poor little Dolly."

They stayed outside for some time, discussing the situation. He suspected she needed to talk about it as much as he did, as if they could somehow make sense of it. "Why would God let a little child's parents die?"

Beatrice tipped her head back and studied him, her gaze intense. He wished it was light enough he could hope to guess what she was thinking. "Weren't you Dolly's age when your mother died?"

"Five. Yes, I was. I hadn't thought about that."

"Perhaps that's why Dolly ended up here—you should be able to understand what she's going through."

"I haven't thought about it in years. But I remember the lonely ache that tore at my innards every night. Not until Maisie came to the ranch to help with me and my two older brothers did the ache abate." He chuckled softly, bringing her questioning gaze to him. They no longer held each other's arms, but he was close enough he could watch her changing expression.

"Poor Dolly," he said, remembering the confusion and pain of those first days after his ma died. "How will she understand her parents going to sleep and not waking up?"

Beatrice took his hand. "I don't suppose there is any way she can, but we must do our best to make her feel safe until her aunt can make arrangements."

He clung to her touch, resisting an urge to crush her hand to his chest. "Pa must have understood how hard it was for me. He brought us a pup. Shep slept on my bed from the time he came and I fell asleep knowing he'd be there when I woke up."

"Dolly has her kitten. She doesn't let it far from her sight."

"I hope it comforts her."

Beatrice smiled gently. "I believe it will and I believe God brought her here so we could help."

They stood hand in hand looking at the house. He couldn't say what Beatrice thought, but he wished there was some way he could ease the pain little Dolly would have to face. "Pa did his best to take care of us boys. He took us with him on whatever job he had to do. Tanner and Johnny reveled in being allowed to ride along with Big Sam, but I often wished I could stay home and play quietly with my toys."

"Dolly will stay with me. I'll do my best to see she gets what she needs." Beatrice faced him squarely. "But I believe you will understand her needs far better than I can so I'm holding you to your promise to help with her."

For a moment he faltered. He had to find the men who were bothering the place. He had chores to look after. He had Charlie to keep an eye on. And she had Maisie to take care of.

Were they doing the right thing in keeping Dolly? Though the sheriff had left them little alternative.

Even in the dim light he could see the challenge in her eyes. He would not let her down. "We're in this together."

Chapter Five

His promise felt like so much more than concern over an orphaned child. For the first time ever, she felt as if she and a man were united in one purpose, together for more than personal gain. Her heart swelled with the idea.

Then she told herself to think sanely. She would accept his help with Dolly. Likely both she and the little girl would need it. But she would not allow dreams of anything more to cloud her judgment.

Standing close to him, holding his hand in the moonlight, surely proved how close she was to forgetting her words of caution and she slipped her hand to her side. "I better get Dolly into bed."

He sprang away. "I brought her things. You'll be needing them."

They hurried to the door, where Levi picked up a basket of little-girl things. "I'll take it to one of the bedrooms." He ground to a halt inside the door and they watched Dolly sleeping with Smokey pressed to her chest.

Levi turned to Beatrice and commented, "She's a beautiful child. So fair." He had taken off his hat and hung it on a hook and rubbed a hand over his head.

Beatrice wondered if he made a comparison between the child's fairness and his own dark skin and hair. From some of his earlier comments she understood him to be keenly aware of his half-breed status. But she could think of nothing to say that wouldn't sound like being a half-breed meant more to her than it did.

With a start she realized that over the hours of this very long day she'd drawn a firm conclusion. It wasn't the outside of a man that she cared about, it was how he conducted himself and how he treated others. So far, she'd seen nothing but kindness and concern from Levi.

She took the basket from Levi and began to search through the garments. "I'll find her nightwear."

"Should I put her things in Johnny's room?"

She straightened and regarded him. "Would you have liked to sleep alone when you were five and had lost your mother?"

"No."

"I doubt she does, either. Put her things in my room. She can sleep with me."

While Levi did so, she slipped the nightgown over Dolly's head. The child barely stirred. How long had she been alone? Lost and frightened? It made Beatrice want to cradle her in her arms and sing lullabies to her. Instead, she hummed as she lifted Dolly and made her way to the bedroom she'd been given.

Levi waited at the doorway until she'd settled the

child. Beatrice glanced up, wondering at his bemused expression as he watched the child.

He shifted and tipped his head toward Maisie's room. "Did Ma waken at all?"

"I haven't heard a sound."

"She took some drops for her pain. They'll make her sleep soundly."

He seemed reluctant to leave. She wished he didn't have to go, knowing the minute she closed the door and he walked away she would have to confront the enormity of what she had agreed to do. Care for an injured woman, run a ranch house and now see to a young child.

"Will your ma mind having Dolly here?" she whispered.

"She'll love it." His gaze sought the child and a smile softened his features. "I bid you good night." He closed the door and his footsteps sounded as he crossed the floor to his own room.

Mindful of the sleeping child, she turned the lamp low and quietly prepared for bed. She'd prayed for a chance to prove herself capable and earn her independence. She smiled to herself. God certainly meant to answer that prayer.

She sobered. So long as she didn't fail.

Rather than get her own Bible out and risk disturbing Dolly, she took the one on the bedside table and opened it to a bookmark. Surprisingly it was the book of Ruth. She read the verses with fresh eyes. Like Ruth she had come to a strange country with unfamiliar customs. Like Ruth, she would do her best to fit in. Though she did not expect to find a man like Boaz, who would care about her needs. Not that her needs meant a thing in comparison to Dolly's. *Lord, help us comfort her and make her feel safe.*

She crawled in beside Dolly. The child sighed and snuggled close.

A strange, long ache tugged at Beatrice's arms.

Beatrice woke the next morning to something tickling her nose and someone giggling. It took but seconds to remember where she was and realize the giggle came from Dolly and the tickling from the kitten who was perched under Beatrice's chin.

"Good morning to you both," she said and turned to meet the dark brown intense gaze of a little girl who had grown suddenly sober.

"He didn't find them, did he?" Dolly whispered.

Beatrice shifted the kitten to the bed so she could pull Dolly closer. "He found the wagon. Your mama and papa are dead. Were they sick a long time?"

Dolly nodded and answered in another whisper. "Mama said I had to be quiet so Papa could get better. I tried to be quiet."

Beatrice closed her eyes against the pain that accompanied the realization that Dolly thought she was responsible in any way for her papa's death. How was she to make the child understand it wasn't her fault? *God, please guide my words.* She had not even finished praying when she heard Levi and Maisie talking and understood he was helping her from her room.

She sprang from the bed. "I have to hurry. Can you find something to wear? Levi brought your clothes." She pulled on a dress and quickly brushed her hair into place, then tied it at the back of her neck. There was no time to fuss with it what with breakfast to prepare, and who knew what else?

Dolly found a dark green shapeless dress that she eased over her head. Holding Smokey, she stood at the door, her eyes wide.

Despite the need to hurry, Beatrice knelt at the child's side. "I didn't get a chance to tell you that you are going to live here until your aunt Martha comes to get you."

"With you?" Another whisper.

"Yes, and with Levi and his mama. She's hurt her leg so can't move around much so we have to help her."

"I'll be very quiet."

Beatrice thought if Dolly got any quieter she would become mute.

"Levi's cousin Charlie might be here, too." She wasn't sure of Charlie's plans. Nor did she know when Big Sam would return and decided it was best to not mention him at the moment. "We all want you to feel happy and safe." She was certain she could speak for the others. After all, who wouldn't want that for a child? "Okay? Are you ready?"

Dolly nodded, but Beatrice noticed that poor little Smokey was getting squeezed extra tight. She rubbed the kitten's head. "She's such a good kitty."

Dolly nodded again.

Beatrice hoped the child hadn't decided to never talk again. She took Dolly's hand and together they crossed the sitting room and into the kitchen, where Levi stood over the stove and the smell of coffee filled the air.

Maisie looked up at their approach. "I heard we have

a little visitor. You must be Dolly." She held out her hand, but Dolly pressed to Beatrice's side.

Maisie wisely ignored the behavior and spoke to Beatrice. "I trust you had a good sleep."

"Yes, fine."

Levi had turned from the stove and watched them.

Beatrice brought her gaze to his, felt the power of his dark eyes and something more. As if their shared experiences of the previous day had drawn them together. She tried to pull her gaze from his, to right her thoughts from thinking that the day had signified anything special. Not that she desired anything special.

He looked away first, then drank his cup of coffee and set it down. "I have to look after chores. Can you manage in here?"

The fragile feeling of the moment lay shattered at her feet. He saw only her inadequacies. She drew back her chin. He would not see another failure in meal preparation. "I can manage just fine, thank you."

Levi had meant his question to be helpful but she'd taken it as uncertainty about her abilities. He strode through the door. Well, if supper last night was any indication, she'd given him good reason to have doubts.

Charlie moseyed from the bunkhouse, still adjusting his shirt. His eyes were shadowed, his hair mussed, but he quickly donned his hat to hide it. He saw Levi and shifted his direction, as if he wanted to avoid meeting him.

Levi changed direction, too, and fell in at his side. "Charlie, I got to say you look like you were trampled by a herd of buffalo."

"Yeah? Feel like it, too. What was you up to last night? I heard you riding in way after dark. Sure makes it hard for a man to get a good night's sleep."

"Sorry." He told of finding Dolly and her dead parents.

Charlie ground to a halt, all annoyance gone from his expression. "Ah, that's hard. So the little girl is staying here until her aunt comes."

"That's the plan."

"A pretty young woman and a little girl. Cousin, it sounds to me like you're growing domesticated."

"I have no such intentions."

"Still missing Helen?"

Levi ignored the hard tone in Charlie's voice. Nor would he ask why Charlie made it sound like Levi was foolish to still be missing her. He would never tell anyone that his pain from missing her was but a fraction of the pain he felt at being rejected for being a half-breed. Though if anyone would understand, it might be Charlie.

"Time you got over her and looked for a decent woman."

Again that hint that Helen had not been the sort of woman Levi deserved. But then, what sort did he deserve? Certainly not a city girl like Beatrice. Or any white woman. And the native ladies considered him too white for their liking.

He'd come to accept it wasn't necessarily his heritage, but he himself that was the problem. "We best get the chores done and head on in for breakfast."

Charlie whooped with laughter.

Levi cringed. Sometimes Charlie was so loud.

"Do you guess we'll have raw eggs and burnt toast?" Charlie asked.

"All that matters is that Maisie stays off her feet."

"Can't say as I agree. A man can only do so much work on poor food." Charlie managed to sound regretful, but Levi suspected he would welcome the excuse to get out of the menial chores he considered beneath him.

"You get the cow milked and I'll check the stock." He strode away before Charlie could voice the argument Levi saw building. As it was, he heard his cousin muttering as Levi rounded the barn, intent on checking the breeding stock first.

His eyes narrowed as he studied the gate. Someone had tampered with it, because it wasn't closed exactly the way he did it. He checked the ground and made out a set of boot prints that were larger than either his or Charlie's boots. The troublemakers had been around again, but had done no harm. It unsettled him. What were they up to? Did they mean only to harass, or were their plans more dangerous and they had simply been interrupted before they could carry them out?

He circled the rest of the ranch, checking gates, checking on the pigs, the chickens and the cookhouse, and peering into every building whether it was empty or full.

Nothing seemed amiss. It should have made him relax but it only made his tension mount. He did not like this constant uncertainty. He must track the troublemakers down and put a stop to this nonsense.

But how could he get away for any length of time with Maisie laid up, a child visiting, Charlie grousing about the chores that needed doing and Beatrice...?

And Beatrice? Her presence was supposed to make it easier for him to get away. He could not explain why it did quite the opposite.

Charlie dumped a bucket of milk in the pig trough, returned to the cookhouse and emerged with a cloth-covered jug. He turned toward the house.

Levi fell in at his side.

"Do I smell bacon?" Charlie asked.

Levi sniffed. "Think you do."

"Does it smell burned?"

Levi sniffed again. "Can't say it does."

They lengthened their strides in a hurry to get to the bacon before it started to burn. "Morning," Charlie said, as they entered the house. "So you're the little girl who is visiting?"

Dolly stood at Beatrice's side and at Charlie's exuberance, shrank into the folds of her skirts. Beatrice lowered a hand to Dolly's shoulder and pressed her even closer.

"It's okay," Levi said to the child. "This is my cousin Charlie and he has a loud voice."

Charlie grunted a protest. "I'm not loud."

"Yes, you are," Dolly whispered.

Levi chuckled and met Beatrice's eyes, feeling pleased when he saw she shared his amusement. What was there about her eyes that made him feel pulled out of himself and into a field of scented roses and golden light?

"Breakfast is ready," Beatrice said. She seemed a little breathless. Or was it that he heard the rapid beating of his own heart?

"Everyone sit down," Maisie said and they did so.

He managed to say grace at Maisie's request, though he could not remember what he said. It was the smell of bacon, he told himself, that had him so confused. After all, supper last night had left him hungry. He slipped four fried eggs from the platter and a generous amount of bacon. The bread wasn't toasted, but that was probably a good thing considering the crispy, blackened edges on each egg. But breakfast was edible and both he and Charlie ate eagerly.

After a bit, they both slowed down and slathered jam on slices of bread.

Charlie held his knife in one hand as he began to speak. "Levi, you should be more careful about closing the gate on the horses. If I hadn't seen it was open, the horses would have gotten out."

"I always close it carefully."

"Well, someone else must have opened it then. 'Cause I didn't." Charlie sounded defensive.

"I didn't mean to imply you did. Just forget it." The sooner the better, as he hadn't told Maisie about the troublemakers. Hoping to divert the interest he saw in his stepmother's eyes, he spoke to Beatrice. "Breakfast is good. Thanks."

Her cheeks blossomed like pink roses. "You're welcome. I'm learning."

"Levi?" Maisie said.

He held Beatrice's gaze a second longer. Not only because he didn't want to face Maisie, but also because he enjoyed how Beatrice's eyes shifted color, revealing her emotions. Right now they were dark as burnished gold filled with a mixture of embarrassment and pleasure.

"Levi, what's this about someone opening the gate?" Maisie's voice was firm, demanding his full attention.

He turned to her. "I might have been a little careless yesterday what with all that happened." He hoped she'd accept his explanation. After all, how often did he rescue a beautiful woman and a little girl in the same day? Not to mention his cousin.

But even before she spoke, he knew from the disbelief in her eyes that he had failed to convince her.

"Levi, you are never careless. Now tell me what's going on."

"Yes, ma'am." There was no point in trying to ignore her. He'd learned that a long time ago.

Dolly left her chair and crowded to Beatrice's side, her eyes wide with concern. "Did he do something bad?" she whispered to Beatrice.

Maisie chuckled. "Levi never does anything bad."

"Never?" Dolly considered him with awe.

"But he sometimes tries to keep secrets," Maisie said, her voice gentle.

Levi knew Maisie's gentle voice carried unyielding stubbornness. He had wanted to spare her the worry of knowing what was going on. But Charlie's careless comment now made that impossible. "It's nothing to concern you. Any of you," he added for Beatrice's sake. "Probably just some youngsters away from home for the first time who think it's funny to get into mischief."

"What sort of mischief?" Maisie asked, insisting on knowing all the details.

He would only give her enough to stop her from asking for more. "A gate left open now and then. I expect whoever is responsible hides somewhere nearby watching for me to discover it and then has a good laugh about the trick they played on me. Just harmless fun."

Maisie studied him with knowing eyes but he held her gaze unblinkingly. Finally she blinked. "It doesn't sound like harmless fun to me."

"Probably city boys who don't understand what they're doing." He reached for his coffee cup, knowing it was empty, and managed to look surprised then glanced at Beatrice. His surprise grew real at the hard look she gave him, her eyes narrowed, her lips pressed tight. What had he done? Or said? He stifled a desire to bang the heel of his hand on his forehead. His comment about city boys could be construed as a criticism of city people in general. "They don't know any better," he said by way of explanation and apology.

Her look did not change.

Charlie nudged him. "I think you put your foot in your mouth, cousin."

"I didn't mean anything by it," Levi said with some despair and rose to fill his coffee cup. Not until he sat down again did he realize it might have been wiser to forget more coffee because now he was forced to drink it, all the while enduring a harsh look from Beatrice and a disbelieving one from Maisie. He dropped his gaze to Dolly. And a frightened one from her.

He forgot the other two and focused on the child, wanting to reassure her. "It's okay, Dolly. No one is angry."

"You sound angry."

He wondered why she never spoke above a whisper.

"I'm not. Ma, are you?"

"No, I'm not angry."

He turned to Beatrice. "Are you angry?"

Her expression softened as she pulled Dolly close. "I'm not angry."

"Me, either," said Charlie.

Dolly relaxed but still pressed to Beatrice's side.

He felt Maisie's continued study of him and knew she had more questions that he didn't want to answer, and especially not in front of the child and the city gal who might construe the situation to be more dangerous than he thought it was. He downed his coffee, grateful it wasn't scalding hot, and pushed away from the table. "I've got to take care of the stock." He hurried from the house before anyone could stop him.

A laughing Charlie caught up to him halfway across the yard. "You can run, cousin, but you can't hide."

Levi slowed his steps. "Who's running?"

"You know Aunt Maisie wants to know more about these city boys and what Aunt Maisie wants, Aunt Maisie gets."

"Huh!" He wasn't going to confess he feared exactly that. "Besides, I don't know if it's city boys. I only suggested that so they wouldn't worry."

Charlie laughed loudly. "I don't think the city girl liked hearing city boys talked about like that."

"I guess not." He wished he could retract the words but he couldn't. And the whole situation reminded him of the vast difference between him, a half-breed cowboy, and her, a well-to-do city girl.

But why was such a girl in Montana and insisting she needed a job?

* * *

Beatrice stared after the departing men. City boys—and by extension, city girls—were spoken of with great disdain. "How many city girls—" she quickly corrected herself "—boys, has he known?"

Maisie chuckled. "Not many. But don't be offended. I was a city girl when I came, a fact that Levi seems to have forgotten. You did well this morning."

"Thanks to your instructions."

"Just remember, no one is born knowing how to run a household or make a meal. They learn. Some sooner, some later. All that matters is you're willing to learn."

"I am." No one had any notion of how desperately willing she was. Even her father believed it was only a matter of time until she returned to Chicago and his plans for her. She eased away from Dolly, who had relaxed somewhat now the men were gone. "I'll clean up."

A little while later, the kitchen was clean, the dishes neatly arranged in the cupboard, the kitten fed and taken outside under Dolly's watchful eyes. Beatrice had swept the floor and made Maisie's bed.

"What's next?" she asked the older woman.

"If you'd be so kind as to bring me the sewing basket, I'll do the mending."

Beatrice did so.

"Thank you. I think a nice stew would be perfect for dinner."

"Stew?" Beatrice swallowed hard.

"It's easy. There's canned meat and a little later you can bring in some vegetables from the garden to add to it. Meanwhile, why not take Dolly and Smokey outside for some fresh air. Feel free to—" Maisie stopped and glanced toward the window. "I hope Levi is right and whoever is leaving gates open is only interested in mischief, but do be careful."

With Maisie's warning ringing in her head, Beatrice and Dolly and Smokey left the house. Beatrice turned toward the barn and other outbuildings. She'd stay close to them in case someone lurked nearby. "Let's have a look around."

Dolly nodded.

Beatrice's curiosity about the child blossomed. "Did you live on a farm or a ranch with your parents?"

"A little farm," she whispered. "Papa said we'd have a great big farm when we got where we were going."

"Where were you going?"

"I don't know."

They reached the trail in front of the barn and continued along it. Beatrice had been this way before with Levi, so she felt safe. "Were you happy to leave your farm behind?"

"Mama said it was for the best and she said I could keep Smokey."

Beatrice had to lean toward the child to catch what she said. "Smokey sure likes being with you." The kitten never complained about being held so tightly. "Do you think she would like to walk for a while?"

Fear darkened Dolly's eyes. "What if she runs away?"

"We wouldn't want that, would we?" She didn't press the point.

They reached the pigpens and Dolly giggled at the animals. "Papa had two pigs. He selled them."

After a bit they moved on, circling the pens. From

out of nowhere, Charlie appeared in front of them. "Hi," he said, his voice extra loud to be heard above the noisy pigs.

Neither she nor Dolly had noticed the man until he stood right in front of them. Beatrice jerked in a breath at the surprise, but Dolly gasped. Smokey, alarmed by the commotion, escaped Dolly's grasp and raced away, disappearing behind a nearby shed.

"Smokey," she wailed.

Beatrice was glad to hear more than a whisper from the child, but would have preferred different circumstances.

Then Dolly raced after the kitten, Beatrice hot on her heels.

They skidded around the corner of the building and Dolly rushed straight into Levi's arms, with Beatrice managing to stop before she collided with him. But only by inches. He steadied her, his hand firm on her shoulder.

"What's going on?"

Charlie reached them. "I didn't mean to scare you. I thought you knew I was there."

"Smokey ran away," Beatrice said.

Dolly sobbed against Levi's neck, the sound tearing at Beatrice's heart, bringing a sting of tears to her own eyes. The tears threatened to overflow when Levi patted the little girl's back and made comforting noises.

"Don't cry, little Dolly. We'll find Smokey. I promise."

Dolly slowly quieted, believing Levi's promise.

Beatrice found herself believing it, as well. What

was there about this man that made her so easily forget that she didn't intend to trust any man ever again?

Levi wiped away Dolly's tears. "Tell me where you last saw her."

"There," she whispered as she pointed toward the shed.

"Maybe she's still there." They knelt down and peered under the wall. "You should call her," Levi said.

"Come here, Smokey."

"She'll never hear you if you only whisper." Levi's gaze came to Beatrice and she understood he wanted the child to speak in a normal tone of voice.

She knelt beside the pair. "Call your kitty, Dolly."

Dolly sucked in a deep breath and called, "Come here, Smokey." Her voice barely passed a whisper, but at least it was out loud.

"She'll surely hear that," Levi said, sounding as proud as if he had taught her to speak a new language.

Dolly sat back on her heels. "Maybe she's not there." Her voice was back to a whisper.

"Call her again. She might only be frightened and need to hear your voice."

She raised her voice and called again.

"Meow."

"I hear her. I hear her."

Beatrice and Levi grinned at each other when Dolly used her normal voice.

"Come on, Smokey. Nobody's going to hurt you."

The kitten poked her nose out from under the shed, then slowly came out, going directly to Dolly.

She picked up her cat and buried her face in the animal's fur.

Charlie let out a sigh of relief and hurried away.

Levi sat on the ground, his back to the wall of the shed. He looked at Beatrice and patted the ground next to him.

She should refuse. She should do something else but she could think of nothing else to do. *You're a city girl. Remember what he thinks of city girls.* But it wasn't like she planned to stay on the ranch longer than Maisie needed her. So she sat beside him.

Dolly found a long blade of grass and began playing with the kitten. Soon they had moved a few feet away.

It was rather pleasant sitting in the shade with a man who took the time to help a little girl. She knew not all men were so kind. Nor were all cowboys. Levi must be a breed of his own.

"You never did tell me why it was so important that you have a job." His words ended her pleasant thoughts.

"I don't think my reasons would matter to you."

"Why not? Because I'm just a half-breed cowboy who doesn't have normal feelings?"

She could not miss the hurt in his voice and shifted to look into his eyes. "I never meant anything of the sort, nor do I think it." She waited as his expression softened. "You give me reason to think someone you cared about said those words to you." Seeing a flash of pain in his eyes, she wondered if she should drop the subject. "Did they?"

"Half-breeds belong in no-man's-land."

"Who says?"

"People."

She waited but from the stubborn set of his jaw she knew she would get no more from him. Nor could she say why it mattered. Normally she would not have shown half so much interest in what a man thought, or why. Perhaps that was why she'd believed Henry St. James truly cared for her.

Thankfully, Levi, too, chose not to press her for her reason for needing a job.

What would she have said if he did? Would he be sympathetic to her plight, or see it as proof she didn't belong in the country?

Chapter Six

How had she guessed so accurately why he believed what he did about himself? Yes, he'd heard it off and on most of his life, but when Helen had said things that made him think being a half-breed made him unacceptable, his heart had taken the words and stored them.

Levi told himself it was time to get back to work but still he sat beside Beatrice watching Dolly play. The only excuse he allowed himself was his concern for the child. "Why do you think she whispers all the time?"

Beatrice told him how the child's mother had said Dolly must be quiet in order for her father to get better. "Maybe she blames herself for her papa's death and somehow, in her childish mind, she thinks if she doesn't make any noise, things will be okay."

"The poor child. Maybe it's wrong of me to encourage her to talk out loud. Am I just adding to her sense of guilt?"

"I honestly don't know."

They contemplated the situation for a few minutes

then Beatrice spoke. "I suppose we should let her find her own way. All we can do is help her feel safe."

Dolly had gotten several yards away and glanced over her shoulder to see where Levi and Beatrice were. She walked back and edged between them.

Beatrice and Levi grinned at each other over her head.

"Seems she feels safe with us," Beatrice murmured.

He grinned at her. "I kind of like knowing that."

"Me, too."

He held her gaze, searching for and finding a sense of belonging even if it was only because they shared a concern for this orphaned child. With a guilty start, he realized he'd never felt this sense of unity with Helen. With her, it had always been about earning her favor.

He broke the eye connection first, knowing his thoughts had gone to dangerous territory. She was a city girl, with secrets. She was only here to do a job then she would leave. And he did not intend to open his heart to more pain.

But his eyes wanted to return to hers, to explore further, perhaps even to let her glimpse something in his own heart. Instead of listening to the demands of his heart, he focused his attention on her hand, resting on Dolly's knee.

Without giving himself time to change his mind, he placed his hand on Dolly's other knee. So much for not listening to his heart.

The three of them sat together. No one spoke. No one moved.

Contentment eased away the sting of Helen's words. He could get used to this feeling.

"Levi, come quick." The urgency of Charlie's call jolted Levi to his feet and he raced toward the sound.

"What is it?" he asked as soon as he was close enough.

"There's something wrong with one of the mares. She's down and can't get up."

He didn't bother to get any more details from Charlie, but raced past him to the horse pasture. He immediately saw the mare Charlie was concerned about. She was in the far corner, stretched out, her legs clumped together in an odd manner.

Levi vaulted the fence and jogged across the grass, alert to any dangers. He suspected the mischief makers had something to do with this. He knew he was right before he reached the mare's side.

"Whoa. Take it easy." He slowed and approached the struggling mare cautiously. Someone had tied her legs with a thin rope and the animal had managed to further entangle her legs. "Whoa. Whoa." He signaled for Charlie to stay back and caught a glimpse of Beatrice and Dolly at the fence, but he remained focused on the horse.

He reached her head and held her until she stopped struggling, then he began to unwind the rope from her limbs, a task that required a lot of pulling and tugging. Finally he freed the mare and spoke soothingly as he rubbed his hands along her legs, searching for injuries or hot spots. She seemed fine but he'd use some liniment just to be sure. Fashioning a halter to put on her, he led her across the pasture.

Charlie waited at the gate and opened it to let them out.

"She doesn't seem to be limping," Levi observed with relief.

"How did it happen?" Charlie demanded. "This is worse than leaving a gate down."

"They must have done it while we were having breakfast." Or while he sat in the shade enjoying his time with Beatrice and Dolly. "Thankfully she hasn't been tangled long." He waited for Charlie to close the gate, not leaving until he was certain the gate was good and tight.

Beatrice and Dolly stood several yards away, observing it all.

How was he to show the little girl she was safe if someone kept causing trouble? He could only hope that, at five, Dolly was old enough to start to put together how bad things happened yet life could be safe, especially if there were people to help you. He hoped she'd seen him as one of those who would help. "You want to watch me rub her leg?" he asked.

She nodded.

"Then come along." He signaled for them to come to his side, feeling again a taste of contentment as the three of them led the mare to the barn. He tied her up and showed Beatrice and Dolly where to stand so they could see and yet not alarm the mare. Then he went to the tack room, found the liniment and returned. He poured the liquid into his cupped hands and smoothed it over first one of the mare's legs and then another until he had done them all. There was something soothing about massaging the animal's limbs, his head pressed to her flank.

"Is she hurt?" Dolly whispered.

"I think she's okay." He'd have to keep a much closer watch on the animals.

"You saved her," Dolly added.

He appreciated the child's approval even though it was partially unwarranted. If he hadn't untangled the horse, Charlie would have. And if neither of them had been nearby? Likely the mare would have realized she couldn't free herself and lain down to wait for rescue.

At least the culprits hadn't used wire.

Dolly climbed off the fence where she's been watching and went to the doorway to play in the sunshine with Smokey.

"I'm just a city girl," Beatrice said. "But I know this animal could have been seriously hurt. Why would anyone do such a thing?"

"I don't know and it's not knowing that frustrates me. I haven't been able to catch anyone in the act. I've seen tracks and I've tried to follow them. That's what I was doing when I came across you in the river."

"I appreciate you rescuing me."

He glanced up in time to catch pink stealing across her cheeks. Was she embarrassed at having to be rescued? Or did she think of him carrying her from the water? He smiled at the pleasure the memory gave him and wondered if she shared any degree of the feeling.

She met his eyes and the pink deepened.

He ducked his head, concentrating on the horse's legs. If the pink meant anything, perhaps she enjoyed the memory.

"I take it you've never caught up to them."

"No. They are smart enough to ride over rocks, or through the river, or otherwise hide their tracks and

I have not found any sign of a camp. They don't do anything very serious. Even this—" he indicated the mare's legs "—was done with rope rather than wire. I just wish I knew what they were up to."

"Are you saying that they are just making a nuisance of themselves? But for what purpose?"

"I don't know."

"Could they be hoping to keep you distracted so they can do something else?"

He sat back on his heels. "I've wondered about that but I can't think what. The cows are all in pastures to the west and there are plenty of cowboys keeping an eye on them. The only thing here is the horses and the people."

She gasped. "Like me? Are they after me?"

He straightened and went to the fence so they stood face-to-face only a foot apart. "This started days before you came but never mind that. Why would you think someone would be after you?"

She shifted so he saw only her profile. "There's no reason. I overreacted."

"Beatrice, are you running from someone? Do I have reason to worry someone might be after you?"

"No, no. Nothing like that."

He caught her chin and turned her face to his. Her eyes darted past him. "Beatrice, I can't keep everyone safe if I don't know what to expect. I think you better tell me what you're afraid of."

Slowly her gaze came to him. "I don't think there is any cause for you to be concerned."

"Perhaps you can let me be the judge of that." He

kept his finger and thumb on her chin so she couldn't turn away.

She swallowed hard. Her eyes begged for mercy.

His almost released her, but if she was in any kind of danger, he wanted to know. Not just for the sake of the ranch, or even Maisie. But for her sake, as well. He would protect her. "I need to know." He spoke softly, calmly, much as he had spoken to the mare, though he didn't feel at all like he had with the horse. And he wasn't about to examine that thought right now.

"I suppose you could say I'm running," she said. "From my father."

His fingers gentled, brushing more than holding as he sensed her pain. "Why?"

She sucked in air. "I wasn't willing to go along with his plans for me."

"Such as?" he persisted.

Her eyes sparked gold daggers. "Marry a man of his choosing simply because he needed a suitable son-in-law, seeing as I did the unspeakable by being born a girl, leaving him without a male heir."

He blinked at her sudden anger. "You didn't care for the man?"

"Men who only wanted to become the Doyle heir." Her eyes filled with hurt that tore at his innards. "I will be more than someone's means of getting ahead. My father sent me to my aunt Opal in the hopes I would come to my senses." She snorted. "I have no such intention. I don't need his money. I will learn to support myself."

A chain of emotions raced through Levi—sadness at how she'd been treated, admiration at her determination to stand on her own and a great urge to pull her into his arms and comfort her. He understood she tried to appear strong but he saw the flicker of uncertainty in her eyes.

She turned and his fingers dropped from her chin to her shoulder. He pulled her toward him but the fence stood between them. If he wasn't mistaken, she leaned into the fence as if wishing it was not there.

"Beatrice, I believe you will find your own way."

"Yes, I will. And that means I'd better tend to my duties. Thank you for…" She waved her hand without finishing. As if not knowing what she was thankful for.

He watched her leave, torn between an urge to run after her and tell her he would help her be the person she wanted to be and the fading warning uttered by his brain that he was not the sort of person she needed to assist her. Perhaps he should tell her so and take her back to town. But how could he? Maisie needed help. Dolly needed a place to learn to feel safe again and he…

Well, he needed nothing but an answer to who was causing trouble on the ranch.

"First, we need potatoes and carrots. They're in the garden. You'll have to dig some for supper."

Maisie's words made it sound so easy. She knew where potatoes came from, but she'd never personally been involved with getting them.

Maisie gave her directions to the garden. "Dolly, do you want to stay with me?" Maisie had given her a bit of yarn to use to play with Smokey.

"Okay," Dolly whispered.

Maisie smiled at the child and continued her instructions. "The potatoes are to the right of the gate, the carrots to the left. The digging fork is by the fence. Take a basin to bring them back in."

Every word made sense until she reached the garden. To the right were all sorts of plants. Which ones were potatoes?

Levi crossed the yard—the last person she wanted to see right now. She did not want anyone to know how truly citified she was. How ill-prepared she was for this job. She did not want anyone to see how much it hurt to know how little her father had valued her. Or perhaps how greatly he valued her, but for the wrong reasons. At least in her mind. Why had she told Levi? She might excuse it by saying she'd been touched by his gentleness with Dolly. By how he seemed content to sit in the shade with Beatrice and the child. Or perhaps it was triggered by watching his careful tending of the mare. But most likely it was because of the way he caught her chin and held it so firmly yet gently, triggering within her a need for more of the same. Not until that moment had she realized she was starved for kind and gentle touches which had been almost nonexistent in her life.

Now she felt embarrassed and exposed before him.

The thud of footsteps came closer.

Go away. Please go away.

"Lose something?"

She straightened. "No. Just looking at—" she kicked at the soil, desperate for a reasonable explanation of her purpose "—at the garden."

He grinned. "See you found it. 'Course it's kind of

hard to miss what with the scarecrow in the middle, the fence around it and all the plants inside the fence."

He seemed to be enjoying this greatly. What did he think of her awkward confession? Oh, if only she could hope someone would see her for who she was, who she wanted to be.

Who was that? An independent, self-sufficient woman who needed no man to take care of her, she firmly informed herself. And best she not forget it.

She hadn't noticed the scarecrow and turned to study it. It stood amidst the plants, a stuffed shirt, stuffed pair of trousers and a face drawn on a gunnysack. The mouth held a corncob pipe. One eye winked. There were even whiskers and scraggly hair. Despite herself, she chuckled. "Could it be fashioned after a relative of yours?"

He laughed. "How did you guess? It's my uncle six times removed."

It took too much effort to remain upset and she turned back to him, a smile cheering her heart.

He grinned, his dark eyes twinkling.

She couldn't remember why she was supposed to be annoyed as their gazes went on and on. *Independent, self-sufficient. Remember?* With a great deal of effort, she tore her gaze away and kicked at the soil.

"Are you here after potatoes?"

"Yes…and carrots." She would not admit she didn't know how to get them, had never in her entire life dug in the dirt. Why, Father would be shocked and Mother would swoon if they suspected what she was doing. However, she thought with some degree of sharpness, their opinion no longer concerned her.

Levi grabbed a digging tool—the fork, she could tell that—and pulled out a green plant, tossed it aside and eased away the soil to reveal a little nest of potatoes.

She fell to her knees, unmindful of the damp earth, and gingerly picked each potato from the dirt. An unusual, though not unpleasant, aroma wafted over her. Closing her eyes, she breathed deeply, filling her lungs and her soul with a scent that seemed to breathe life itself.

"There's nothing like the smell of freshly turned soil. Makes a person grateful." Levi stopped suddenly.

She understood he wondered if she shared similar thoughts and likely imagined all she cared about was not getting her hands dirty. She meant to disabuse him of the notion and rose to face him, nothing but the mound of potatoes separating them, and told him of her thoughts regarding the soil.

He chuckled. "'Breathe life itself.' I like that. Are you by any chance a poet?" His words tingled her brain. No one had ever before admired her way with words. In fact, Father had often told her men didn't fancy a woman who spoke of things that should only interest a man. She took that to mean they didn't care for a woman to be too intelligent...maybe afraid it would make them feel less so. But Levi had approved. Said he liked it. And she liked that he liked it.

Remembering he'd asked a question, she answered. "Not a poet, though I do admit to liking words."

He chuckled. "That might mean a number of things. It could mean you talk a lot or that—" He shrugged and looked slightly embarrassed.

"Or what?" She longed to know what he thought.

"I was going to say the first thing that popped into my mind but perhaps it isn't appropriate. You being a city gal and high-society and me being a ranch man and working-class." She didn't care for the way he drawled the words, as if mocking her opinion.

"Here I stand in the middle of a garden, my hands soiled from picking potatoes from the ground, and you call me a high-society girl? Surely you jest."

He grinned, obviously pleased with her response. "I confess it's hard to think of you as such at the moment."

Warmth trickled through her heart at his approval. "So tell me what you were going to say."

"Okay. I might have been going to suggest you are deeply touched by nature." He looked to the right of her ear as if the words made him uncomfortable.

But they filled her with a strange wonderment. She tipped her head and considered what it meant. "You might be right. I found the drive out here exceedingly—" She paused as she sought for the right word.

His gaze came back to her. "Yes?"

A smile warmed her eyes. "Fulfilling. Yes, it was fulfilling to see everything. The trees, the flowers, the mountains…even the grass. I had no idea it grew in such a variety of colors. Sage, fern, moss, mint, olive—" She lifted her hands to indicate she couldn't express herself the way she wanted to. "So many. Of course, my opinion changed somewhat when the heavens opened and poured out rain."

"Indeed." His smile did not mock or belittle. No, it filled his eyes and made her want to stand there until darkness fell. "Oh, no." She pressed a hand to her mouth. "I forgot I'm making dinner." She gathered up the rest of the potatoes, took the basin and hurried away.

"Don't you need carrots, too?" His voice stopped her in her tracks and slowly she retraced her steps.

"I forgot."

Levi gave a brief nod of understanding and stopped at a row of feathery ferns.

She stared as he dug out bright orange carrots. "All these are carrots?" There were several rows of them.

"We store them for winter use. Remember, what we don't grow or produce ourselves, we don't eat. That's the way it is out in the country." He studied her, as if waiting for a response.

If he thought she would say it was much easier to get things at the market or from a street vendor, he would have to wait a long time, especially considering she usually got them served on a china plate. "It must be so satisfying to produce what you need."

"Yes, it is."

"I expect I'll know the same satisfaction when I know I can take care of myself."

His gaze went from her eyes to her chin, as if remembering, then he nodded. "I suppose so."

"Thanks for your help." She started to leave but then hesitated. "I'm grateful for this opportunity to learn more."

"Think nothing of it."

She hurried back to the house, pausing at the door to glance back.

He leaned against the garden gate, watching her.

She stood at the door without reaching for the doorknob. Why was he still looking at her? She wished she could see his face better and perhaps read his expression.

Then she realized she was watching him, as well. Why? It wasn't like his kindness meant anything except he was a kind man. She entered the house wondering who had made him so certain that being a half-breed meant a woman wouldn't be interested in him.

That didn't mean her, of course. She had other ambitions. But surely others found him as attractive and appealing as she did.

She shut the door firmly behind her as if by doing so, she could shut her thoughts to such nonsense.

Chapter Seven

Levi watched the door for several seconds after it had closed then slowly, reluctantly, turned away. She'd liked the smell of the earth and the greens of the grass. He'd never heard anyone speak of it in such terms before, giving him a new appreciation for the things he'd known every day of his life.

Maybe she'd like to see more of the colors of nature. Wouldn't she enjoy the blue valley to the west and the dark pines a little higher up? Then there were the mountains. Of course she'd seen them already. She couldn't be in Western Montana and not see them but they changed as one got closer. She'd like that. And what about the waterfalls by Johnny and Willow's home and the trees where Ma had liked to worship God. He'd surely have to take her those places, too.

Whoa, right there. Have you forgotten who you are?

Had she?

He hurried to the barn to start cleaning it.

But a little later, when the dinner bell rang, he had

not succeeded in putting an end to dreaming of all the places he'd like to take her.

He took his time about emptying the wheelbarrow and putting away the shovel.

Charlie waited at the barn door. "I'm hungry enough to eat burned chops and half-cooked potatoes, though at the speed you're moving, the potatoes will be cooked to mush by the time we get there."

"Just putting stuff away."

"Where you figure it's gonna go?"

He ignored Charlie's insinuation that he was stalling. "I'm ready." They fell into step as they crossed the yard.

"You trying to avoid Beatrice?" Charlie asked.

"Why would I want to do that?" Little did Charlie know that it was all Levi could do not to break into a run and see Beatrice a few minutes sooner than their current pace would allow.

Charlie chuckled. "I didn't say you *wanted* to. In fact, ever since you spent half the morning entertaining her I kind of think you *want* to see her even though since Helen you've avoided women like they're poison."

Levi didn't answer. He could hardly deny it and he sure wasn't going to admit it, although there had been Fern, but their friendship had been short-lived, hardly worth mentioning.

"Beatrice seems awfully nice, doesn't she? What with how she tries so hard to get things right and how she takes care of little Dolly."

Levi hoped Charlie was done but his cousin slid in one more jab.

"Not at all like Helen."

They reached the house, saving Levi from having to respond. Yes, Beatrice was different from Helen, but he couldn't say for certain just how. Nor if that meant she saw past his mixed heritage. Not, he firmly informed himself, that it mattered one way or the other.

They entered the house. Levi did his best to keep his attention on everything but Beatrice. He saw that Maisie looked comfortable, with a book, her Bible and the sewing basket on a stool nearby so she didn't have to move about to get her things.

Dolly stayed close to Beatrice, cautious of the men. Levi blinked as he realized she didn't seem to be afraid of him…only Charlie. It took only a tiny shift for his eyes to go to Beatrice. Their gazes crashed together, hers as full of interest and uncertainty as he figured his was. He might have stood there all day, staring and wondering what this strange connection meant, except Charlie nudged him.

"You gonna sit down?"

Levi found his confused way to the table and sat. He somehow managed to ask the blessing. He took the serving bowl as it was passed to him and spooned thick stew to his plate. He ate it but his thoughts were not on his food. How could they be with Beatrice sitting across the table from him?

She hadn't put her hair up today and it hung down her back in a pale brown tumble. Strands fell about her face.

"Stew is sure good. Right, Levi?" Charlie's question jerked Levi's attention back to reality.

"Yeah, it's good. Thanks."

Did she blush at his faint praise?

They finished the meal without him saying anything to make Charlie sit up and take notice. But Levi didn't relax until Charlie excused himself and left the house, saying he had something to do. He never thought to ask what Charlie's plans were. Nor did he care. He savored another cup of coffee as he watched Beatrice wash dishes and Dolly dry them.

As Charlie had noted, she was very good with the girl and Dolly seemed to feel safe with her.

Maisie yawned. "I'm tired. Levi, help me to my bed, then you and Beatrice take Dolly out and amuse her for an hour or two."

"Yes, Ma." He let her lean on his arm as they went to her bedroom. "How is your leg, Ma?"

"It's a little sore but it's not bleeding. Beatrice checked to make sure." She settled herself on her bed and closed her eyes. "You run along and take care of her and the girl."

Dismissed, he returned to the kitchen, where Beatrice and Dolly had finished the dishes. "Maisie wants us to leave her alone to rest. What would you like to do?"

Dolly picked up Smokey from where the cat sat by the stove lapping up milk. "Mrs. Harding told me about the mice in the loft. Smokey really wants to see them."

He wanted to tell Dolly she didn't have to keep whispering, but he glanced at Beatrice, saw her silent warning and nodded.

"Are you ready, then?" he asked, holding out his hand to Dolly, half expecting she would shrink back from him. When she took his hand and gave him a shy smile he couldn't help but grin. Beatrice took her other hand and gave him a smile of understanding.

Feeling as if they were a three-person unit, they edged from the house and went to the barn.

Dolly went directly to the ladder to the loft then paused, looking from Smokey to the ladder.

"Do you want me to hold your kitten until you get up there?"

She nodded and solemnly released the kitten to him.

Feeling honored by her trust, he cradled the cat in his arms.

Dolly scampered up the ladder with the sure-foot-edness of a child who had done it before. She reached the top and held out her hands to receive the kitten.

He climbed three rungs and placed Smokey in her hands, then climbed the rest of the way and turned to Beatrice. He'd expected to have to urge her up but she poked her head through the opening before he said a word.

He held out his hand to help her to her feet and kept her hand in his as she stood and looked around. The loft doors stood open letting in a blast of sunshine.

Beatrice breathed deeply then sneezed.

He laughed. "It's dusty up here."

"Look at the dust floating in the light. It looks like it's dancing."

Dolly had gone to the far corner and put Smokey down to explore.

Levi led Beatrice to the doorway that allowed a wide view of the mountains to the west.

Her grasp on his hand tightened and she stared at the sight. "You can see forever."

"Only as far as the mountains," he amended with laughter in his voice.

She sighed. "I could never tire of a view like this. It makes me feel—" She stopped and cleared her throat. When she continued, she sounded choked. "Like a part of a great plan."

"Let's sit." He had to release her hand to allow her to sit on the floor, her dark purple skirt fanning out about her.

He sat cross-legged at her side and they both looked out the door. He pointed out various landmarks and enjoyed her comments about them. It was hard to believe she was a city girl.

Harder still to remember he was a half-breed and could never be accepted in her world.

Dolly squealed, bringing their attention to her.

"I wish she would feel safe enough to talk out loud," he said.

"She's been through an awful shock. Bad enough to lose your parents, but to be there as they died..." She shuddered. "I can't even imagine it. Sometimes I wonder if she will be permanently affected, but then I watch her playing and think she seems resilient."

"I expect she'll need lots of love and patience. I pray her aunt will provide it."

"Me, too." She turned her gaze to him, full of rich gold and caring. "Let's agree to each pray for her every day."

He nodded. He couldn't have said no to her if he wanted to, which he didn't. He had already been praying for Dolly, but to know he and Beatrice had a pledge to both do so forged a bond between them.

He reached for her hand just as she reached for his and they squeezed each other's fingers. Never mind that she was white and a city girl and he was dark-skinned and a country boy. They were united in this one thing.

Likely the only thing they would be united on, he warned himself.

That evening, Beatrice watched Dolly sleeping, then crossed to the window and looked out at the silvery landscape. She saw such beauty around her that, at times, she felt overwhelmed. If only she could paint what she saw or find words to describe it.

Or that she could find words to describe Levi.

She closed her eyes against the tremor racing along her veins.

What had happened to her vow to never again trust a man? To become entirely independent so no man could ever think she needed him so badly she would be co-erced into marriage like her father wanted.

It seemed every time she was with Levi she forgot the pain of learning her value to others, thinking only of the way the skin about his eyes softened just before he laughed, enjoying the way he described various places and things they saw, or, most telling of all, finding his touch so reassuring.

Only when she was alone did she hear the insistent warning voice that she knew she must heed.

She sat on the chair next to the bed and opened her Bible. *Lord God, I need comfort and guidance. Help me not to lose my way. Show me the path I should take.* Glancing down, she saw that God had answered her prayer most directly and read the verse: *No man, having put his hand to the plough, and looking back, is fit for the kingdom of God.* She had no idea what Jesus had meant when He spoke the words, but they drove a spear through her conscience. She'd prayed for a way to gain independence and God had provided this job. She must not let her silly thoughts distract her from her goal.

Her mind settled as to what she must do, she finished preparing for bed and climbed in beside Dolly and Smokey. As usual, the child murmured in her sleep and curled up against Beatrice.

Beatrice wrapped her arms about Dolly and held her close. She trusted God had brought her here for another purpose besides learning how to run a household. Dolly needed whatever comfort and security Beatrice could offer until her aunt was able to make arrangements regarding her.

Going to family was certainly the best, most comforting thing for Dolly, but Beatrice had already grown exceedingly fond and protective of the little girl and would miss her terribly when they parted.

Her plans were solidly in place the next morning when she and Dolly hurried to the kitchen—Dolly to take her kitten outside and Beatrice to start coffee and prepare breakfast. But they slid sideways at the sight of Levi by the stove, watching her approach.

Her footsteps slowed and she veered to her right straight to the cupboard, opened it and tried to think what she wanted.

Levi poured a cup of coffee for himself, another for Maisie, and went to the table.

Beatrice continued to stare into the cupboard. How was she to keep her mind centered on her work, her goals and protecting her heart when he filled the room? Filled her thoughts. Threatened to fill her heart.

She grabbed the nearest object, glad to see it was a jar of jam. At least taking that from the cupboard would make sense, but she stood holding the jar and still staring at the shelves as behind her Levi and Maisie discussed Big Sam.

"I wish he would get home," Maisie said.

"I wish he would stay away until your leg is better," Levi countered. "He's not going to be happy with either of us."

Maisie chuckled. "His anger won't last long. I will see to that."

Levi laughed. "I best get the chores done and make sure Charlie is okay."

"He's doing better, isn't he?" Maisie asked, her voice rife with concern.

"So far." Levi pushed away from the table.

Beatrice could not continue to keep her back to him—she must know if he would look her way—so she slowly turned.

He stood at the door, his hat in hand. Their gazes caught with such force, she forgot to breathe. His smile began at his eyes and then caught his mouth. "I'll be back for breakfast." With a tiny nod, he was gone.

Her lungs filled with a whoosh. Her thoughts took a little longer to begin working and might have taken even longer if Maisie hadn't suggested making porridge for breakfast.

By the time the meal was ready and she stepped

outside to ring the bell, Beatrice had herself firmly in hand. She would not forget the plans she'd formulated for her life.

She made it through breakfast without being side-tracked and spent the rest of the morning cleaning the house. She realized that it was hard work to mop floors, but she discovered a great deal of satisfaction from see-ing the floors gleaming.

Dinner turned out quite well. She would soon be confident enough to manage a few meals on her own so that when she left here she would qualify for an-other job.

Pain grabbed at her insides. She held very still until it passed, determined to ignore it. Yes, she would leave here. She'd known it from the beginning. Nothing had changed.

She might have continued to hold her feelings in check except Maisie sighed wearily. "I really need a rest. Levi, help me to my room then you and Beatrice take Dolly out for an hour or two again."

No, Beatrice wanted to wail. Yes, her heart sang with joy. Only, she argued, because she loved seeing the scenery and animals. Not, she insisted, because she looked forward to another outing with Levi. And Dolly, she added quickly.

Dolly looked pleased at the idea and grabbed a towel to dry the dishes.

Beatrice could not refuse…not with the suggestion coming from Maisie and with Dolly anticipating the outing. Besides, who was she to argue about a few hours in the company of the very man whose presence made her forget every promise she'd made herself about guarding her heart?

Levi returned grinning widely. "Ma says we should go see the burrowing owls. Would you like that?"

Dolly nodded. "Can I take Smokey?"

"I think she better stay here this time. The little owls might not come out if they see a cat." His gaze slid to Beatrice's. "Do you want to see the owls?"

She couldn't keep the joy and anticipation from her lips, nor from her voice. "I'd love to." She put away the last dry dish, hung the towels to dry and waited while Dolly made sure Smokey was content on a blanket by the stove.

Levi led the way outside and guided them eastward, past the ranch buildings and across a grassy pasture. They came to rocky soil and Levi reached out a hand to help Beatrice. She tried to convince herself she hadn't been hoping he'd do exactly that, but gladly took his hand as her shoes slipped on the rocks.

He was close to her side and murmured, "This is one of the places where I lose the trail of whoever is responsible for the mischief on the place." He slowed and looked about. She did the same and saw nothing to give her cause to be concerned.

He sighed. "They seem to be able to vanish."

"You'll catch them one of these days."

He chuckled. "Thanks for the vote of confidence." Dolly had been examining the rocks and picking up small ones to stuff in her pocket. Levi called her to them. "We're almost there and we'll have to sit and be absolutely quiet if we want to see them." He indicated a good-sized boulder and he and Beatrice sat side by side with Dolly leaning against their knees.

Beatrice squeezed one of Dolly's shoulders and chanced a quick glance at Levi. The quick glance turned into a long considering look. She felt as if he had walked through a door in her heart and found himself at home. Or was she talking about her own feelings of having found herself at home in his heart?

"Where are they?" Dolly asked in her usual quiet whisper.

Levi broke the connection and pointed to the grassy knoll a hundred feet away. "Over there," he whispered. "They've gone underground at our approach but will come back out if we're quiet. They're very curious little fellows."

Beatrice followed the direction he pointed. The only thing to see at the moment was a mound of dirt but their patience was soon rewarded. One little yellow-eyed head poked from the hole. Then four owlets crowded out and stood at attention. They bobbed their heads, danced and jostled for position. One twisted his head sideways as if wondering what the world looked like from a different angle. One seemed to be scolding the others. Several minutes later, a shadow passed over them and they scurried back into the hole, almost getting stuck as they tried to all get in at once.

Beatrice laughed softly. "What little clowns. Thank you for showing them to me." She didn't recall taking his hand again, but somehow or other their fingers were intertwined and he squeezed.

"My brothers and I always enjoy watching them. When we were younger, it was hard for all three of us to be quiet." He lowered his head to talk to Dolly. "You did very well. Did you like them?"

She nodded vigorously. "Will they come out again?"

"Maybe. But only if we are very quiet. Why don't we move farther away so we can talk without them feeling threatened?" He got to his feet and pulled Beatrice after him. They retreated several yards to sit on another boulder.

If she wasn't mistaken this one was considerably smaller than the other. Their shoulders pressed together.

Dolly watched the burrow for a while then lost interest and turned her attention to rock hunting.

Beatrice studied the scenery. From where they sat, a vista of rolling grass, crisscrossed with trees, lay before her. Yellow and gold dotted the groves. "The leaves are beginning to change color."

"Fall is almost upon us."

"Is it a busy time of year for you?" She wanted to know everything about ranch life. Even more, she wanted to prolong their sojourn in this place.

"It is. We have to round up the cows and brand the calves that were born over the summer. We move the cows down from the high pastures so they don't get snowed in. As winter deepens the stock is moved into pastures by the barn so we can throw feed out for them if we need to."

She chuckled. "It sounds to me like you enjoy the season."

He shifted to look directly at her. "I love all the seasons."

She studied his dark intensity. "Tell me about the other seasons."

He told of the excitement of spring when everything was burgeoning with new life. He spoke of the more busy days of summer, when they rode the range, keeping an eye on the herds, worked with new horses and put up feed. "Winter is our slow time unless we have to deal with a snowstorm."

"What do you do to pass the time?"

"Fix harnesses, take care of the animals in the barn. The winter evenings are long. We read a lot. And play checkers." He laughed. "Big Sam considers himself the reigning champion so when one of us boys beats him, he won't let us go to bed until he wins." He laughed again, causing Beatrice to think he enjoyed the competition with his father. "I've lots of times let him win just so I could get some sleep."

She chuckled. "It sounds like fun."

"What did you and your family do for entertainment?"

The joy of the moment evaporated at his question. Her life seemed so barren and artificial. Her former life, she corrected. Realizing he waited for her answer, she gathered her thoughts. "We entertained a lot." Always those who were socially suitable and, in hindsight, dreadfully dull. "There were teas and literary gatherings."

"Wait. What are literary gatherings?"

She looked past him, almost embarrassed to admit what they involved. But he waited. "People would take turns reading from different books in the hopes of interesting us in the book of their choice."

"That might be interesting."

"Sometimes. But often it was simply a way of trying to look superior to others so those who read would pick books that were dreadfully dull." She brightened as she remembered one man who never followed that trend. "Mr. Munroe always read from really popular books like those by Mark Twain or Robert Louis Stevenson."

For a little while they talked about the books they enjoyed.

Suddenly, Levi bolted to his feet. "Look where the sun is. We better get back before Maisie worries about us. And what if she tries to get to the kitchen herself? She'll start that wound bleeding again." They called Dolly to join them.

He held her hand as they crossed the rough ground and continued to hold it even when they reached the grass, but more, she thought, to make certain she kept up a good pace than because he enjoyed the contact.

They reached the house and he bolted through the door and strode to Maisie's room. Beatrice heard the relief in his voice when he saw she was in bed, waiting for him to help her.

Beatrice solemnly turned her attention toward supper preparations. Levi's sudden switch from interested to remembering his duties was exactly the reminder she needed to bring her thoughts back to where they belonged.

How could she so easily let them wander down a forbidden trail?

Chapter Eight

Levi hurried from the house and trotted to the barn. What had he been thinking to sit out in the sun for half the afternoon? If Maisie had tried to get up... He shuddered. He would blame himself if something happened to her. Even worse, Big Sam would also hold him responsible

He'd left Charlie with the task of oiling the harnesses and went to the tack room to check on his cousin. "Charlie?" Only the rustling of mice overhead and the gentle lowing of the milk cow. Levi checked each stall. No Charlie.

He jogged to the bunkhouse. Evidence of where Charlie had slept but no Charlie. Perhaps he'd gone to the cookhouse for something. Levi turned his steps that direction, his nerves growing more tense with each step. He knew Charlie would be feeling the lack of strong drink by now. He should have been around to help his cousin through the yearning.

He opened the door to the cookhouse, not expecting to find anyone there. Nevertheless, he called, "Charlie, are you here?" A quick glance revealed nothing. He was about to turn and look elsewhere when he heard a scuffling. He crossed the floor to look on the other side of the cupboard. "What are you doing?" His cousin was on his hands and knees as if searching for something. "You won't find a bottle here."

Charlie sat back on his heels. "I'm not looking for a bottle."

"Then what are you doing? Praying?" He didn't mean to mock but Charlie had never been a praying man.

"Maybe I should. Or maybe you could."

Was Charlie trying to warn him of something? He squatted down beside Charlie. "Why? What's wrong?"

"Why do you care?" Charlie scowled deeply. "You expect everyone to be perfect, just like you."

"I do not."

Charlie nodded. "Yes, you do. Levi, you're my cousin and all, but you're a hard man."

The unfair accusation stung. "Hard? How can you say that? I consider myself kind, gentle and caring."

Charlie continued looking at the floor.

"Tell me what you're looking for and I'll look with you." He'd prove Charlie wrong by helping him.

"I lost my special five-cent piece. I took it out to look at and I dropped it. Now I can't find it."

Levi eased his breath out. Fine, he'd crawl around on the floor looking for five cents if that's what it took. They crawled the length of the floor. They poked under the cupboard. "I'm sorry, Charlie. I don't see your coin. Look, I'll give you five cents."

Charlie stood up and faced Levi. "I knew you wouldn't understand."

Levi tossed his hands upward in frustration. "Explain it to me."

"My pa gave it to me. He said, 'Charlie, there will be times you forget who you are and why you matter. When you do, you take this coin out and remember that you matter to me and your ma. You matter to God.' So long as I have that coin all I has to do is look at it and remember I matter to someone even if I am a drunken half-breed like you say."

Levi's heart smote him. "Charlie, I didn't mean it that way. You are somebody and you matter. Now let's find that coin."

They both returned to their hands and knees and again searched the floor. The light under the cupboards was poor, so Levi lit the lantern and held it to shine light along the floor.

"I see it," Charlie said and eased the coin from under the cupboard. Grinning widely, he stood to his feet. "Thanks, Levi. You're a good cousin." He tucked the coin into his pocket and left the cookhouse.

Levi watched out the window as Charlie crossed the yard to the bunkhouse. Despite his final words, Charlie's accusations burned deep inside. He wasn't a hard man.

Something else Charlie had said earlier burned through Levi's brain. He'd said that Levi acted like women were poison. He rubbed his finger along the dusty window ledge. Beatrice wasn't like poison in any way. More like roses and perfume. She seemed friendly and accepting of him.

But if Helen had proved anything, it was that it was okay to be friends with the likes of Levi when they weren't in the company of others.

He wasn't hard, he mentally argued. He was careful. After all, a man didn't step on a cactus without getting spines in his foot. And he wasn't likely to be so careless again about trusting.

Nor would he forgive Helen for the way she'd hurt him.

Maisie's voice immediately sounded in his head. "Boys, there will always be people who offend us." She said basically the same thing many times, but Levi recalled an incident when the boys were on the cusp of adulthood and had gone to town on their own. Tanner had been set upon by three bullies and came out of the fight with a battered face. He reported to Maisie all the ugly things the trio had said about him. Tanner bore the most resemblance to their mother's kin and usually got the brunt of the cruel comments. Not that he ever walked away from the insults.

"We can keep track of all those offenses and they will soon become a burdensome weight on our shoulders. Or—" She kissed each of them on the forehead at this point. "We can forgive, leaving our offenders in the hands of a righteous God who judges all men fairly. Forgiveness is the only way to get rid of that load."

"How can I forgive?" Tanner had asked, his words harsh with anger and pain.

"Only by trusting God's fairness. And remember how Jesus so freely forgave each of us. Not because we deserve it."

He didn't know if Tanner ever truly believed those words until he met Susanne.

Levi wondered what it would take for him to be willing to forgive and forget the past.

Realizing it had been some time since he'd checked the entire ranch site, he hurried from the cookhouse and circled the buildings, looking for any sign of mischief. He completed his tour at the horse pasture. All the animals grazed contentedly. Their trough was full of water. He'd have to thank Charlie for that. The gate was securely fastened. Seeing everything was as it should be should have made him relax.

It didn't. He knew the troublemakers were only waiting for a time when they could sneak in without being caught. Having Charlie here had limited such opportunities, but Levi was certain the culprits were lying low, biding their time.

What did they want? Why didn't they simply knock on the door and tell him?

Beatrice managed to keep occupied throughout the next day with extra work in an attempt to keep from thinking of Levi. He'd come for breakfast and lunch but hurried away after each meal. And Maisie hadn't suggested they take Dolly out so she could rest.

"We do little work on Sunday," Maisie said, and then she chuckled.

Beatrice had lost track of the passing days so Maisie's announcement caught her off guard. Uncle Elwood would be working on his sermon for tomorrow. At least if he was able to get a break from caring for the sick. And Aunt Opal would be busy making soup to deliver to the ill. She missed them. With a start, she realized she missed them far more than her own parents, who had always been distant. The realization made her miss Aunt Opal and Uncle Elwood even more.

Maisie's voice brought her back to the work she must do today. "At least the men don't do anything but the essentials. But they still expect meals, so the women work. However, I've learned to do as much as possible on Saturdays so I can enjoy a quiet Sunday." She instructed Beatrice on how to make a huge pot of soup full of several kinds of vegetables and some chopped meat.

"Enough for Sunday or in case Sam comes back." Throughout the day, Maisie looked often at the door. When Big Sam hadn't returned by nightfall, she grew worried. "Things must be worse than they thought."

Dolly yawned widely.

"Come along, little one. I'll put you in bed." Beatrice waited, wondering if the girl would agree. Until now, she had refused to go until Beatrice did.

"Will you tell me a story?" Dolly whispered.

"Of course. It's my favorite part of the day."

Dolly beamed. "Mine, too." She stood, shyly watching Levi. She waited for him to notice her.

He looked about the room until his gaze found Dolly and he jerked as if surprised to see her. "Who are you?"

"I'm Dolly," she whispered then covered her mouth as she giggled.

"And what's that you have in your arms?"

"My cat, Smokey."

"Well, she looks like a very special cat."

Dolly nodded, dancing from foot to foot as if recognizing the teasing in Levi's eyes.

"I'm happy to hear she's special because…" Levi edged forward on his chair. "Because…" He sprang forward and swept Dolly into his arms and hugged her just tight enough to make her squirm. "Because a special girl like you deserves a special cat."

He rubbed his rough cheek against hers, bringing more laughter.

And then they both grew serious and studied each other with solemn expressions.

"You have a good sleep now, you hear."

"Will you be here when I get up?"

"Here or outside. I won't be far."

Satisfied with his assurances, she smiled. "Okay."

He put her down and patted her back.

Beatrice reached for her hand. "I'll put Dolly to bed then help you," she said to Maisie.

Maisie had told her that she wished Levi would marry. "He is so good with children. He deserves a good woman and a family of his own."

Beatrice agreed but understood she wouldn't qualify even if she was interested, which, of course, she wasn't. A good woman would know how to run the ranch home, how to ride a horse, certainly how to grow a garden. Hadn't he said what they didn't grow, they didn't eat? And likely a good woman would know how to rope and brand and any number of things that were only words in Beatrice's mind. She had no idea how to do any of those things.

She took Dolly to their room and handed her the nightgown she'd worn every night. She'd love to take the child shopping for a new fine cotton nightie. It wasn't her right and she didn't want to offend the aunt. Dolly changed and waited for Beatrice to get positioned in the rocking chair Maisie had insisted they needed. She was right. Sitting and rocking the child proved soothing for both of them.

"Tell me a story," Dolly asked, once she had cuddled into a ball in Beatrice's lap, with Smokey in her arms.

"In the beginning, the earth was empty and dark." She told the story of creation.

Dolly sighed as she told how God made man and woman. "Then He gave them children, didn't He?"

"Yes, He did, but that's a story for another night."

Dolly didn't move and Beatrice waited. It was in these quiet moments that Dolly often opened up.

"What if He made the children first?"

Beatrice silently prayed for wisdom to answer the need of Dolly's heart. "God knew babies and little children need help. He sends children to families so they have someone to take care of them. Like Smokey. You aren't his mama but you take good care of him. Your aunt will do the same for you." She wished she could offer more but she couldn't. "Do you understand?"

"I guess so, but it won't be the same as Mama and Papa."

Beatrice had to swallow back the pain she felt at what this child would have to endure. "No, it won't. You will always miss your mama and papa and that's the way it should be. But God will never leave you. He will provide others to care for you and to love you." *Oh, God, please be sure she is loved.*

"Like you?"

It took a moment for Beatrice to realize what Dolly meant. "Yes, like me." It thrilled her to know the child felt her love.

"And Levi? And Maisie?"

"Yes, and Levi and Maisie." How wonderful that Dolly felt secure in this home.

She listened to the child's prayer then tucked her into bed. Dolly's eyes closed immediately. Despite the loss of her parents, Dolly seemed happy and secure.

If only she would start to speak not just in a whisper.

Beatrice tiptoed from the room. Levi had helped Maisie to her room and Beatrice went there to change Maisie's dressing and help her get comfortable in bed.

As soon as she was done, Maisie took Beatrice's hands. "Pray with me that the men are safe."

Understanding that Maisie needed someone else to do the praying, Beatrice asked God to keep and guard the men and bring them back soon.

"Thank you," Maisie murmured.

Beatrice slipped away to her own room, where Dolly already lay asleep. Levi had disappeared without saying good-night. It meant nothing, she assured herself. Besides, didn't she want to do her job and not be side-tracked by forbidden feelings?

Yes, she did.

But disappointment lay heavy on her heart as she fell asleep.

She wakened the next morning to a kiss from Smokey and a giggle from Dolly. She laughed and hugged the little girl before she scurried from bed. She dressed, did her hair and smoothed her bedcovers, then tiptoed to Maisie's room and tapped on the door. The older woman called for her to enter. Beatrice helped her dress then assisted her to the chair in the kitchen.

Levi entered the room. His black hair had been slicked back. He wore clean jeans and a black shirt with a bib yoke held in place by silver buttons.

He must have noticed the widening of her eyes. "Thought I could do with some cleaning up. Yesterday, Charlie said I was a sorry-looking mess."

"You clean up nicely." Oh, my. Why had she blurted out the first words that came to her mind? It wasn't as if she didn't know to guard her tongue.

He grinned and Maisie chuckled.

"Beatrice was about to fry up eggs for breakfast."

She was?

"Fry up some of those cooked potatoes first," Maisie said and Beatrice forced herself to concentrate on the task before her. She would not burn this meal. Maisie had taught her how to control the heat in the stove, but it proved harder to do than Maisie's words led her to believe. However, she was determined there would be no charcoal-flavored food today.

The potatoes browned nicely. The eggs were a little too hard but they weren't burnt.

She would not meet Levi's eyes as she concentrated on serving the food.

Maisie took Dolly's hand after she'd seated herself. "Levi, would you please ask the blessing?"

Beatrice reached across the table for Charlie's hand. As she bowed her head, she stole a glance at Levi from under the protection of her eyelashes.

He looked directly at her. She shut her eyes in a hurry.

"Dear God," he prayed. "Bless this food, bless the cook and bless all those we love. Amen."

Bless the cook? Did he mean it personally or was it simply a rote prayer? She again stole a look at him and was trapped by his dark-eyed intensity. She couldn't swallow. Couldn't tear away her gaze.

"Levi, pass the eggs to Charlie." Maisie's words enabled Beatrice to pull her attention to the food before her.

She would not let herself look at him the rest of the meal, though it took a great deal of effort, especially when he spoke.

"I wonder if I should check on Big Sam and the others."

"There's a crew up there. They'd let us know if they needed anything," Maisie said, but she sounded worried.

"I suppose you're right."

Maisie sighed softly. "Though I had hoped your pa would be back by Sunday."

"The job must have been tougher than they expected."

"Maybe they'll make it home yet today."

They finished the meal and Levi was about to push away when Maisie spoke again. "I'd like to have a little Sunday service."

"I thought you might want to," Levi said. "Charlie and I will come back after the kitchen is clean." The two of them left.

Beatrice drew in a deep breath for the first time since the meal began. Why did she let Levi's presence bother her so much? It didn't make sense to her. She'd been the subject of many a young man's attention back in the city, but none of them had made her cheeks burn, her lungs close off and her mouth say inappropriate things. Even though it was true that Levi looked good all cleaned up.

Heat rushed up her neck and pooled in her cheeks.

As she cleaned up the kitchen she struggled to keep her thoughts from continually harkening back to Levi. Levi and how his black shirt made him look so strong. And bold. Not like Henry St. James, who didn't make her heartbeat quicken. Nor her cheeks burn. She had never watched out the window, looking for him to appear.

Realizing her hands had grown idle and she was staring out the kitchen window, she jerked about and forced herself to think no further than the dishes that needed washing.

The job done, she carried the water out and poured it on the rosebush. She inhaled the lovely scent, closed her eyes and leaned over the nearest blossom. Every few days Levi brought in a fresh rose and put it in the bowl by Maisie's table and the scent wafted to Beatrice as she went about her work.

The Doyle house back in Chicago often had huge bouquets of flowers in the rooms but never had she noticed such a powerful aroma from any of them. Why was that? Did flowers growing in the wilds of Montana develop more perfume? The thought went deeper. Did men and women on the ranches of Montana develop more character? Henry St. James certainly seemed weak and colorless in comparison to Levi.

Levi? Why was she even thinking of him? Let alone comparing him to Henry?

She straightened and stared into the dark eyes of the very man she tried so hard to forget. He wasn't more than ten feet away. "I didn't hear you approach."

"Just coming for the church service Maisie wants."

"Of course. I'm just finishing up the kitchen." She waved the dishpan as if he wouldn't have noticed it.

"Here comes Charlie." The other man trotted from the barn. "Let's go inside."

She realized she stood rooted to the spot and made her feet move. What was wrong with her? Or was there something about him—his dark looks, his powerful presence—that was responsible for the fact that every time he was near, she forgot how to think, how to act?

She rushed into the kitchen, wiped the dishpan dry and hung it behind the stove. She carefully draped the towels over the drying bar, then wiped her hands on the apron she wore. She stared at the white fabric. Shouldn't she remove it if they were having church? She untied the strings and hung the apron beside the stove.

"I'd like to go outdoors," Maisie said, and held up her hand before Levi could voice his protest. "However, we'll go to the living room instead." Levi helped her upright and held her arm firmly as they hobbled into the other room.

Charlie hung back. "Ladies first," he said.

Beatrice took Dolly by the hand and followed the pair. Maisie patted the chair next to hers and she sat there. The five of them sat in a circle, Dolly wide-eyed and uncertain. Beatrice understood her confusion. How could this possibly be considered church? Where was the choir? The pews? The congregation? Things truly were different in Montana.

Maisie spoke. "Beatrice and I practiced a song yesterday. We're going to sing it for you."

Beatrice tried to collect her thoughts. Yes, Maisie had suggested they might sing in church. She'd never envisioned this was what she meant. Straight across from her sat Levi, his dark eyes seeing too much, probing too deep, turning her carefully constructed world into a tangle.

"Are you ready?" Maisie asked.

Beatrice nodded, clasped her hands together in her lap and looked past Levi to the scene outside the window. Maisie hummed. Beatrice turned toward her so they would stay together.

"Fairest Lord Jesus, Ruler of all nature—"

As they practiced yesterday, Beatrice realized she'd never before been so aware of God as ruler of all nature.

"Beautiful Savior! Lord of all the nations!"

This God was hers. He had brought her to this place in answer to her prayer. She would not waste this opportunity.

"Glory and honor, praise, adoration. Now and forever more be Thine."

Silence filled the room. She allowed her gaze to seek Levi. He sat motionless, revealing nothing in his expression. Had she done poorly? She tipped her chin. It didn't matter. She had enjoyed singing with Maisie and the words were deeply felt.

The song was to God's honor and glory.

Levi smiled and nodded. "Very nice."

Her insides mellowed. It didn't hurt to feel man's approval, either.

"Levi, could you read a favorite passage of yours?" Maisie's voice jerked her back to her surroundings as Maisie handed Levi her Bible.

He opened the pages tenderly, as if afraid to tear the well-worn paper. "Isaiah chapter forty-three, verse two. 'When thou passest through the waters, I will be with thee. And through the rivers, they shall not overflow thee. When thou walkest through the fire, thou shalt not be burned, neither shall the flame kindle upon thee.'"

He closed the Bible.

Maisie thanked him, took the book and opened it again. "I'll read the previous verse for without it, the second verse is a lot of doom and gloom. 'But now thus saith the Lord that created thee, O Jacob, and he that formed thee, O Israel, fear not, for I have redeemed thee, I have called thee by thy name—thou art mine.' You see, we are made by God and held in His hand, sheltered by His love."

Maisie closed in prayer. "Levi, why don't you take Beatrice for a walk so she can see some of the meadows robed in beautiful garb?"

Beatrice's heart leaped at the thought and then she forced sense into her thoughts.

It was only a walk. It meant nothing. He was only agreeing to please Maisie.

Just as she would go only to please her.

Levi glanced at Beatrice and saw the way she seemed to withdraw, the look of joy on her face shifting to guarded and distant. She ducked her head to study her fingers. He'd watched her bend over the roses. Had seen her fascination with the ducks. Had listened to her colorful description of the ordinary things around her. So he knew it wasn't that she had no interest in the beauties of nature.

But Helen's words of rejection came back to him, telling him she wouldn't want to share the rest of the morning with him.

Her head came up. Her eyes blazed. With longing to share time with him?

With a mighty struggle he brought his thoughts into line with reason. She only wanted to see more of the outdoors. He was simply an escort. He wanted nothing more. It mattered not in the least what she thought of him.

Except it did. Wounded male pride, he assured himself. Nothing more.

"Would you care to take a walk?" He kept his voice cool, to prove to himself he cared not whether she said yes or no.

"I'd love to. Would you mind waiting while I get my bonnet?"

Yes, he minded. A bonnet would hide her hair so he couldn't see the sun shining off it. "Of course not." He turned to Charlie. "Do you want to come, as well?" *Please say no.*

"He can keep me company," Maisie said. "You, too, Dolly. I'd like to hold your kitten, if you don't mind."

Charlie grinned widely. "You know what they say. Two's company, three's a crowd."

"Never crossed my mind." At least not in those exact

words. Thankfully, Beatrice had gone to her room and didn't hear Charlie's comment.

She stepped from the room, a pretty blue bonnet tied under her chin and kidskin gloves upon her hands. "Shall we?" Her gaze went to the door.

He hurried to throw open the door and stepped back so she could go ahead of him.

"Where are we going?" she asked, looking about.

"I thought you might like to see a different part of the ranch."

"That sounds fine to me."

They kept a leisurely pace as they passed the bunkhouse, the cookhouse, the barn and the corrals. The whiff of the pigpen reached them.

He glanced at her. She wrinkled her nose. Her eyes met his and the skin around them crinkled. "Sorry. I don't mean to be rude but the smell is really quite obnoxious."

The tension he felt in her presence melted away. A chuckle rumbled from deep inside. "Never before heard anyone apologize for the smell of pigs."

"Sure seems someone should have long ago."

He laughed. She had a way of putting things that drove amusement deep into his heart.

They reached the end of the ranch yard and before them stretched a narrow trail, rolling hills with bluffs of trees and scattered flowers. They continued down the dusty tracks of the trail that Johnny and Willow used.

"What lays ahead of us?"

"More of the same. But Johnny and Willow live three miles down this trail."

Another few steps. She seemed deep in thought about something. Would she share it with him? He wouldn't mind if she did. He'd like to learn more about her.

"Can I ask about the Bible passage you read?" she asked after a bit.

"Ask away." No harm in discussing the Bible.

"It talks about going through the water and the fire. I take that to mean personal pain and trials. I know you lost your mother when you were young and that certainly had to have been painful, but may I be so bold as to ask if you have personally experienced other instances?"

They had stopped walking and faced each other.

His insides clenched with remembered pain. "Not fire as such, but water, yes."

She waited as if understanding he needed time to sort out what he wanted to tell her.

"The cabin where Johnny and Willow live was built by a man named Sy Hamilton. He had a daughter about my age. Helen." Once the flow of words started he seemed unable to stop it. "Two years ago we developed quite an interest in each other." The flow stopped as suddenly as it began.

Beatrice touched his arm. "Something happened, didn't it?"

"She drowned."

Beatrice gasped. "How dreadful." Her fingers remained on his arm and the gentle pressure calmed his heart.

He stared past her, though he saw nothing of the

landscape, only the dark regrets of his thoughts. "I should have known better."

A tiny gasp came from her. "You had something to do with it?"

It was almost laughable that she thought the worst. "No. I wasn't even there when it happened."

"Then I don't understand your meaning."

"I should have known better than to let myself care." His gaze jerked to hers. *I won't let myself care again,* he silently warned.

"Why? Are you afraid of being hurt? Aren't some things worth the risk of pain?" Her words were as soft as butterfly wings, and just like butterfly wings made their way into forbidden places. They landed softly in his heart, making it difficult to guard his feelings.

He shook himself. He needed to deny he was afraid. "After a few hurts, a person learns to guard their heart."

"A few? I don't understand."

"We almost lost Maisie years ago." Why did her gentle questions race straight for his heart without giving his brain a chance to censure what he would say? "Forget it. It wasn't important."

"Obviously it was or you wouldn't still be naming it. What happened to Maisie?"

Rather than answer, he strode along the trail again. She scurried to keep up. He slowed to accommodate her. "Us boys didn't know what was wrong with her. We understood afterward that she had lost another baby she hoped to have. But she stayed in bed. Never got up to look after us. Pa said she had a broken heart. I asked if a person could die from a broken heart and he said it was possible. Even though I was only ten at the time I thought if that happened I would die of a broken heart, too."

"She obviously did not die. What happened?"

Tension eased away as he thought of what he'd done. "I decided I wouldn't let her go without doing everything I could to bring her back. So every day I took her a gift. A flower, a feather, a cookie baked by the girl who came to help, anything to make her interested in life again."

"Levi, that was so kind of you. It must have meant a lot to her."

"She said afterward that my visits helped her see how much she had to live for." Silence followed his confession. "I suppose you think me a little foolish."

"Not at all. But…"

Did he want to hear her *but*? Two steps later he had to know. "But what?"

"Rather than make you afraid to care about someone I think it would make you realize how much you can do for those you care about."

"I let myself care about Helen. That didn't turn out so good, did it?" He wouldn't tell her of the cruel, heart-twisting words Helen had said.

"No, it didn't. I'm sorry for your loss. But I think it's because you want love that you fear it. You know how powerful it is but you want assurances at the same time. Life doesn't come with such assurances but you chose the Bible reading this morning. God says He will be with us so we're not overwhelmed."

A patch of bright flowers in many colors came into sight. Glad of a diversion, he pointed it out.

She fell to her knees at the brown-eyed Susans. He

expected her to pick them but she closed her eyes and breathed deeply. "I can almost hear the earth sing with joy. Without the ability to use words, it sends out beautiful flowers."

"You certainly have a way with words." He listened hard. She was right. A person could hear something deep and primal. But not from the earth—from his heart. What would it be like to share life with someone like Beatrice, who saw life in such a beautiful way? Would it make him able to believe in the goodness of others? He scoffed at his wayward thoughts.

He sat on a grassy spot nearby and watched as she opened her eyes and touched several of the blossoms. Almost reverently.

After a bit, she sat back. "Thank you, Levi," she said, her expression serious. She plucked a tall slender harebell. "I did not mean to make light of the pain and distress you have felt over your losses. First, your ma. Then fearing you might lose Maisie, then Helen's drowning. I realize it's a lot and I did not mean to be unsympathetic." She handed him the blue flower then brushed her gloved hand along his shirt-covered forearm, sending a flood of sensations up his nerves. It felt good to have someone acknowledge his feelings. He pressed his hand to hers and smiled into her eyes.

"Thank you." The words failed to express what he felt but then what words would? He tucked the harebell flower into his hatband.

The smile she gave him washed away a dark stain in his heart. He didn't even bother to think what he meant by that observation. Her unusual way of saying things must be catching.

He must bring things back to the reality of his life, but her look went on and on, seeming to challenge him. And then something shifted. Whether in her or in him, he couldn't say, but the air between them shimmered like a summer mirage and yet he felt he could see into the distance more clearly than ever.

"Levi." Her voice was so low he had to bend forward to hear her. She kept her head down as she talked. "You are a sweet man who deserves to love and be loved."

Her words melted his hard heart. "That's what Maisie says," he blurted out.

"There you go. How can you argue with her? She's wise and caring and sees a lot."

"Yeah, but she's my ma. She's expected to say those things." Why was he pushing for more? And what did more look like?

"I'm not your ma." She faced him, her look driving deep into his soul. "We always have choices as to whether or not we are going to dwell in the past or put our hope in the future. Maybe love is a risk that's worth taking."

He wanted to believe the future could hold all the things he secretly longed for—belonging, acceptance, love and family. But was he willing to pin his hopes on those fragile things? "Sometimes our choice is to accept our lot with grace and dignity."

Her eyes shifted, no longer meeting his, looking into the distance as if seeing her own choices. He longed to ask what they were. She talked about independence, freedom. Didn't that void her talk of following after the things her heart longed for? He wasn't sure he wanted to know and sprang to his feet. "We best get back before Maisie worries."

His heart settled back to normal and the locks around it fell into place.

Chapter Nine

Beatrice couldn't believe she'd been talking to Levi of love. He must have loved Helen a lot for her loss to have affected him so profoundly. What pain that man had suffered. Such bitter losses. And yet it hadn't made him hard. Quite the opposite. He had a gentleness that touched a chord within her. Made her yearn to be the recipient of such fierce, loyal love.

She would not be so foolish as to expect it. Nor was it what she wanted…though at the moment she couldn't remember why not.

They lost no time in hurrying back to the ranch, both in a rush, it seemed. No doubt he was anxious to get away from her and her foolish suggestions. As soon as they reached the house, she dashed inside. Charlie tended the pot of soup simmering on the stove.

"I'm sorry," she said to everyone but mostly to herself. "I should have been here."

"Nonsense," Maisie said. "I appreciate your help but I have no wish to take advantage of it. Besides, Charlie and I have had a good visit."

Dolly sat at Maisie's feet, playing with Smokey. Beatrice felt a sting of guilt that she'd left both the child and the meal for others to take care of.

"Thank you," she said to Maisie, then grabbed the plates. Levi did not look in her direction, confirming her feelings that she'd ventured into forbidden territory. As she set the table, she continually stole looks at him, wishing he would meet her gaze. And do what? It was time to set her thoughts on her duties and he concentrated on setting the table.

As they shared the meal, Maisie asked about their walk.

"I took her to a field of flowers," Levi said. "She said she could hear the earth sing." His dark eyes held her gaze. She could not guess what he thought. Did he consider her foolish, or did he like the way she described what she saw and felt?

Her cheeks burned as she remembered the other things she'd said.

"That's lovely." Maisie's voice grew distant. "I wish Big Sam was here. He'd love to hear how you describe the land he loves. Levi and his brothers love the land, too." She glanced at Levi. "It's almost as if she has fallen in love with the ranch."

Before Levi could answer, Beatrice pushed to her feet and gathered up the dishes. "I'll wash these up." Thankfully no one commented on her sudden desire to start cleaning up after the meal.

"Levi, would you help me to my bed? I believe I'll rest a while."

Levi sprang to Maisie's side and assisted her to her room.

Dolly took her cat outside.

Charlie wandered outside, too, leaving Beatrice alone with her rambling thoughts. Love the ranch? It would be easy to do so. But there was no place for her here. As soon as Maisie's leg healed, she'd leave and find a job elsewhere.

She'd be independent. Just as she wanted to be.

"Have you?" Levi spoke from behind her.

She hadn't heard him return to the kitchen. Her hands stilled but she would not turn around. At the moment she felt too uncertain of her feelings. About the ranch. And about him.

She hotly denied there existed any confusion about her feelings.

"Have I what?"

"Have you fallen in love with the ranch?"

She couldn't move. Couldn't breathe. Could not think.

He waited a moment but she could not answer him, so he strode to the door, closing it quietly behind him. She watched him cross the yard and enter the barn. He came back out carrying his saddle, then caught up his horse, saddled it and rode away without a backward look.

Her lungs emptied in a whoosh.

The afternoon spread out before her. What was she to do? Maisie napped. Levi obviously did not wish to keep her company. Never mind. She could amuse herself.

She went outside. "Dolly, do you want to come for a walk with me?"

Dolly shook her head. "Smokey wants to play in the dirt," she whispered.

She would enjoy the woodlands and the river by herself and she started down the trail toward the river. The same one that Levi had accompanied her on her first day here. Hadn't she been impressed by his self-assurance even then? A strong, kind man.

The blue of the water flashed before her. The rumbling song of it soothed her. *God, I feel so close to You here*. She meant on the ranch. Or did she mean in nature? And shouldn't feeling close to God make her feel less restless? *I don't understand why I feel this way. I don't even know what it is I feel. You do, though. You know me and my thoughts. Please make them less tangled*.

Reaching the river, she sat on the bank and watched the ducks. The sounds and scents of her surroundings sifted through her, soothing away her confusion. She had come to help Maisie and she would do that without letting thoughts of love, the allure of nature and especially not her silly reaction to Levi divert her from that task.

Having decided her course of action she tried to relax and enjoy her surroundings. She might have succeeded if her thoughts hadn't kept returning to the morning scene. And the flowers, she tried to make herself believe. Like the blue harebell she'd given him. She lifted her face to the sky. Why had she done such a thing? Examining her actions now, it seemed almost romantic. She'd only meant to express sorrow over his losses.

She sank over her knees, feeling very lonely.

He belonged here, surrounded by people he loved and who loved him in return.

She didn't know where she belonged. In fact, she was a lot like Dolly. Yes, her aunt and uncle had given her a home, but she couldn't stay there forever. Nor did she want to.

Never mind. She would not feel sorry for herself.

The thud of an approaching horse jerked her to attention. Who was it? Perhaps the men who were responsible for the mischief around the place. She glanced around, seeing how alone she really was and how far from the house. No one would hear her if she called for help. She bolted to her feet and raced for the trail. But wouldn't the rider or riders be more likely to see her if she ran? Instead, she drew into the shelter of a tangle of bushes and hunkered down, hoping she was out of sight and praying God would hide her.

Levi tasted the sourness on the back of his tongue and tried to convince himself the cause was knowing the scoundrels had taken advantage of the simple church service and his absence as he entertained Beatrice. It was not, he silently repeated, because Beatrice had not answered his question about what she thought of the ranch.

Had he really thought she might say she loved it and would gladly spend the rest of her life living in Western Montana? It wasn't as if she hadn't been clear about how she saw her future. Independence was what mattered to her. He supposed he could understand after the way her father had treated her. Couldn't the man see the treasure he had? No. Instead, all he cared about was having a son and heir—and having failed at that, a son-in-law and heir.

He pulled off his hat and smiled at the drooping harebell. Then he planted the hat squarely back on his head and turned his full attention to the trail left by the mischief makers. Though this time the mischief had been a little more serious. They had gone into the cookhouse and tossed the contents of the cupboards on the floor. If Soupy got his hands on them they would regret their actions.

Levi had been able to follow the trail easily…too easily. They had crossed the yard as if taunting him, then the trail had gone up a hill turning toward the river. He lost it at the water's edge, knowing they had gone into the river. He kept to the bank, hoping to pick up the trail again when they left the water.

He must concentrate or he'd miss the signs.

He stopped and hung over the back of his horse, staring at two footprints. Small. Like a woman's. The skin on the back of his neck tightened. Only one woman would be here. Beatrice. If the rogues had discovered her alone and unprotected…

His fists curled.

If they harmed so much as one hair on her head…

He didn't finish the thought. Suffice it to say they'd be very sorry.

He sat up to study his surroundings. There was something odd about the bushes to his left. They should be dark green. But he caught a glimpse of light. That didn't make sense. He squinted at the area. Wasn't that the exact color of the dress Beatrice had been wearing? Not white, but not brown. Sort of in between.

The tension slid from his shoulders and he grinned. How long would she stay there thinking no one could see her? Maybe he'd just wait and see and he leaned back in his saddle.

The bushes rustled. She sniffed and then sneezed— a barely there wheezy sound.

Still she didn't move. Someone should tell her she couldn't stay hidden after she'd sneezed.

He waited.

She remained in the bushes.

He waited some more. Yes, he should be trying to track the troublemakers but this was more urgent. More interesting. And a whole lot more fun.

How long before she'd know her hiding place had been discovered and stepped into the open?

All his anger at her—or was it at himself for wanting things he knew to be out of his reach?—vanished in amusement at how she stayed hidden, in relief that she was safe, and in something bigger, better and way beyond reach. He allowed himself only a quick acknowledgment of how much he enjoyed her company.

The bushes rustled. The patch of not-white, not-brown shifted. She peeked out from behind a branch. He could only see one eye and it widened and she poked her whole face out.

"What are you doing here?" She stepped from the bushes, brushing her hair and her skirts.

"Waiting to see how long you would stay there thinking you were hidden."

She favored him with an annoyed look. "But why are you *here*?" She jabbed her finger toward the ground as she moved toward him.

He knew what she meant, but rather than answer, he swung his leg over the horse and dropped to the ground, watching her approach. His grin pulled up the corners of his heart.

She stopped two feet from him, her eyes narrowed. "You're really enjoying yourself, aren't you?" Her voice contained just enough sharpness for him to know she found his enjoyment annoying.

He nodded, not one bit repentant.

"Did you follow me?"

He shook his head.

"Are you going to tell me what you're doing here or do I have to guess?"

"Guess."

She studied him long and hard but he didn't mind one bit.

"You came for a swim?"

"Nope."

"You're going fishing."

"No fishing pole."

She rolled her eyes upward. "Do I have to do this until the sun sets?"

He relented marginally. "I was practicing my tracking skills." Remembering the troublemakers, he lost all sense of amusement and glanced around. Perhaps even now they were watching, waiting. His skin crawled at the thought of being spied on.

"Those culprits?"

"There were up to mischief while we had Sunday service and afterward." No need to mention the time he'd spent studying flowers with her, especially when he fully intended to forget the whole episode. Especially the flower tucked in his hat. He crossed his arms to keep from reaching up to see if it was still there.

"What did they do?"

"They tossed the contents of Soupy's kitchen to the floor. I would hate to be in their boots if Soupy ever gets ahold of them."

"Did they take anything?"

"Not that I could tell. Just made a mess."

Somehow they had fallen in side by side with the horse following and started up the trail toward the house.

"What do they hope to gain by making trouble?"

"I wish I knew." They came to the yard. Dolly sat by the rosebush, playing with Smokey. She grabbed the kitten when they approached and held it so it wouldn't run from the horse.

"Do you want help cleaning up the cookhouse?" Beatrice asked.

He'd thought to do his best at tidying up before Soupy returned and wasn't looking forward to it, but now it seemed a pleasant way to spend the rest of the afternoon. "You sure you don't mind?"

"Not at all." They crossed to the cookhouse. He tied the horse to the nearest post and they stepped inside.

Beatrice gasped at the mess. "This is vandalism."

"I suppose it is, but to what purpose?"

"Did you make someone mad? Offend them?"

He snorted. "I offend a lot of people simply because I'm half-Indian."

"I cannot believe anyone would do this simply because of your mixed blood. There has to be more to it than that."

"Well, if there is, I wish someone would tell me what." He handed her various items and she arranged them on the shelves.

"Soupy is going to roar like a mad bull when he sees things have been moved." Levi couldn't stop imagining how upset the cook would be.

"You're not to blame."

"He might not see it that way. He'll say I was left in charge and why didn't I guard his domain?"

She laughed. "I'm sure he'll understand if you explain."

"You haven't met Soupy."

"I don't think I want to."

Levi picked up several small sacks of spices. Would she be around long enough to meet Soupy? He was out with Pa and the crew. Like Maisie said, they should be back any day. But if they were delayed…well, Beatrice would only be here until Maisie's leg had healed.

It was not nearly long enough.

He handed the sacks to her. Their fingers brushed and a shock went through him. Why did he react to her this way? She had made it plain that she wanted to live an independent life. Wanting to be clear as to what she meant, he said, "Will you go back to Chicago at some time?"

She grew still. The amusement fled from her eyes. The skin on her face seemed to sag. "My father will allow me to return on one condition. If I marry one of the men he deems suitable." She shook her head slowly, obviously saddened by the prospects.

"And you will only marry for love?" He had to know her feelings. A horse in the nearby pasture snorted. A crow cawed from the trees. But between Beatrice and himself, there hung a long silence.

She stared past him, though there was nothing behind him but the wall. "I see no reason to marry. I plan to be independent."

Her words twisted through his heart. He wondered if she knew how sad and lonely she sounded. Recalling her earlier words, he raised a question. "Didn't you say love was worth a risk?" Why did he want to defend love? Maybe because of Maisie and Big Sam. Their love was beautiful and grew more so as time passed. He would wish the same for Beatrice. But not for himself? No! Because he knew love was a dangerous thing. It broke hearts. And yet he wanted to prove otherwise to her.

He almost missed the look of fear and pain in her eyes before she quelled it.

"I guess I'm a coward. I'm not willing to trust love again."

"Again? You've been in love?" The idea stung deep inside.

She stared into the distance.

"I'd really like to know," he said softly, invitingly. He caught her hand, knowing a sense of rightness when she didn't pull away.

Beatrice wanted to run. Go to her bedroom and hide behind the closed door. Go anywhere but here, where she teetered between protecting her heart and opening it to Levi. It was the gentle pressure of his hand on hers that riveted her to the spot and opened the floodgates of her pain.

"I fancied myself in love with a man. Henry St. James. He did not meet my father's requirements for a suitor, but I thought our love was strong enough that Henry would defy my father in order to court me." She dreamed of even more—marriage, love, family and being valued. "I was wrong. My father gave him a sum of money to stop seeing me and he took it only too gladly."

Levi squeezed her fingers. "The man must have been blind. Not to mention greedy."

She nodded. Hearing his words, believing them did not ease the pain. Nor did it soften the shell encircling her heart. Though she thought she detected cracks in it and quickly mended them. "How can I trust love? My suitors are looking at monetary reward. I thought a man unlike the ones my father chose for me would be different, but he also saw me as the source of financial benefit." That wasn't the only reason she couldn't trust love. Deep in the bottomless pit of her heart she found the real reason and admitted it. Her parents didn't value her for just being her. Her suitors didn't see her as who she was. Henry had only pretended he cared about the person she believed herself to be.

Could she trust anyone to see her for what she was?

Did she even know who or what she was, apart from the role her parents had fashioned for her? She could only be certain if she proved to herself she was a person in her own right and she could only do that by standing on her own two feet. "I need independence. Not love or marriage." Even as she said the words, the shell around her heart threatened to shatter. She wanted love but could she trust it until she was confident of her own value?

Why was it the very thing she wanted she must reject or else live the rest of her life wondering if she was capable of being a real person?

Levi dropped her hand. "I forgot about poor old Scout. I need to unsaddle him." He went to his horse.

She'd disappointed him by denying she needed love. But she could not say otherwise. Life was too uncertain.

He never made it to the horse but returned to her side and caught her by the shoulders. His dark eyes held hers like a vise.

She tried to swallow. Couldn't. Her throat had constricted. Her mouth had gone dry. She felt his look clear to her heart. Felt dormant areas there springing to life.

She tried to reason away those thoughts but failed.

He lowered his gaze to her lips.

She knew his intention. Knew she should stop him. But something inside called for affection. Maybe even love.

He lowered his head, caught her lips in a tender, sweet kiss that made no demands and offered no promises. "I think you want more than you will allow yourself. Maybe love is a risk worth taking," he said, his voice husky, and then he caught up Scout's reins and crossed toward the barn.

She clutched her hands to her chest as pain and hope knifed through her. Never before had she felt such a jolt in her heart. His words and his kiss had split her protective shell wide open. Why had he thrown her

own words back at her when he didn't believe them?
Or was he starting to think love was worth the risk?

Did she?

She heard her father's words. "You're of no use to
me as a girl. The least you can do is marry a man who
will become my son," he'd said. She had to be more.
Not until she proved she could manage on her own
would she believe it.

Thunder shook the ground. She glanced upward.
Not a cloud marred the blue sky. And it didn't feel
like thunder. It kept increasing in volume. She looked
toward the sound. Dust rose from a bunch of horses,
with men on their backs.

Maisie was home alone and Dolly sat undefended
in front of the house. Beatrice picked up her skirts and
ran. Before she reached the house she saw a dozen or
more horses milling around the barn. Several men had
dismounted.

Her heart lodged in her throat. Her steps faltered.
Were these the men responsible for the damage she and
Levi had just cleaned up?

Were they going to hurt Levi? She wanted to call
out a warning but must protect Dolly and forced her
feet to continue.

Dolly sat in the yard, her eyes wide as moons,
Smokey clutched in her arms.

Beatrice scooped her up and rushed to the door. A
big man reached for the handle. She almost stumbled.
"Wait. Who are you and what do you want?" Where
was Levi? Or Charlie? How could she defend herself
or Dolly and Maisie against all these men?

The big man looked her up and down. "I might ask you the same thing."

Her knees buckled. She insisted they stand firm. Levi left the barn and headed toward them. Never before had she been so glad to see a man and so certain he would protect her.

Levi went to the big man's side. "Pa, welcome home. May I introduce Miss Beatrice Doyle, niece to Pastor Gage's wife. And this is Dolly. Beatrice, meet my father, Big Sam."

His father! Her fear leaked out so quickly that she had to stiffen her arms to keep from letting Dolly slip to the ground.

"Pleased to meet you." The big man held out his hand.

She shifted Dolly so she could reach out to the man. His engulfed her smaller hand.

"Levi, what's going on?" Big Sam asked.

"Maisie…"

Big Sam leaned forward. "What about Maisie?"

"Sam? Sam, is that you?" Maisie's voice came from inside the house.

"Where are you? Why aren't you here?" Not waiting for an answer, Big Sam burst through the door. "What's going on?" His roar made Beatrice want to cover her ears.

Dolly shuddered and buried her face against Beatrice's neck. "It's okay," Beatrice murmured. "No one will hurt you." She'd make sure of that. She glanced at Levi.

He patted Dolly's back. "That's my papa. He wouldn't hurt anyone." He rocked his head back and forth. "I wouldn't care to be in Maisie's shoes right now. Big Sam won't be happy."

If Levi meant to reassure Dolly, Beatrice thought, he shouldn't sound so morose. She could not make out the words of Maisie's gentle reply. Then a deep rumble as Sam answered. She grinned. "I think Maisie has calmed him."

He rolled his eyes. "That's love for ya."

She laughed. Their gazes caught and held. She knew hers revealed more than it should. The longing to know the kind of love that conquered anger and turned into quiet concern. That gave a person the confidence to be themself. She tried to stem the thoughts. Love was not for everyone.

She read his own denial of love. How strange that each of them tried to convince the other to believe in love, yet were unwilling to do so themselves.

Levi indicated they should enter the house, where she saw Big Sam lean over Maisie and kiss her. The color in Maisie's cheeks matched the rose bouquet in the middle of the table and her eyes sparkled.

Big Sam turned to Beatrice. "Maisie tells me you've been a great help. I thank you. I hope you'll find it in your heart to stay until she is able to get around again."

Beatrice tipped her head. "I'll stay if you want, though I warn you I am inexperienced." If he let her stay she would do her best to leave the place able to say otherwise. She ignored the sting behind her heart at knowing she would leave.

"Maisie says you're a quick learner and she's enjoyed your company."

Somewhere in the distance a door slammed and an

angry voice could be heard. Big Sam looked out the window. "Soupy is waving the broom like he's on the warpath. Something going on I should know about?"

"Yeah, Pa." Levi filled him in on the mischief the intruders had caused. "They always seem to know when me and Charlie are away. I've tracked them but their trail always disappears in the river or on rocks."

"Who is doing this?"

Levi lifted his hands in an I-don't-know gesture.

Big Sam crisscrossed the room in long strides until Maisie caught his hand.

"Stop pacing. Sit down." She patted the chair beside her and he sat, though he looked like he would jump up any minute.

"I don't like it," Big Sam said. "I'll post a guard at all times. Let's go have a look and see what they've been up to." He grabbed his hat and headed for the door.

Levi didn't immediately follow but crossed to where Beatrice stood, Dolly in her arms. He touched the little girl's head. "You're okay?"

Dolly nodded and gave him a shy smile.

Levi waited.

Beatrice realized he wanted a response from her, as well. "We're fine." Did he think she would be changed after their kiss? Dare she admit, even to herself, that she might be? Not that it made any difference to what she must do.

Oh, if only she could trust that anyone would see her the way she wanted to be seen.

Levi turned and followed his father.

Beatrice drew in a satisfying breath then realized

she had another mouth to feed and surely Big Sam must consume a lot of food.

"Dolly, how would you like to help me make supper?"

Dolly nodded and Beatrice put her down.

"What shall I make?"

Maisie gave her directions and she began to prepare the meal. She needed to concentrate on what she was doing, which left her little time to think about the afternoon.

Even so, she managed to glance out the window many times, watching as Levi and his father toured the place, often stopping to study something and talk.

From there, it was only too easy to think about the way Levi had kissed her.

What did his kiss mean?

What did she want it to mean?

Nothing, she told herself again and again. She would not allow herself to again believe a man could see her for who she was.

Chapter Ten

Levi followed his pa around the place, pointing out the mischief the intruders had done. All the while, his thoughts kept returning to the cookhouse, where Soupy was still slamming things. Only it wasn't Soupy he thought of. It was Beatrice and the way he'd kissed her.

If not for the fact that it would invite questions from Big Sam, Levi would have pounded the heel of his hand on his forehead. What had he been thinking? It wasn't as if any romance could exist between them. She was very clear that she meant to pursue her own goals.

Not that he had any interest in a romantic relationship. There were far too many reasons to avoid it. She was a city girl. He a half-breed. She'd soon enough learn that association with him would mark her. She was used to being part of high society and he would never be welcomed into that circle.

He'd meant the kiss to make her realize how much she deserved love. And to somehow make up for the way her parents and her former beau had treated her. As if she was nothing more than a valuable object.

But his mental arguments did nothing to eradicate the way his heart had bounced up and down at the gentle kiss. Nor did it stop the way his heart continued to jump at the mere thought of the kiss. And the possibility of another.

No. There would be no other kiss. For his sake and for hers. He must remember how vastly different their lives were.

The supper bell rang and Big Sam left off his questions about the intruders and headed for the house like a man who hadn't eaten in days. Levi knew better. Soupy had gone along with Pa and the crew and their meals would have been more than adequate.

No, Pa was in a hurry to get back to Maisie.

Levi kept in step with Big Sam. Not that he was in a hurry to see anyone.

If only he could convince himself of that fact.

The next morning, Pa decided to check all the fences around the place and make sure all the doors on the barn and outbuildings were secure. Levi could have told him he'd already done that, but he didn't mind being kept busy within sight of the house, which allowed him to watch Beatrice work without her being aware of his attention.

It being Monday, she tackled the laundry. Laundry was hard. He knew she'd never done it before. When she dragged a heavy sheet to the line he almost went to her rescue even though he knew she would not welcome his interference. She had a need to prove she could manage on her own.

She wrestled the sheet to the line, pinned it there and steadfastly continued.

He let his waiting lungs release air.

A sweet sound reached him. He tipped his head to listen to her sing as she worked. She had a lovely voice. Sweet and rich, like thick cream on warm chocolate cake. He could listen to her sing all day.

"Levi, did you reinforce those hinges?" Pa called and Levi turned away from watching Beatrice to return to his task. Listen to her all day? How could he think such a thing knowing she had plans that took her away from the ranch? And he had no such plans.

She did not belong on a ranch. And most decidedly did not deserve a place in his heart.

No piece of his heart would ever again be given to another. It was a matter of survival.

He added another nail to the door hinge, the pound of the hammer drowning out her voice. When he finished he could still hear her. He stopped and listened. He might deny a lot of things but he couldn't deny the pleasure of listening to her sing. Nor could he deny the pleasure of spending time with her, hearing her description of the world around them, watching the way she smiled at Dolly, enjoying the way she moved about the kitchen as she worked. Nor could he deny the pleasure of kissing her.

He needlessly pounded at a nail. If he let himself grow more interested in her he would soon enough find his heart ripped to shreds. He'd survived losing his ma. Survived almost losing Maisie. Barely survived losing Helen and, worse, hearing the truth about her feelings toward him. He would not survive another heartbreak.

Or more accurately, didn't want to test the idea. No, he would guard his heart against further rejection and hurt. Not only that, but he would also protect Beatrice from the cruelty of the comments that association with him would bring.

Pa decided he wanted a smaller pen for the brood mares and over the next few days, Levi poured his thoughts and energy into building fences. He might have succeeded in pushing Beatrice from his mind except for the fact she was there when he went in for meals. And she went from the house to the garden, from the house to the pigpen to dump the slop bucket, from the house to the chicken house to gather eggs, from the house to a growing spot inside his heart, where she seemed to have taken up residence against his better judgment.

He'd ask Pa to send him to one of the far line cabins, but something stubborn and stupid inside him wouldn't allow him to do so.

Friday dawned bright and clear. Since breakfast, Levi had laid out planks for the fence, driving long spikes into them with deadly blows of his hammer. He'd worked so hard at not looking toward the house that his back ached and he used the pain as an excuse to straighten. Could he help it if the house was in his line of sight? Beatrice bent over the rosebush, smelling one of the pink blossoms. She wore a pink dress that matched the color of the roses. Her blond hair had been twisted into some kind of pretty roll at the back of her head, but strands of it drifted about her face. She tucked a strand behind her ear as she straightened.

She turned and looked in his direction.

Even across the distance he felt her golden-brown eyes searching. For what, he could not say. He'd done his best to avoid her, running from his feelings, pretending his kiss hadn't meant far more than he meant it to. To him, at least. He couldn't say what it meant to her.

Was she aware of his avoidance or did she put it down to Big Sam's return?

He gave a little wave and bent over his work again.

Had he ever felt so keenly aware of everything Helen did? Been so attracted to her voice, her movements, her observations of nature and her assessments of the ranch?

Of course not. She knew the ranch and ranch work as well as he. Things in nature that Beatrice commented on, Helen had known all her life.

Another demanding question surfaced. Had he ever missed Helen the minute she stepped out of sight? He would not answer the question.

Aren't I supposed to be guarding my heart?

He would continue to do so. He must.

He might have succeeded in pretending he wasn't so keenly aware of Beatrice except he heard the concern in her voice when she called, "Dolly?"

His hammer dropped to the ground as he straightened to stare across the yard to her.

She hurried from one spot to the next, calling the child.

His nerves twitched and he trotted to the house. "What's wrong?"

She grabbed his arm, her eyes wide. "I can't find Dolly. She was here a moment ago."

"She won't have gone far." The child never wandered. She only left Beatrice's side to play outside with the kitten and even then remained by the door. He called her name. "We won't hear her if she answers. Not unless she decides to speak above a whisper."

"What if...?" They looked at each other with the same thought. What if the intruders had taken her?

"They've never done anything more than mischief." Somehow he felt it was a personal attack directed at him. The fact there had been no sign of them since Pa returned reinforced the thought. Someone seemed to delight in tormenting him.

Of course, if they'd seen him playing with Dolly, they might understand he cared about the child and think to hurt him by taking her.

He bent over and studied the tracks in the dust. It wasn't hard to pick out Dolly's. "She headed for the trees here. Let's see where she went." He reached for Beatrice's hand, relieved when she took it. He'd wondered if she might try to keep a safe distance between them after he'd kissed her.

Just as he meant to. But present circumstances overrode the need.

They entered the wooded area behind the house. The ground crackled under their feet—it was dry and dusty after a long, hot summer. It yielded no sign of Dolly.

"Can you see her tracks?" Beatrice asked, her voice thin with worry.

"She was headed this way." He pushed aside a low-hanging branch and held it for Beatrice to follow. Her pink-rose scent wafted to him and he turned. "We'll find her." He would do anything to ease the pinched look about Beatrice's eyes.

She searched his gaze, at first uncertain and afraid, and then she nodded, confidence easing the strain in her eyes. "Then let's do it. The poor child will be so afraid."

Squeezing her hand, they forged onward, calling Dolly but more often pausing to listen, knowing they would never hear her whisper. Crows flew from the trees, cawing a loud protest. Overhead, a flock of geese honked as they flew by in a V.

But they heard no little girl.

He stopped. "I can't believe she would have gone this far. Let's search closer to the house."

They searched through the tangled underbrush. But back at the yard, they had not found her.

"I'm worried," Beatrice said.

"Me, too. But we will find her. I promise you."

"What if...?"

His jaw clenched. "We will find her." If those men had taken her, he would follow them to the ends of the earth. "Let's try that direction."

She tugged on his hand and stopped him. "We need help."

He glanced past her toward the barn. Pa was nowhere to be seen and the cowboys were all away. "There's only Soupy."

She looked toward the sky. "We need God's help."

"You're right." He clasped both her hands to his chest as he bowed his head. "God of all creation, You see everything, including a lost little girl. Please guide us to her. Amen."

"Amen," Beatrice repeated.

They stood with hands together for another heart-beat, strength and assurance flowing through him. And something more. A fierce protectiveness toward Dolly. He would keep her safe. He'd do the same for Beatrice, only he didn't have the right. And she would not give it to him.

They again entered the trees, searching for the child.

He stopped and looked at a bent branch. "She came this way."

"Dolly," they called in unison, their gazes catching as they waited for any answer, even though they didn't expect one.

With a jolt, he realized he had never felt so connected, so in tune with anyone before as he did to Beatrice at this moment. It was only mutual concern for a frightened child, he insisted. But it was more. It was like they could communicate without the use of words.

Like Maisie and Big Sam did.

The thought slammed into his mind and he jerked his gaze away. He caught a movement in the distance. "That wasn't leaves." He pointed in the general direction. But it was too far above the ground to be Dolly. Were the intruders lying in wait for him?

He drew Beatrice behind him and eased forward. In twenty feet he knew what he saw and it wasn't intruders. It was one little girl huddled in a branch about ten feet from the ground.

Beatrice saw her, too, and would have rushed forward but he held her back. "We don't want to frighten her and make her fall."

She stopped and called softly, "Dolly, are you okay?"

Dolly shook her head no.

Levi and Beatrice edged closer.

"Can you get down?" he asked.

Again she shook her head.

He reached up toward her. "Jump and I'll catch you."

She shook her head. "Smokey," she whispered, pointing above her head.

Smokey sat on a branch higher up. Levi couldn't tell if the kitten was afraid to come down or content to be sitting there. "You come down first and then I'll get the kitten down."

"You don't need to be afraid," Beatrice soothed. "You know Levi will keep you safe."

His insides swelled at her confidence in him. He would keep both of them safe if he had the right.

And if he didn't mean to keep his heart from danger.

Ignoring the obvious that Dolly could have been hurt and that would have touched his heart deeply, he lifted his arms toward the child. "Let go and let me catch you."

Dolly edged forward.

Beatrice gasped. "Please be careful," she whispered, more for her sake, Levi thought, than for the child's.

Dolly clung to the trunk of the tree.

"You have to let go to get down."

Dolly's eyes widened and she shook her head.

"I'll have to go get her," Levi told Beatrice.

She caught his arm. "Please be careful."

He took a minute to enjoy the concern in her eyes before he stepped on the lowest branch and pushed upward. He edged between branches and climbed to another. The branches were far enough apart to allow Dolly to climb upward, but didn't allow much room for a grown man.

A branch caught his hat and sent it spiraling to the ground, where Beatrice picked it up.

He shifted and a dry branch jammed into his cheek. He felt the wet trickle of blood. He was now close enough to reach Dolly and pried her from her perch. With a whimper, she wrapped her arms around him and held on.

The poor child trembled with emotion. He realized he did, too. If something happened to her...

He could not let that thought go any further and he held her close with his free arm, her breath warm against his neck. It took a few seconds for his heart to beat normally again, sending strength to his limbs.

The way she clung, he was free to use both hands in descending.

He dropped to the ground in front of Beatrice and pried Dolly from his neck. "You have to let me go so I can get Smokey."

Dolly shifted into Beatrice's arms, clinging to her neck as she'd clung to Levi's.

Levi cupped his hand over the little girl's head, gave Beatrice a smile full of promise then climbed the tree again, careful to avoid the branch that had scratched him on his first ascent. He reached Smokey.

"Come here, kitty."

Smokey meowed.

Levi glanced down. Both Dolly and Beatrice looked up at him, hope and fear mingled in their expressions.

He liked to think at least some of the fear was on his behalf. He managed to get his hand around the kitten and lifted her from her perch. She dug her claws into him, afraid of falling. He wasn't sure how he'd hold her and still hang on to branches as he descended. Only one way he could think of, so he stuck the kitten inside his shirt.

The kitten turned around twice, realized it was safe and curled into his body. Now he could climb down.

"Where's Smokey?" Dolly whispered as he stood in front of the pair.

He patted his shirt at his waist. "Right here." The lump wriggled and meowed.

Dolly leaned from Beatrice's arms, and Beatrice set her on the ground. Dolly held out her arms to receive the kitten.

Levi pulled his shirttail from his waistband and lifted Smokey to her owner.

"Thank you," Dolly whispered, then sat down, drew her knees up and buried her face in the kitten's fur.

Levi smiled at Beatrice. "It's good to see them both safe and sound."

"Thanks to you." She set his hat upon his head and drew her finger down his cheek. "You're bleeding." She pulled a beautiful white, monogrammed hankie from her pocket and dabbed at the wound. "It must hurt."

"It's nothing." Indeed, the touch of her fingers had erased all pain.

She caught his chin and turned his face so she could see the scratch better.

His heart kicked into a gallop that stole away his breath.

"I think it's stopped bleeding."

He swallowed hard. "I expect I'll live."

"Good to hear."

The husky tone of her voice brought his gaze to hers and he felt as if he had missed the last three steps of a stairway and hung suspended in air. He knew he'd hit bottom, and reality, with a thud, but for now he let himself enjoy the sensation. The sounds of the woods were distant, like something in a dream. All that mattered was the warm look in her eyes. Like sunshine poured from her. To him.

Her gaze shifted to his mouth.

Was she remembering the way he kissed her? Was she hoping he'd do it again?

He dipped his gaze to her mouth then back to her eyes. She watched him. "Beatrice." His throat was so tight the word barely escaped.

She looked toward Dolly. His gaze went the same direction.

There would be no kissing with the child right there.

In fact, if he cared to remember his earlier decision to guard his heart, there would be no more kissing at all.

"Let's get them back home," he said, and despite every word of warning he'd ever given himself, he reached for Beatrice's hand. His heart rejoiced when she did not resist.

"Come on, Dolly," Beatrice said and the child followed them, the cat safely cradled in her arms.

Beatrice had watched Levi climb the tree, her heart stuck in her throat. What if he fell and injured himself?

What if Dolly fell? She held Levi's hat, somehow finding strength and courage in the warm felt between her fingers. Levi was a man of the West, used to all sorts of challenges. In fact, his mixed race uniquely prepared him to face any number of things, such as city girls stranded in the river or a kitten and a little girl stranded in a tree.

She knew with her mind that he was safe and Dolly was in good hands, yet she couldn't pull in a satisfying breath until he stood in front of her.

She had placed his hat on his head, almost hugging him in the process and wanting so much to hug him because he'd saved Dolly and because he was safe. But she must remember her goals. And remember she didn't belong here. She was only helping Maisie and then she'd move on. It was what she wanted, what she needed, but oh, how hard it was to believe that at the moment.

With a muffled cry she had realized he bled and tenderly wiped at his wound. And if her fingers should linger longer than necessary, who was to know? Except her.

It was getting harder and harder to remember why she had come west and what she must do.

And yes, when their gazes had locked, she had wished for another kiss. There had been something about the gentle way he'd kissed her that had…what?

She tried to convince herself it had done something she didn't welcome—like shatter the walls she had erected around her heart. But the truth was, his kiss had melted the walls.

It must not be. Neither of them wanted it. Yet when he reached for her hand, she took his willingly.

Only, she firmly informed herself, because both of them had been frightened by Dolly's disappearance.

They reached the house. "I best get back to work," he said.

"Me, too." Yet neither of them moved.

"I'm relieved she's safe and sound." His gaze went to Dolly and then back to her.

"Me, too." She crumpled the soiled hankie in the palm of her hand.

"Sorry to ruin your pretty handkerchief."

"It will wash."

"You'll be okay now?" His gaze drifted from her eyes to her mouth to her chin and back again, as if assuring himself she hadn't suffered because of their adventure.

"We're fine. You're the one that got hurt." She resisted an urge to touch his cheek again.

"It's nothing."

Somewhere in the far distance, a pot banged against another.

He blinked. "Soupy's making supper. I better get my work done." He slowly eased away to return to whatever he'd been doing.

And she must return to her work. She would take Dolly inside with her to make sure she didn't wander away again, but before she did, she knelt before the child. "Honey, what happened?"

Dolly's eyes were big as she whispered, "Smokey ranned away and climbed the tree. I tried to get her down."

"Next time Smokey runs away, you tell me or Levi and we'll help you find her. Okay?"

"Was you scared?" Dolly said.

Beatrice tried to think what the child meant. Scared Dolly was lost? Or scared the kitten was stuck in the tree? She settled for an answer that would address both issues and reassure Dolly and herself. "I knew Levi would take care of us."

Maisie looked up from her mending as they entered the kitchen and smiled. "I heard Levi out there."

"Yes, Dolly followed Smokey into the trees and they both got stranded up a tree. Levi helped me get them down."

Maisie turned to the child. "Are you okay? Were you frightened?"

Dolly clung to Beatrice's side. "I thought no one would find me." Her whisper was barely audible.

Tears sprang to Maisie's eyes. "You poor child. But if you got lost everyone here would search for you day and night until we found you."

"Levi found me." Her whisper was stronger, more confident.

"Levi knows how to find people," Maisie assured Dolly.

Dolly settled nearby, content to play with her kitten, and Beatrice turned her attention to preparing supper. *Levi knows how to find people.* The words echoed in her head. Could he find her? How could he when she hadn't found herself?

Chapter Eleven

"I've asked Big Sam to send messages to Johnny and Tanner and their families to join us on Sunday. It's been far too long since I've seen everyone."

Beatrice stared at the dishpan full of Saturday breakfast dishes without seeing them. She'd heard about the lovely, practical, courageous and hard-working wives the older Harding boys had married. If they came here, she would be exposed as the opposite. A city girl with city ways and little experience at practical things that they would take for granted.

"I've asked them to bring food so don't worry. You won't have to cook for them all."

Beatrice smiled and nodded as Maisie continued, little knowing preparing a meal was but a fraction of things she felt incapable of doing. And now her ignorance was to be revealed before the whole family.

Unless she could find a way to escape the gathering.

"Big Sam is bringing in a roast. I'll show you how to cook it. We'll have it hot for supper tonight and slice the rest cold for tomorrow." Maisie rattled on about cooking potatoes and boiling eggs for a potato salad. She mentioned the things Susanne and Willow would bring. "They are both fine cooks. You'll enjoy meeting them."

Beatrice wondered how Maisie could voice both thoughts together.

"I'll help you make a chocolate cake."

A cake? Beatrice had barely managed muffins and her first attempt at bread had been a failure. Now Maisie wanted her to bake a cake.

Maybe she should go back to Chicago, where she knew how to fit in.

But of course she wouldn't. She would learn how to bake a cake, make bread, cook a meal and whatever else she must know to survive in the country.

So she could be independent? A thin little idea crept in. Or so she could fit into ranch life?

Ranch life, town life—what did it matter so long as she could prove she could take care of herself? That she was more than a pretty little reward for people using her to achieve bigger and better plans.

"That's Levi's favorite," Maisie said.

Dolly had been listening to the conversation. "My papa liked chocolate cake best," she whispered.

Beatrice looked at the child, seeing tears pooled in her eyes. She knelt and pulled Dolly into her arms. "Then you must help me make a chocolate cake for Levi and his family. Okay?"

Dolly nodded.

Beatrice allowed herself just a tiny hope that the cake would turn out and Levi would be pleased to have known she'd prepared his favorite. She pulled a chair to the table for Dolly to perch on, got the ingredients Maisie listed and, with Maisie directing them, she and Dolly mixed up a cake and stuck it in the oven. Beatrice held up crossed fingers. "I hope it turns out okay."

Maisie chuckled. "It's never failed."

Indeed, it looked just like a cake should look when Beatrice pulled it from the oven a short time later and set the pans on a rack to cool.

"Now you'll have to make the icing."

Beatrice gulped. "Don't you think you're expecting the impossible to think I can make a cake and the icing?"

Maisie only smiled. "Not at all."

And so Beatrice, with Dolly's eager help, mixed together the sugar and cocoa and cream in a pot and set it to boil. She cooked it, cooled it and beat it according to Maisie's instructions, then spread it on the layers of the cake. Done, she stepped back and admired her creation.

"It wasn't hard, at all, was it?" Maisie asked.

"Not with you guiding me." Would she be able to do it again on her own? She hoped so. She ticked off on her fingers the things she now knew how to do—make a few meals, make biscuits, do the laundry, clean the house and now, bake a cake. She was getting downright domestic. Her victory faded a bit. Likely no one else would think so.

As she worked throughout the day, she thought of meeting Johnny and Willow for the first time, and their children—baby Adam and his two sisters, Celia and Sarah. They were twelve and ten respectively. She'd also meet Tanner and Susanne, and Susanne's two nieces and two nephews, whom they were raising. She had asked Maisie to repeat their names and ages several times, determined to keep all the children sorted out. Frank, eleven, Liz, ten, Janie, six, and Robbie, five.

In the afternoon, she took Dolly outside and sat in the shade to talk. Every time the visitors were mentioned throughout the morning, Dolly had grown stiff. Beatrice hoped she could prepare the child for the upcoming day.

Or should she take her and the two of them could go elsewhere until the visitors left? The thought was tempting, yet she felt honor-bound to help Maisie take care of the meal. Plus she was eager to see Levi with his family and watch his reaction when he tasted the chocolate cake she had made.

"Two of the children are your age so you'll have someone to play with."

Dolly stared at a spot on the ground, not moving, not saying anything.

Beatrice glanced toward the barn, saw Levi standing in the doorway watching. A smile tugged at her lips. Try as she might, she could not forget the few tender moments they had shared—one when he'd surprised her with a kiss and another when they knew Dolly was safe. She wondered if he felt the same way. But right now, her concern was Dolly and she sent him a silent plea for help.

He must have heard her unspoken request for he ambled toward them and sank to the ground on the other side of Dolly. He smoothed Dolly's hair. "What are you fine ladies doing this afternoon?"

"I was telling her about your brothers and their families visiting tomorrow."

Dolly stiffened.

Levi shared a look of concern with Beatrice and then bent his head close to Dolly's. "Are you scared of so many people?"

Dolly nodded.

Levi chuckled. "Can't say as I blame you."

Beatrice wanted to warn him his words were only adding to the child's worries, but he continued before she could speak.

"Did you know Tanner caught a bunch of horses and is taming them to start a new herd?"

Dolly shifted a bit as if interested.

"Funny thing is he caught himself a pretty young woman with four orphaned children at the same time."

"Their mama and papa are dead?" Dolly whispered.

"Sadly they are. But they had their aunt Susanne and now they have Tanner. One big happy family." He paused to let her digest the information. "And then there's Johnny."

"What's he do?" Dolly asked in her quiet little voice.

"He's raising horses, too, only he's raising those big horses that pull heavy wagons or plows. They're very nice horses. Gentle and easygoing. You'd never guess where he found his wife."

Dolly rolled her head back and forth.

"She was in a rickety wagon with her little baby boy trying to get to her orphaned sisters."

"No mama and papa?" Dolly said again.

"No, but they have their sister, Willow, and now Johnny, and they live in a very pretty spot."

He'd once told her that was where Helen had lived and Beatrice wondered if it hurt to see his brother and family living there.

Dolly studied Levi for several seconds, looking for and finding encouragement to face children who had suffered the same sad loss of parents she had, and then Dolly turned to Beatrice.

"Will they tease Smokey?"

At a loss to know how to answer, Beatrice looked to Levi for direction.

He smiled, turning her heart all mushy soft. "I think Maisie would let Smokey sleep on your bed while they're here. If Beatrice thinks that's a good idea."

Beatrice hugged Dolly to her side. "It's fine with me."

Her arm brushed along Levi's side and she remained there, content for this small contact and happy to know Dolly felt safe with them.

"Can I take her to the room now and tell her she will have to stay there when your family comes?" Dolly asked.

Even though the kitten spent every night in the bed and was welcome anywhere in the house, Beatrice understood Dolly needed to prepare herself and answered, "Yes, you may."

Dolly got up and took the kitten inside.

Neither Levi nor Beatrice moved.

Levi was the first to break the silence between them. "I'm going to miss her when her aunt takes her."

"Me, too." She couldn't keep the pain from her voice. "I've grown to love her."

He squeezed her hand. "I pray the aunt will be loving and understanding."

Just like he'd promised. "Me, too."

He pushed to his feet and reached down to pull her up. Gaining her feet, she stood but a few inches from him, close enough to see how the pupils of his eyes disappeared into his irises. She was drawn into his gaze, floating like a leaf in the wind. She knew all her longings and dreams showed on her face, but at the moment she couldn't think why she should care that he saw them. But would he? Would he understand what she wanted when she wasn't even certain herself? Was it independence or acceptance? Would she know what she wanted if she found it?

He still held her hands, folding them to his chest.

He shifted his gaze past her to the barn and the fence he was working on and pulled his hands free. "Pa wants me to finish the new enclosure before Johnny and Tanner come." His gaze did not return to her as he murmured a quick goodbye and hurried away.

She sucked in warm air, sweet with the scent of roses, and willed her heart to stop fluttering. He'd been clear that he wasn't interested in caring for another woman. Not after Helen. Why that knowledge should sting she couldn't say...or admit.

As soon as she felt she had schooled away every hint of her wayward reaction, she returned to the house to finish the meal preparation under Maisie's instructions.

Somehow she managed to avoid looking directly at Levi when he came in for the evening meal, but when they went around the table to tell of their day, she let her hungry eyes find satisfaction.

He looked at Maisie as he spoke, his gaze drifting to Beatrice where it stalled as he talked of his day.

She heard not a word of what he said, trapped by the look in his dark eyes.

Did he intend for her to see longing, or was she only seeing the reflection of her own thoughts?

The next day was Sunday and she dressed in a stylish gown. One in dark gold that she thought emphasized her eyes and hair in a becoming fashion.

Dolly scrambled from the bed. "What I wear?" she asked in an anxious whisper.

Beatrice had gone through her clothes and decided she liked the purple dress she'd worn when she and Levi found her. She'd washed and ironed it. Again she thought how much pleasure it would give her to take the child shopping. She handed it to Dolly and helped her with the buttons, then brushed and braided her hair.

She talked as she did so. "Remember all the people who are coming to visit. You'll have friends to play with. I'm sure you'll have fun."

Dolly listened carefully as if trying to believe that Beatrice was right.

As soon as they were ready, they went to the kitchen, where she made and served a simple breakfast. She was so nervous she couldn't hold a thought for more than a second and her gaze darted from one thing to another throughout the meal. Nor did her tension ease when the men went outside.

Her hands were in soapy dishwater when a wagon drove into the yard. She stared out the window as a man as dark and handsome as Levi swung to the ground and reached up to take a little boy from the woman's arms then helped her down. The woman took off her hat and shook her long, dark hair free. It tumbled down her back.

Two girls jumped from the back of the wagon.

This must be Johnny and Willow and their family.

Levi and Big Sam greeted them and then Big Sam ushered them to the house while Levi took care of the wagon.

As they drew closer Beatrice stared at the woman. Her dark, bold look made Beatrice feel mousy and colorless. So much for thinking she looked fine in her dress.

They stepped inside and all of them kissed Maisie on the cheek then turned to Beatrice.

"Johnny and his wife, Willow," Big Sam said. "Their children, Adam, Celia and Sarah. This is Beatrice Doyle, who has kindly been helping Maisie." He smiled down at Dolly as he introduced her.

"Pleased to meet you," they all said in a flurry of greetings.

The sound of another wagon drew Beatrice's attention back to the window to watch the newcomers. Tanner was darker than Levi. Susanne as blond as Beatrice but with dark-fringed eyes. Tanner lifted her to the ground, the look between them so warm with love it made Beatrice's eyes sting.

Four children jumped from the back of the wagon.

She smiled at how the two littlest ones bounced up and down. She squeezed Dolly's shoulder. It would be nice for the little girl to have some playmates.

The family trooped in and Beatrice and Dolly were again introduced.

"What's this I hear about you?" Johnny asked and Maisie explained about her accident.

"But enough about me. I want to hold our church service outdoors." She reached for Sam, who picked her up and led the procession from the house.

Beatrice followed them outside, purposely staying a distance behind. She was not a part of this family. She clutched Dolly's hand, feeling every bit an orphan as the child beside her.

The family sat on a slight knoll. Beatrice sat two feet away with Dolly clinging to her side but Maisie would have none of it. She patted the spot beside her. "Sit by me."

Beatrice could not refuse without drawing attention to herself and she and Dolly slid over. She tucked away a sigh of relief when Levi sat down beside Dolly and smiled at them both. She'd never been part of such a large family gathering and struggled against a desire to belong. She ought to write across her brain in large and bold letters *Must Find Independence*, more for her sake than for anyone else's.

She kept her attention on Big Sam, who stood before them to lead the service. She joined in as they sang two hymns, then Big Sam opened his Bible. "Maisie asked me to read these verses in Jeremiah chapter twenty-nine." He read aloud. "'For I know the thoughts that I think toward you, saith the Lord, thoughts of peace and not of evil, to give you an expected end.'"

Beatrice's thoughts stalled. Hadn't she decided to trust God to take her to the place she needed to be?

God, forgive me my wayward thoughts and guide me to my expected end. She tried to envision that as a woman earning her own living, proving her worth, but the plan faded until she couldn't see it clearly anymore.

Big Sam finished reading and closed the Bible. "You've all heard Maisie say it but I believe it bears repeating. God can be trusted to guide us even through surprising and unexpected circumstances."

"Amen," Tanner said and earned himself an adoring look from his wife.

Big Sam continued. "Often we fight against surprises and think we've made a mistake when rather we need to stop and pray and seek God's will in a situation." The simple service ended in prayer.

The men moved off and conferred with one another.

"Big Sam is worried about the mischief that has been going on here," Maisie said.

Beatrice's gaze followed Levi across the yard. When he disappeared into the barn, her heart continued to follow him.

She shook her head. Romance and heart-rending love was not in her carefully planned future. Planned by whom? A doubt crept into her mind. Was it God's expected end for her? If Levi came to her and confessed the same kind of love she saw between his brothers and their wives, what would she do? She brushed her skirts as if they were dusty. They weren't. She simply needed to keep her attention on something she could touch and see.

Levi would never let himself fall in love with an incompetent city girl.

But if he did?

She couldn't answer the question.

Levi followed his pa and brothers to the new set of corrals. He would not glance back to see if Beatrice noticed him leaving, perhaps even regretted it, but the effort to keep his face forward made his neck hurt.

He'd noticed how she'd hung back as if she didn't want to be part of the family gathering. Part of him resented her attitude but a much larger part wanted to draw her into the family, let her see how welcomed she'd be, how she'd fit in like a missing member if she would let herself do so. But the stubborn set of her chin let him know that she wanted only to follow her own plans. He vowed he would not think of her the rest of the day.

"Have either of you seen any sort of mischief like we have?" Big Sam asked of Levi's brothers after he'd filled them in to what was going on at the ranch.

The brothers said they had not.

Big Sam thumped his fist to the top plank of the fence. "I don't like it. What is the purpose of all this?"

Tanner studied Levi. "Sounds personal to me. What have you done to offend someone?"

The question brought Levi's full attention to the conversation. "Me? You're the one who always used to walk around with a chip on your shoulder looking for someone to be mad at."

Tanner shrugged. "You've got the wrong man in mind."

Levi and Johnny looked at each other and chuckled.

It was true. Since Tanner had met Susanne, the chip on his shoulder had vanished.

Big Sam held up a hand. "Let's concentrate on the matter at hand."

The brothers nodded. For the next few minutes, they tried to think why anyone would want to bother the ranch, but no one could come up with anything that made sense.

"Looks like the women are putting out the meal," Tanner said, and the men all looked that direction. Both Johnny and Tanner hurried to help their wives.

Levi hesitated about five seconds, then trotted toward the house, catching Beatrice just as she reached the door. "Can I help carry anything?"

"Yes, please." She handed him a box of dishes.

"What do you think of my family?" he asked.

"There's lots of them."

He tipped his head back and laughed. "Must seem like it to an only child. To me, too. Until a few months ago I had only two brothers. Now look at the family. How is Dolly doing?"

"She was sitting close to Maisie when I left." Her expression grew troubled. "I hope she doesn't find it all too overwhelming."

"We'll keep an eye on her and make sure she's okay." He liked the way Beatrice's eyes filled with sunshine at his offer to help.

"Maybe playing with the others will help her find her voice again." She took a full platter and a bowl of potato salad and they headed back to the others.

Soon a tablecloth was spread and food laid out. The children sat with their parents. Dolly sat between Levi and Beatrice. He caught a knowing glance between Johnny and Tanner and they each flashed a grin at him. He wanted to warn them not to tease Beatrice. She wasn't used to brothers or sisters and wouldn't know how to respond.

When Big Sam got to his feet, Levi removed his hat and tossed it to the side as his pa prayed.

It took a few minutes to pass the food around. He laughed at Beatrice's wide-eyed wonder at all the food. Baked beans, mustard beans, sliced meat, potato salad, bean salad, coleslaw, buns so light they could almost float and pickles galore.

"It looks like everyone has had good gardens," he said by way of explanation to Beatrice, but it set off a flurry of comments about garden produce, the best way to pickle beets and how soon they should dig the root vegetables.

He glanced at Beatrice, saw the confusion in her eyes and chuckled. He leaned close so she alone heard his words. "Don't look so surprised."

"I'm amazed and overwhelmed. I had no idea there were so many things to learn about living in the country."

He sensed her discouragement and wanted to ease it. "That's the key."

Her eyebrows rose, asking for clarification.

"Everything is learned."

"I suppose so, but I can't hope to ever catch up to all this." She tipped her head toward the food to indicate what she meant.

"Don't sell yourself short. You've already learned a lot."

She shrugged and he knew she was unconvinced.

"Levi," Tanner called, "how is Charlie doing? Until I saw him over by the bunkhouse, I haven't seen him since he staggered to Susanne's farm and frightened her."

The others demanded an explanation and between Tanner and Susanne they told an amusing story of Susanne keeping guard at the farm, not knowing if Charlie was friend or foe.

Tanner chuckled. "She stood guard with a rifle but didn't have the gun loaded." His gaze went adoringly to Susanne. "After that I made sure she had a few lessons in handling guns."

The way Susanne blushed, Levi wondered if the lessons had included more than loading and discharging a firearm. Maybe he should teach Beatrice how to shoot.

Dolly pressed hard to his side. He saw the fear in her eyes and the warning in Beatrice's gaze and guided the conversation to talk of the horses and the gardens.

"I tried to convince Charlie to join us for the meal," Maisie said. "But he said he didn't want to intrude."

"He's family. It wouldn't be an intrusion," Big Sam said.

Beatrice pushed to her feet. "I'll go get the cake." Levi's sisters-in-law produced pies and cookies.

Levi watched Beatrice go. Had Maisie's comment about Charlie intruding made her feel out of place? Would it look odd for him to follow her and assure her she belonged? If she wanted to.

He might have gone despite the speculation that his leaving would bring, except Dolly sat so close. He put an arm about her and drew her to his knee. He realized his brothers watched him with undue interest.

Let them think what they wanted. He only meant to comfort a frightened little girl.

Beatrice returned carrying a cake covered in chocolate icing.

Chocolate. His mouth watered.

She cut the cake into enough pieces for everyone to have some, placed slices on small plates and passed them around.

"Umm, this is good," he said, after one bite. "My favorite cake. Thank you." He ignored the teasing looks from his brothers.

"It's my first attempt at baking a cake," she admitted then glanced around, perhaps slightly regretful that she had admitted it.

"I would have never known," Susanne said.

"Nor I," Willow added. "It's delicious and so tender."

"It's good," Celia and Liz both said.

The children all chorused their approval.

Beatrice's cheeks were pink but she looked pleased at the praise. "I didn't do it myself. Maisie and Dolly helped me."

Another round of approval for the little girl's contribution.

Dolly hid her face against his shoulder but not before Levi saw her smile.

He felt Tanner watching him. Tanner looked from Levi to Beatrice to Dolly and his gaze came back to Levi.

Something in his eyes told Levi he thought he saw something special. Levi could have told him he didn't.

Not that he expected Tanner would believe him if he didn't want to.

The truth was he was finding it harder and harder to believe it himself.

Once the pies and cookies had been shared, the women began to gather up the dirty dishes and left-over food.

He rose to help Beatrice.

"I have something for you." Willow stood before him.

"Really?" He tried to think what it could be but came up blank.

She reached into her pocket and withdrew a bit of red-and-white fabric. She shook it out.

His lungs froze. It was the bandana that Helen had often worn. "Where did you find that?" The words croaked from his throat.

"It was shoved behind a shelf. I guess no one noticed it." She handed it to him.

He couldn't remember lifting his arm and taking it but the bandana lay across his palm. It was worn on the corners, frayed along one edge. Helen had always worn it when out riding.

But never in town. When in town, she dressed more ladylike, as if she didn't want people to associate her with the ranch.

As if she wanted to be something other than what she was.

Just as she wanted Levi to pretend he didn't know her when they were both in town.

She'd worn it about her neck when she'd told him they could only be friends in secret.

She'd made him feel less than a person, less than a man.

Only a shameful half-breed.

He stuffed the bandana into his pocket. "Thanks," he managed to say, though it wasn't thanks he felt. He did not welcome the reminder of who Helen was or how she felt about him. Worse, how she made him feel about himself.

He grabbed a stack of dishes and strode toward the house.

Chapter Twelve

Beatrice had seen the flash of pain in Levi's eyes. The poor man still hurt from Helen's death. She followed him to the house. "Levi—"

But Susanne and Liz had entered, carrying food to put away, and she couldn't say anything at the moment.

Levi hurried away.

She'd wait until the others left.

The women returned to sit by Maisie.

Frank followed Tanner and Johnny around as they looked at Big Sam's horses.

Little Adam fell asleep in Willow's lap.

Liz, Sarah and Celia wandered away, enjoying each other's company.

Janie and Robbie raced back to the women. "You want to play with us?" Janie asked Dolly.

"You can go play," Beatrice urged the child.

Dolly considered it a moment then shyly followed the two children. They wandered away.

Beatrice leaned back on her elbows content to watch

Dolly. She didn't quite join in the play, but seemed happy to be with the other children.

Her gaze slid toward the men at the horses. Levi stood elbow-to-elbow with his brothers, but it seemed to her from the way he stared into the distance that he was only there physically. She ached for him. If only she could do something to ease his pain.

The women shared news of the past few weeks and Beatrice let her thoughts drift away.

"Tell us about yourself."

Beatrice sat up as she realized Susanne meant her. The two younger women leaned forward as if eager for information. She glanced to Maisie.

"Tell them about yourself," the older woman encouraged.

Beatrice couldn't think how to describe her life to these women, who were surrounded by love and acceptance. "I'm from Chicago," she finally managed to say.

Susanne touched Beatrice's brocade skirt. "I knew you must be from a big city. Your dress is very fashionable."

"Thank you." She would trade every inch of fine fabric for what these women had—love, acceptance, family and worth.

"Why have you come out west?" Willow's voice was gentle, not a hint of judgment.

Beatrice looked past the women to Levi. He alone knew of her real reason. What would they think if they knew it was to avoid being used as bait for a suitable son-in-law? Why, she wondered, didn't Father simply take a suitable man into the business? But he insisted he must be part of the family. Did he think Beatrice owed it to him for her failure in being born a girl? Realizing the women still waited for her answer, she said, "I felt the need of a change and thought what better place than Montana?"

"How do you like it here?" Willow asked.

Beatrice didn't know if she meant here at the ranch or here in Montana and settled for the latter. "Montana is beautiful."

"And wild," Susanne said.

"Just like the men. Until they meet the right woman." Willow and Susanne grinned at each other then they turned their gazes to Beatrice.

She looked from one to the other and shifted her gaze to Maisie. Why did they all watch her so intently? Surely they didn't think… Her and Levi? They were wrong. She must clear up any false ideas. "As soon as Maisie is well enough she doesn't need help, I will return to Granite Creek."

"Are you planning to return to Chicago at that time?" Willow asked.

"No, I'm not. Aunt Opal is looking for a position for me."

The women blinked as if surprised.

"What sort of position?" Willow asked.

Anything, she thought. "A nanny. A housekeeper." Embarrassed, she ducked her head. "I admit I don't have much experience. But I'm learning."

"She learns very quickly," Maisie said.

"Thank you."

"What about Dolly?" Susanne looked at the little girl playing with her younger nieces and nephews.

Beatrice explained about the aunt. "As soon as she

makes arrangements, Dolly will be going to her." A lump in her throat choked off her voice.

Willow patted her hand. "I'm sorry. It's obvious you've grown fond of her."

Susanne nodded. "Levi has, too."

The pair shifted to look at their brother-in-law.

"I would have never brought that bandana if I'd known he'd be so upset," Willow said.

Maisie reached for Willow's hand and squeezed it. "You had only good intentions. But when it comes to Helen, Levi is very closemouthed."

They all watched Levi, making it possible for Beatrice to study him without drawing attention to herself.

The conversation turned to other things until Adam stirred and wakened with a smile.

Willow hugged him. "I can still hardly believe how God has blessed me. My son has a loving father. My sisters are safe and sound. We are a happy family." Her eyes glowed with joy as she looked to where Celia and Sarah played with the younger children, then sought out Johnny still talking to his father and brothers.

Beatrice jerked her gaze away as her lungs tightened and tears pressed at the back of her eyes. Oh, to have what Willow had. But she wasn't even sure what it was Willow had that she wanted.

"I feel the same. I'm so blessed." Susanne's eyes sought Tanner's.

Their gazes met across the distance and Tanner straightened, a smile upon his lips, and strode toward them. Susanne was on her feet before he reached them.

"We should get the kids home," Tanner said. "Thanks

for everything, Ma. You, too." He nodded toward Beatrice. "And thanks for taking care of her."

Johnny had followed and scooped up little Adam, who held out his arms to the man.

Johnny added his thanks and soon the children were gathered up and in their respective wagons.

Big Sam went to each wagon and bade them goodbye. Levi did, too, but as soon as the wagons left the yard, he returned to the horse pasture to watch the animals grazing.

Dolly pressed to Beatrice's side or she would have gone to Levi immediately. She understood Dolly's need for reassurance, but could not speak frankly with the child present, so instead she folded the tablecloth and took it to the house. Big Sam carried Maisie in. "Do you want to rest?" he asked her.

"No, I'm fine. Put me in the chair if you don't mind."

"I don't mind." He settled her in the comfortable chair and kissed her cheek. "I just don't want you to overdo it."

Maisie patted his cheek. "I am well taken care of thanks to you and Beatrice."

Beatrice turned away, unable to watch the love between them without choking up. It seems these Harding men loved well and deeply. She glimpsed Levi, who was still at the corrals. Loving deeply meant hurting just as deeply when something went amiss.

"Dolly, why don't you get Smokey and play with her?"

Dolly rushed to get the kitten from the bedroom.

As Beatrice waited for her to take the kitten outside, she did her best not to look continually out the window, then realized she wandered restlessly about the kitchen and forced herself to stand still before the cupboard, though she must have looked like she was lost, for she had no reason to study the contents.

Dolly returned and Beatrice turned to Maisie. "Can I leave Dolly here while I go for a walk?"

"Of course you may. And don't hurry back. Take all the time you need." Maisie was about to add more, but Beatrice spoke before she could, not caring for the knowing look in the older woman's eyes.

"Thank you." She hurried from the house.

She got as far as the rosebush and stopped. What did she think she could say that would make any difference? But she must try. She bent over one of the pink blossoms and breathed in the scent, finding it gave her a touch of courage. If only she had shears, she would take a blossom with her. She tried to break off one of the delicate blooms, but succeeded only in pricking her finger. She pulled a handkerchief from her pocket to blot the drops. It was the same handkerchief as she'd used to wipe away Levi's blood. Now it had stains from both of them.

She told herself it meant nothing but her heart believed otherwise.

Levi shifted. She must hurry before he left, so she crossed the yard to stand at his side.

He glanced toward her, then went back to studying the horses. "I hope you enjoyed the day."

"Yes, I did. Your family is not like any I've seen before."

He slowly came around to face her. "Because we're half-breeds?"

She stared at him in total surprise then quickly recovered. "Technically only three of you are half-breeds. And no, that is not what I meant. Your family is so loving and accepting and so…" She shrugged, not able to find words to express the feeling that hovered at the edges of her thoughts.

He shrugged as well and looked again at the horses.

She knew what she wanted to say to him, but she didn't know the words and simply followed her feelings. She touched his arm. "Levi, I am so sorry for the pain you still carry over the loss of Helen. Willow regrets bringing that bandana. She thought it would comfort you. Instead, it upset you."

He yanked the red material from his pocket. "This? She thinks this upsets me?" His words were harsh, his expression harder. He tossed the bit of fabric to the earth and with the heel of his boot ground it into the muck. "Everyone thinks I sorrow over her death and of course I do." His eyes bored into hers. "But she left me weeks before she died because she didn't want to be associated with a man who was part Indian. She said we could be friends in secret, out here in the country." His gaze circled the landscape and came back to her, full of an ancient pain.

Her hand went to his arm, but she kept her fingers still despite an urge to squeeze them and offer what little comfort she could. She sensed he would shake her hand off if he realized it was there.

"She did not want people to judge her poorly because of me." The agony in his voice sliced through her like a sharpened knife.

She silently prayed for the right words to say to him.

To make him understand that it was who he was inside that mattered, not what others thought of him. "You are fearfully and wonderfully made." The words were from scripture but she didn't know if she quoted the verse correctly or not. "Can't you see that?"

He grew very still. His breathing slowed. "Can you?"

Oh, if only he knew that she saw him as a man with strengths that she'd ached for all her life. A man who showed gentleness and kindness, sought the well-being of others, who—

His eyes burned a hole through her defenses and she felt exposed and vulnerable.

She jerked away, afraid he would read her thoughts. Yet she had to answer his question, if only to prove to him he was acceptable in her sight. "Levi, I think it matters less what I think of you than what you think of yourself."

He caught her by the shoulder and turned her to face him. "Beatrice, listen to yourself. Take your own advice and stop seeing yourself as insignificant and useless. Stop seeing yourself as your father taught you to. You, too, are fearfully and wonderfully made."

Her cheeks burned. He meant did she see herself as she wanted him to see himself.

Levi had thrown her words back at her only to divert the conversation from him. As soon as he'd spoken, he realized how true the words were, but seeing the way her cheeks colored and her eyes glistened, he wished he could pull them back. He had no desire to hurt her.

How could he make up for it?

He caught her hand and tucked it around his elbow. "It seems we both have to learn to see ourselves as God sees us." He didn't know if he could ever do that. Or perhaps, he meant he would never be able to believe others could accept him fully. "Weren't you about to tell me what you thought of my family?" He wanted to hear more. And mostly, he wanted to turn their thoughts toward more pleasant things.

For a moment he thought she might withdraw and then she relaxed, her hand warm in the crook of his arm.

"I am amazed at how kind and loving they are to each other. It thrills me to think of the children in both families finding such loving homes."

They had begun to walk down the little trail by the horse pasture.

She lifted her face toward him. "I wish and pray for Dolly to find the same kind of love and acceptance."

He caught her shoulder with his free hand. "I do, too, though I will be sad to see her leave. I wonder how long before the aunt replies."

"I will miss Dolly more than I ever expected to."

He nodded agreement. "I wonder if she'll feel safe enough with her aunt to start talking aloud."

Beatrice chuckled. "I've gotten used to her quietness. And after an afternoon with seven rowdy kids, I think I appreciate it."

They shared a laugh then fell into step again.

He longed to know more about her. What was her childhood like? Had she known accepting love from anyone? The kind Levi and his brothers had known—from both parents and then a loving stepmother?

"What sort of things did you do to amuse yourself as a child?"

She got a faraway look in her eyes. "I read lots. Did needlework. I'm quite good at it, actually." Her smile was faintly apologetic. "I spent two winters working a picture of a parrot atop flowers." Her smile deepened, easing tension from his throat.

She continued, her voice slightly mocking as if she realized how bland her life sounded. "I love the bright colors in it."

Although he enjoyed watching the play of emotions in her eyes, he had hoped for more insight into her childhood than picturing her bent over her needlework, shut indoors, watching life from a nearby window. "Didn't you play?"

She shifted her gaze past him. "I once had a friend, Isabelle. She was allowed to run and jump and play. I joined her until my parents discovered my activities." She let out a soft sight. "After that Izzy no longer came to play and I was taught how a young lady should properly conduct herself."

Levi didn't realize his jaw had clamped like a vise as his imagination of her childhood grew even more depressing. Beatrice made it sound as if she was not allowed to enjoy normal childhood play.

"That's sad. Maybe here you can learn to have fun again." Maybe he'd make sure she did. Like time spent on the swing or exploring wildflowers. But there were so many other enjoyments he'd like to introduce her to. And he could start right now.

He grabbed her hand and broke into a trot, pulling her along with him. He had to slow down when they reached the trees, but as they navigated the narrow path he did not release her hand. They reached the river. "One of the things me and my brothers liked to do was skip rocks."

"How do you do that?"

He chuckled at the bewildered look on her face. "You choose a flat rock." He picked up a suitable one. "And hold it like this then throw it to the water." His rock skipped twice before it sank. He found another rock and handed it to her. "You try it."

She threw the rock and it sank immediately.

"Try again."

She tried again and the rock again sank.

"You need to throw it sort of sideways. Like this." He reached around her and guided her hand. She fit perfectly in his arms, her shoulders just below his chin. Her hair tickled his nose, the scent of roses filled his senses. He might have fallen in the sun-warmed water in a nearby pool left in the eddy of some overhanging trees for the way everything else melted away.

He tried to remember what he was supposed to be doing.

Showing her how to skip rocks. Yes.

He eased her arm back, then propelled it forward quickly. "Release the rock now."

She did and it skipped once. "I did it!" She turned about in his arms to grin triumphantly at him.

His arms circled her.

Her eyes darkened and her smile faded.

They looked into each other's eyes. He let her see all his hopes and dreams and wishes for her. And if some of them were his own…

He blinked, not wanting her to see his own longings.

A smile unlike any he'd ever seen before—full of sweetness and longing, trust and caution, and things he couldn't, wouldn't, identify—filled her eyes and gently curved her lips.

"Levi." His name was so sweet on her lips that he couldn't think.

A crow flew overhead, cawing harshly. The sound jerked Levi to his senses and he forced his unwilling arms to release her. He must remember that he was a half-breed, and she was a city girl whose plans were bigger than a ranch in Montana.

"Try it on your own now." He chose a flat rock and handed it to her.

She plucked it from his palm, her eyes on his.

He read the hurt and uncertainty in her gaze but he could do nothing to erase it. She deserved so much more than he could ever offer her.

She lowered her gaze and tossed the rock. It sank. She crossed her arms over her chest. "I'm no good at this sort of thing." She shook her head when he handed her another rock.

He skipped it himself. But no bouncing rock would ease the regret that stole away the pleasure of the moment.

"Can you let me know the next time someone goes to town? I need to send a note to my aunt." She continued to stare at the rippling water.

She couldn't make it any plainer that she was anxious to make other arrangements. "Of course." He might wish no one would go for several weeks but what would it change?

Chapter Thirteen

Beatrice returned to the house. Maisie assured her there was plenty of food left over from the picnic to provide supper. "Take the rest of the afternoon off and play with Dolly. The poor child has been moping about the place since you left."

Beatrice fell on her knees before the child. "Did you think I had left?"

Dolly nodded, her eyes full of unshed tears.

Beatrice folded the child into her arms. "I'm sorry. I would never leave you. I only went out for walk."

Dolly's tears wet Beatrice's neck as she rocked the child back and forth. Oh, if only she could ease the pain this child carried. She got to her feet and took Dolly's hand. "Let's go outside for a while."

Maisie smiled her approval as they left the house.

Beatrice looked around. She must avoid Levi at all costs after that scene at the river. She rubbed her arm with her free hand, trying to erase the feel of Levi's arms about her. The way he'd held her had made her feel so safe…so hungry for more. She hadn't meant to turn to him, or at least, she hadn't realized how quickly her excitement over skipping a rock would change to something more. Something erupting from the depths of her being, something so unexpected, so vast, she had called out to Levi like a drowning woman would call out for help.

He'd only been interested in showing her how to skip rocks.

It had taken several minutes for her to compose herself.

She wasn't sure her composure could bear seeing him face-to-face at the moment.

To her relief, he led his horse from the barn and rode away.

To her sorrow, he didn't so much as glance toward the house.

It was for the best. Now she could relax and devote her attention to Dolly. She led the child past the barn and up the hill. "Shall we pick flowers and take them to Maisie?"

Dolly nodded and they spent several minutes making a bouquet of wildflowers.

Their arms were full but Beatrice didn't care to return to the house yet. She didn't belong here and it seemed fitting to sit on the hillside and look at the ranch from a distance.

Dolly sat beside her and pressed her head to Beatrice's arm. Beatrice lay the bouquets on the ground beside them and wrapped her arms around the child and simply held her, knowing no other way to offer comfort to a five-year-old child.

Dolly began to speak in her quiet whisper and Beatrice held very still, afraid anything she said or did would make the child stop talking.

"Mama said we would have so many flowers when we found our new place. She said we would have a nice home and maybe even a baby brother or sister."

Beatrice waited, wondering if Dolly would say more. She was no expert on dealing with grief, especially in a child, but she sensed Dolly needed to talk about what happened instead of keeping it all inside. Maybe then she would begin to talk aloud.

Just when she wondered if the child was done, Dolly spoke again.

"Papa got sick and we had to stop. I asked if this was our new home but Mama said we weren't there yet. Then Mama got sick." Dolly shuddered. "I tooked care of her."

Beatrice had helped Aunt Opal with the sick and wondered how a child would manage.

"I guess they died."

Beatrice had to stop her arms from tightening too much. She'd assumed, everyone had, that the child knew her parents were dead. Even Dolly had said they were gone. But did she understand the finality of death? She pulled Dolly to her lap and caught her chin so their eyes connected.

"Your mama and papa are buried in the churchyard in Granite Creek. I'll take you there when we go to town, if you like."

Dolly nodded again. She lowered her gaze. "When are we going?"

"As soon as Maisie is well enough that she doesn't need my help every day."

"Okay." The little girl continued to search Beatrice's eyes. "Can I stay with you?"

A lump the size of a horse lodged in her throat. "I wish you could, but you have an aunt. Do you remember her?"

Dolly shook her head. Tears gushed silently from her eyes.

With a groan from the bottom of her heart, Beatrice hugged the child close. "Oh, my sweet child." At a loss as to how to comfort her, Beatrice rocked back and forth. After a bit she began to sing, as much for her sake as Dolly's. But after a few minutes, the little girl relaxed in her arms.

Beatrice stopped singing.

"Sing some more," Dolly said. "I like it."

So Beatrice sang, grateful she could offer this one thing. And she prayed for Dolly. *Please may her aunt be kind and loving and fill this child's life with joy.*

A horse crested a nearby hill and pulled to a stop.

It was Levi and she watched him, wishing things could be different, but that would mean she would be a different person. If only that was possible. She'd been born a Doyle, her family rich, but Beatrice herself was of no value.

She bowed her head over Dolly's and let her tears flow.

Beatrice woke in early morning silence the next day with an aching heart. She'd grown too fond of Levi. How could she have let this happen? She'd felt so safe in his arms and had silently asked for more. But nothing had changed between them. He still guarded his heart. And she still didn't fit into ranch life.

Would he ever believe he was fearfully and wonderfully made?

Dolly lay beside her, Smoky curled up at her side.

Was it her imagination or did the child seem more relaxed since they'd talked? The pain in Beatrice's heart was not imagined as she thought of life without Dolly.

As she dressed, she acknowledged she would never be the same woman who had left Chicago a few weeks ago. But who would she be and where would she go?

Whatever and wherever the good Lord led her, she would do her best to prove she could handle the situation. She would pen a note to Aunt Opal this afternoon and ask if there was any position available for her yet. If not, she would assist Aunt Opal until she found one.

Her resolve in place, she headed for the kitchen to prepare breakfast.

Big Sam carried Maisie to her chair. "She says she feels completely better and I checked her wound. There's no sign of infection." He kissed Maisie on the nose. "You continue to be a good girl."

Maisie chuckled.

"I'll have a quick look around before breakfast." He strode from the room. Levi had already gone out. They were both anxious about any mischief the intruders might perpetrate.

Maisie sighed. "It's nice to be cared for so faithfully but I'm getting a little weary of it. As soon as Big Sam leaves after breakfast, I want you to look at my wound and give your honest assessment. I think it should be getting better enough I can start to move around."

"I don't want to be accused of aiding and abetting," Beatrice protested. "Big Sam would never forgive me."

"Pshaw. You leave him to me."

Beatrice shrugged and turned back to the stove. She'd have a look at the wound but she wouldn't go against Big Sam's opinion.

Big Sam stomped on the step, spoke to someone. She recognized Levi's voice. Tension flooded through her.

Would he remember how she'd leaned into his arms and practically begged for a kiss? More than that… she'd ached for his acceptance. She kept her back to the men as they took their places at the table.

Beatrice finished serving the meal, then sat down. Big Sam reached for her hand on one side, Maisie reached for Dolly's and Beatrice and Dolly clasped hands. She stole a glance at Levi. He had his head bowed.

She wasn't disappointed that he didn't look at her. Nor was she disappointed when he left the house with a barely there goodbye. At least he gave Dolly a hug. Big Sam paused to kiss Maisie before he left.

Beatrice set her attention on the dish pan and the dirty dishes so she could hide from Maisie the way her mouth pulled down in sadness and confusion.

"They're gone. Now look at my wound."

Beatrice hesitated. "Big Sam won't be happy."

"Leave him to me."

Levi wouldn't be happy, either. He'd hold Beatrice responsible if anything happened to Maisie.

"Beatrice, please."

She sighed. She could hardly disobey Maisie and she went to the woman's side, waited for her to shift so Beatrice could discreetly look at the wound.

"It's looking very good."

"Are the edges mended together? No open areas?"

"Yes and no." She answered several more questions.

"Good, then it's safe to get up. Otherwise I'm going to get as stiff as a board."

Beatrice admired her for taking her time and moving cautiously. After she returned to her chair, Maisie had Beatrice check the wound again to see if there was any sign of bleeding. There wasn't.

"Good. That means it's okay for me to be up a little bit."

Beatrice wondered how long she meant to keep her activity a secret from her husband. Her question was answered at the noon meal.

Maisie smiled across table. "I got up and walked around this morning."

"What?" Big Sam roared and came to his feet.

Levi looked at Beatrice then, his brow raised in disbelief as if to ask how she could have let it happen. How she could be so bold as to challenge his pa and put his mother in danger.

Big Sam turned to Beatrice. "Why didn't you stop her?"

Maisie laughed softly. "Do you really think she could?"

Big Sam settled back in his chair. "No, but I do expect you to listen to me."

"If I listened to you I would be in this chair for a

year. I didn't do anything foolish. I had Beatrice look at my wound both before and after I was up. She assures me there was no change. I promise I will take it easy, but Sam, I will not let you turn me into an invalid."

Maisie gave Levi an equally penetrating look. "Nor you, either, son."

Both men looked a little sheepish.

"Now then, that's settled." Maisie seemed quite pleased with herself.

Beatrice contemplated the event as she did the dishes. Had Maisie always been so confident in confronting Big Sam?

After dinner, Maisie got up again and insisted on helping with some of the work. Beatrice would not be needed much longer at the ranch.

"Let's go outside," she said to Dolly and took her hand. They both faced an uncertain future.

Levi had to stay away from home. He was thinking of Beatrice far too often and far too long. The fact the intruders had done nothing for the past few days provided the perfect excuse.

"Pa, I think I should have a look around and see if I can spot these fellas. I might take along my bedroll in case I end up too far to return."

Big Sam had given him a moment's hard study. "For a week you would hardly leave the place. I had to send Charlie to check on the line cabins to the north. Now you want to go. Might this have anything to do with the way Beatrice jerks her gaze away from you so fast?" He didn't give Levi a chance to answer. "Son, you can't keep running from your feelings."

Levi swallowed back a hot reply. "Didn't I say I was going to look for those men that have been causing trouble?"

"Yup, you did. Go ahead. Don't stay away too long."

"I won't." But even as he said it he knew he would find an excuse to stay away.

He rode to the west, searching both the landscape and the ground in front of him for any clues. He saw nothing. He stopped at a little hollow not more than five miles from the ranch buildings and found evidence of a campfire. The grass was flattened where men had sat. Horse droppings nearby indicated they'd been there long enough for the horse to graze.

He hunkered down and studied the place. Why would they leave this obvious sign of a camp when they'd been so careful to hide their tracks until now? He stood up and carefully studied his surroundings. Nothing to indicate the intruders. Were they deliberately taunting him? But who? And why?

Leading Scout, he climbed from the hollow and circled the area, carefully looking for clues. For about ten yards, he followed a trail but then it disappeared on rocks. He swung to Scout's back and rode in the direction the trail had taken. Not a sign. It was like they had vanished.

It was like they'd been trained like Levi and his brothers on how to hide their tracks.

The sun dipped toward the west. He pulled to a halt and considered his options. Pa wouldn't expect him back. But what if this was a trick to get Levi away from the buildings?

Most of the cowboys were away from the ranch,

though Pa had ordered a man to keep watch at night. But if Pa rode away to take care of something, the women would be alone and unguarded.

What if Beatrice wandered down to the river, or up the hill to look for flowers?

Who would make sure she was safe?

He galloped toward home.

Pa stood at the barn door as he approached.

Levi ignored the knowing smile on his face. "Saw a sign of where they camped but no sign of the men."

Pa grunted. "The men haven't seen anyone hanging about. Could be they were just passing through and bored with themselves. If there's nothing in another week, I'll relax the guard."

Levi wanted to ask him to keep a guard posted until Beatrice returned to Granite Creek, but his throat tightened so much he feared his voice would give away his worry. Now that Maisie was getting up, it wouldn't be long until Beatrice left.

Then he could forget her and return to his normal life.

He closed his eyes for a moment as he led Scout into the barn. His life would never be normal again. He grabbed the saddle and flopped it to the stand with more force than it required.

Big Sam had followed him inside. "No need to beat up your saddle because you're in a knot."

"I'm not in a knot." If only he could make himself believe it.

"Levi, you've been running from your feelings ever since Helen died. I know her drowning was tragic and we all feel bad, but, son, life does go on. It's okay to let yourself care about someone else. I loved your ma but I sure am happy to be able to love Maisie." Pa grinned widely. "You can love again, too, son." He slapped Levi on the back and stood back, as if pleased with himself for setting Levi straight on matters of the heart.

Levi was sorely tempted to clear up Pa's misconception. But telling him that he had been rejected because of his mixed blood would only hurt his pa, so he grabbed a curry brush and tended his horse without answering.

After a bit, Pa realized he didn't intend to say anything more on the subject, so with a grunt he pushed away from lounging against the fence and moseyed out of the barn.

The supper bell rang and Levi groaned. If he had a lick of sense he would have stayed away until after the meal.

Instead he followed Pa inside, kissed Maisie on the cheek, happy to see she sat with her leg on the stool. Maybe she'd found being up did more harm than she thought it would.

Dolly stood by with an expectant look on her face. His conscience stung. In avoiding Beatrice, he had also avoided the little girl. That wasn't fair. She had already dealt with enough loss and uncertainty. He swung her into his arms and rubbed his whiskery chin against her cheek, earning him a joyful giggle.

He couldn't help himself. He looked at Beatrice, wanting to share his joy in this child.

She watched him but ducked away when his gaze reached her.

"How's your leg?" Big Sam asked Maisie.

Maisie waved away his concern. "I'm fine and I'm not doing anything foolish. You can ask Beatrice."

Levi's gaze went to her.

She looked at Big Sam. "She's being very cautious."

"Good. Now let's eat."

Levi carried Dolly to her chair, lingering there until Beatrice had no choice but to move to his side. He pulled out her chair and held it as she seated herself. Her shoulders pressed to his hands as he guided the chair into place.

She did not pull away.

Mentally kicking himself for noticing and caring, he hurried to his place.

He would leave as soon as the meal ended and stay away until everyone was in bed, but first he had to get through supper.

As usual, they went around the table to tell of their day. When it was her turn, Dolly looked straight at him as she spoke in her usual whisper.

"My mama and papa are in the cemetery at the church. Beatrice says I can go see their graves. Maybe you could take me."

His gaze jerked toward Beatrice. Had she had this conversation with Dolly? He should have been there to hold them both. He returned his attention to Dolly. He would not give a promise he couldn't be sure of keeping. "I will take you if I can but no promises. Okay?"

She sighed, her disappointment evident in the way her shoulders sank. "Okay," she said with resignation.

He had to make up for it as best he could. "Would you like to go for a walk with me after supper?"

She nodded and smiled as if he was forgiven. "Beatrice, too?"

"Of course." It was the last thing he wanted. And the first.

"I'll do up the dishes first," Beatrice said after a half beat of silence.

He ended up helping. Only so he could get this outing over with, he insisted. But he could not deny the truth. He was eager to spend time with Beatrice and Dolly.

Try as he might, he could not fight the feeling. So why not enjoy it, even knowing it was temporary.

So he teased Dolly as they dried dishes. He told jokes that had them all laughing. He nudged Beatrice as he shared a laugh with her.

After tonight he would go back to fighting his attraction to her.

They finished dishes and left the house. Dolly walked between them, holding hands with both of them. She swung their hands and giggled.

He glanced at Beatrice. "Let's give her a swing." He lifted his hand to indicate what he meant and they swung her off the ground, earning them happy laughter.

It felt so good and right that he laughed, too.

Beatrice joined in, her eyes shining with what he could only think was joy.

Careful, he warned himself. *Don't be thinking it means more than it can.*

They wandered past the barn and the pigpens.

He and Beatrice glanced at each other and smiled at a shared memory.

Reaching the end of the buildings, he stopped and had a good look around. Was that smoke he saw in the distance or only a bit of cloud?

He searched for the cowboy who was to be on guard and saw him looking in the same direction.

If it was smoke and it came from a campfire of scoundrels that had been plaguing them, they would not find it easy to slip in and out and do mischief.

Just the same, he meant to be careful. "Let's go back."

Tomorrow he would investigate.

He took Beatrice and Dolly back to the house and retraced his steps to watch the smoke. It had all but disappeared. Big Sam joined him. "I'll ride out there tomorrow and see who it is. You stay here and make sure everything is okay."

"Yes, Pa." He welcomed the decision. He'd feel better if he was here to make sure Beatrice and Dolly and Ma were safe.

Never mind that everything he did threatened the safe-keeping of his heart.

Chapter Fourteen

Beatrice poured herself into work the next day. She told herself it was to keep Maisie from doing too much, but mostly it was an attempt to block her wayward thoughts.

Levi had been away most of yesterday. She didn't blame him for wanting to avoid her. After all, she'd practically fallen into his arms, practically begged him to love her.

She should know better than to think he could. She wasn't sure anyone could love her.

About the time she thought she might be able to live with the fact that she wished in vain for the kind of love she saw between Maisie and Big Sam, the kind she'd seen between Tanner and Susanne, and Johnny and Willow, Levi had been charming and amusing. Certainly his attention had been for Dolly. But Beatrice had felt included.

How was she to keep her thoughts straight—focused on her future and the life she meant to create for herself—when he was so nice to her?

However, he'd been distant this morning and left in a great hurry.

She could have ignored him successfully except Maisie had sent her outside on one errand and then another. Dig potatoes. Ask Soupy for more milk. Take the slop to the pigs.

Every time she went outside, she saw Levi.

And even though she ducked away, pretending she didn't see, she felt him in every pore.

While she still tried to sort her thoughts, the men trooped in for dinner.

"By the way," Sam said, "I ran in to a family heading for Idaho and invited them to join us for supper."

Maisie sat up, then grimaced at the pain her movements brought. "I'll have to get up. I can't entertain sitting like this."

"Now Maisie, they won't care. You sit right there and make them feel welcome as you always do and they won't even notice that you can't get up." From the tone of Big Sam's voice, Beatrice knew he meant his words as a warning for Maisie to take it easy.

"It might help to know how many to expect," Maisie said with some degree of frustration.

"I think I counted four children plus their parents. Will that be a problem?" He glanced from Beatrice to Maisie.

Six more. Beatrice barely managed a few meals for five people. Now almost a dozen. It was impossible. She ducked her head so no one would see the shock in her eyes. How easily they all seemed to forget she was not used to this kind of work.

But Maisie said yes. "We'll manage just fine. Where did you find these people?"

Big Sam helped himself to the potatoes before he answered. "I saw smoke from their campfire last night and went to investigate."

That brought Beatrice's attention to Levi, but it was not her right to voice her question.

Thankfully, Maisie did. "Are these the people who have been hanging about causing trouble?"

"Hardly think so," Big Sam said. "For one thing, it's a little hard to hide a wagon."

Relief flooded through Beatrice. Still her gaze stayed with Levi as she saw the worry in his eyes. Not knowing who was responsible, and not being able to stop them, understandably left him concerned.

Was Levi in danger from these people?

She jerked her gaze away to hide the fear that made her want to clutch at her middle.

Thankfully she was too busy the rest of the after-noon to dwell on the matter. She made a huge batch of biscuits and fried meat covered with gravy and put it all in the oven to stew. She dug potatoes and carrots and prepared them.

"You'll need to make a dessert," Maisie said.

Beatrice jerked to a halt. "Are you sure you want me to? I might ruin it."

Maisie laughed. "You haven't ruined anything."

"Have you forgotten the blackened meat, the half-cooked potatoes, the bread that I had to throw out—" She tossed her hands upward. "So many things I've ruined."

"And so many things that turned out just fine. You

have learned very quickly. Now let me tell you how to make apple pandowdy. I'd do it myself except my leg is a little sore although I hate to admit it."

"You rest and I'll do my best." Though she wondered if Maisie was simply forcing Beatrice to try something new. But even if that was true, she was here to help and she would. So she measured and poured and mixed, letting Dolly help with each step. She put the dessert in the oven.

It had baked to perfection—in Maisie's estimation—and Beatrice put the heavy pan on the cupboard. If it tasted as good as it looked she would proudly serve it.

At the sound of wheels rumbling, she glanced out the window. A wagon pulled in by the barn and was soon surrounded by a crowd. Big Sam had said six people, but it looked like a lot more. Maybe because they were all big people. She'd assumed children meant little people.

She checked her reflection in the mirror over the washstand. She had flour on her nose and splattered across her front. "Goodness, I'm a mess." Good thing she wore a big apron to cover her dress. She removed her soiled apron just as Levi hurried in.

Big Sam entered on his son's heels, leading the visitors. "This is my wife, Maisie. I'm afraid she can't get to her feet. She's injured her leg. My son, Levi. Little Dolly and Miss Beatrice Doyle, who is helping out."

Big Sam then indicated the visitors. "This is Stu Bagley, his wife, Trudy, their sons, Morgan, Konrad and Ray." The boys were all a good size though the youngest might not yet be fourteen. "And their daughter, Emma."

The young lady stepped from behind her brothers. Her dark brown hair hung in ripples down to her waist. Her dark blue eyes brought to mind the river on a moonlit evening. She was tiny and well-shaped.

Beatrice greeted the newcomers.

Levi couldn't stop staring at Emma. Not that she blamed him. The young lady was exceptionally beautiful, though with eyes as old as her mother's.

There was a general shuffle as everyone found a place to sit. Beatrice managed to get her place next to Maisie with Dolly between them and stared across at Levi. His gaze never left Emma, who sat beside Beatrice.

Beatrice didn't care that he had never given her that sort of attention. Maybe if she'd left her hair loose and wore a dress with a neckline that revealed a lot of skin—

No reason for her to be snippy. He could drool over anyone he wanted to. It wasn't like it mattered to her. Her plans here were short-lived. Never mind that she shuddered inwardly at the idea.

"I'll say grace," Big Sam said as Mr. Bagley reached for the potatoes. Big Sam held out his hands, as did Maisie. Hands joined around the table.

She quickly bowed her head as Big Sam prayed.

The next few minutes she kept busy passing food. Then it was quiet, save for the sound of much chewing, which was very audible seeing as the Bagleys chewed with their mouths open.

One of the boys, she thought it was Morgan, glanced around the table. "You and him getting married?" he asked, indicating Beatrice and Levi.

Heat flared in her cheeks. "No. I'm just visiting."

Morgan persisted. "He ain't courtin' you?"

She shook her head. What an impertinent young man. A glance at Levi revealed he still had his eyes glued to Emma.

He swallowed loudly. "I'm not courting anyone. I don't plan on getting married."

The young lady tittered. "I can hardly believe that."

Beatrice barely kept from rolling her eyes. She didn't look at Emma but figured the girl would be batting her eyelashes at Levi. She knew she was correct when his skin darkened with a blush.

"Pa," Emma said, her mouth full of half-chewed meat. Somehow she managed to make herself understood anyway. "Maybe we should take a break here for a few days. You know, explore the possibilities."

Levi almost choked.

Beatrice finished her food and glanced around. Most plates were empty. "I'll prepare dessert."

She was about to gather up the dishes when two of the boys and Mr. Bagley took another serving of potatoes. They cleaned out the bowl and took the last half-dozen biscuits. Ray or Konrad—she couldn't remember which was which—ran his finger across the empty meat platter and licked up the last fragments.

It might be impolite but Beatrice stared. These people were sadly lacking in manners. She turned back to the cupboard to dish out the pudding. She filled a pitcher with thick cream. Would it go around the table? Maybe she should start it—where? There were Bagleys everywhere.

A short time later, the food gone and coffee served,

Maisie signaled for attention. "We have a custom here. We go around the table and tell about our day. Big Sam always starts."

Big Sam nodded. "I went and had another look at the coulee where the cows had been trapped. I think we could create a dam that would catch the spring runoff and give us a water supply for the summer. It will be hard work but I think it will be worth it."

Rather than embarrass anyone by going by age, Maisie simply proceeded around the table. Mr. Bagley said how fortunate they were to encounter Big Sam and be invited for a visit. Mrs. Bagley said she surely did appreciate some good victuals. Beside her, Morgan said he wanted to ride one of the ranch horses. Big Sam didn't comment.

One of the Bagley boys said he had seen some owls in a nearby tree.

Levi told about watching the burrowing owls with Beatrice. "She said she could hear the earth breathe."

The Bagleys laughed and Beatrice's face grew hot. Why had he said that? Did he want to see her mocked?

Levi held up a hand to silence the merriment. "If you sit on the ground and listen closely, you really can hear it."

Six Bagleys shook their heads but Morgan put words to their thoughts. "That's a peculiar thing to say." Beatrice smiled on the inside. Nice to know he didn't share the Bagleys' opinion.

Maisie was next and told of something Dolly said. Dolly refused to speak before so many strangers.

Then it was Beatrice's turn. What could she say that

wouldn't invite ridicule? But before she could speak, Emma did.

"This here is a nice ranch. How big is it? How many cows you got? Never mind. We're going to Idaho, where Pa has his sights on farming. 'Course, we'll have to work hard to make it succeed but one thing us Bagleys is good at is work. We know how to work. That's for sure."

Beatrice kept her gaze on the table in front of her. She dare not look at Levi for fear she would see him all calf-eyed at Emma again after her passionate speech.

Two of the Bagley boys talked about snaring gophers.

Beatrice felt Dolly's shock and wanted to cover her ears against the gory details the Bagleys provided. She'd cover her own, too, but wouldn't give any of them the satisfaction of seeing how she felt about the story.

Thankfully the meal and the sharing ended.

"Emma will help with dishes," Mrs. Bagley said. "Thank you for the nice meal." And with that the Bagleys trooped from the house.

But Beatrice couldn't relax. Not with Emma suddenly rushing around, stacking dishes right where Beatrice meant to put the dishpan, then shoving all the pots and pans into a corner almost as if she wished they could be forgotten.

Beatrice took her time about filling the dishpan and starting the dishes. Perhaps Emma would get bored and take herself elsewhere. Big Sam carried Maisie into the other room. Dolly took her cat and slipped outside. Beatrice hoped she wouldn't go too far away but then she never did.

"You don't know much about farm life, do ya?" she asked, taking a wet plate from Beatrice. "You a city girl?"

"I am."

"Huh. I guessed it."

Beatrice steadily washed dishes, offering nothing in way of conversation.

Finally the last dish was washed and dried and put away.

"Thank you for your help," Beatrice said.

Emma had her hand on the doorknob. "I could tell ya needed someone with experience." She left without a backward look.

Beatrice filled her lungs slowly and deeply. She grabbed the slop bucket and headed for the pigpen, welcoming the chance for fresh air.

Only after she was within smelling distance did she laugh at the idea of finding fresh air while feeding pigs.

She dumped the bucket's contents over the fence. Not anxious to return to the house and the possibility of encountering any of the Bagleys, she lingered to watch the pigs shove their snouts into the food. Pigs had no manners. People should, though, but she would not let unkind thoughts fill her mind and instead turned to watch the activity in the yard. Three cowboys sat on the bench under the verandah roof of the bunkhouse. Soupy leaned against the wall of the cookhouse, smoke clouding around him as he puffed on his cigarette.

She couldn't see the Bagleys' covered wagon from where she stood, but glimpsed one of the boys in the area. The others would likely be preparing their space for the night.

She knew Big Sam to be in the house with Maisie. A movement toward the barn caught her attention. Emma walking with purpose.

Beatrice stayed where she was, not moving, wondering if she would be noticed. But Emma had her sights fixed on the corrals closest to the pigpen. Why was she interested in them? Then Beatrice caught a flash of black. Like Levi's shirt. She watched closely and detected another movement. Levi hiding? She grinned at the possibility. She could have warned him he couldn't hide from a girl with such determination as she sensed in Emma.

The girl slipped through the narrow opening at the gate. "You waitin' for me to find you?" She giggled. "Here I am."

"I wasn't waiting for you. Just looking for some time alone."

Another giggle. "You're joshin'."

A beat of silence.

"How come you say you aren't getting married? You're good-looking and all."

Beatrice did not want to be privy to this conversation and looked around for escape, but any movement would draw their attention to her. They'd guess she'd overheard them. She drew back against the fence, wishing she could be invisible.

"I got other plans."

Beatrice tried to decide if Levi sounded dismissive or uncertain. Maybe a girl like Emma would cause him to reconsider his attitude about marriage.

"Maybe you could change your plans. Pa could always use another man to help start a new farm."

Beatrice could almost picture Emma batting her eyes and trying to be coy.

"It kinda looks to me like you could use a woman around here with some experience. That city gal isn't good for squat."

All sense of gentle persuasion disappeared when she spoke of Beatrice.

Beatrice held her breath. How would Levi respond? Not that he didn't agree. Nor could she. She was inept with the work expected of a ranch woman.

"She's managed fine so far despite the challenges. I wonder how we would function in her world?"

Beatrice smiled. He'd defended her.

Emma made a rude sound. "Who'd want to live in a city and be a sissy? Not me." Her voice changed. "I don't think you would, either. You're a farm boy. I could tell that right off."

"You might be right. I belong here on the ranch. Don't have any plans to change that."

"Why? You a mama's boy?"

Beatrice came away from the fence. How dare she? She sank back. She would not be the one to explain Levi to Emma.

"I am who I am."

Beatrice grinned at the dismissive tone of Levi's voice.

Emma's voice turned syrupy again. "I might persuade ya to think of leaving the ranch."

Beatrice couldn't see enough to know for certain that Emma had moved closer and maybe tried to get Levi to hug her, but she followed the black of his shirt and knew he had stepped away in rather a rush.

"Fine. Ya don't need to think yer the only good-looking man in this here country." Emma flounced out of the corral and marched to the Bagley wagon and out of sight.

Beatrice held her breath as Levi followed slowly and at a distance. He stepped out of the pen and looked around.

She tried to disappear into the wood of the fence, but it was impossible. She could only hope he wouldn't notice her.

But he looked steadily in her direction and then closed the distance between them.

Her cheeks burned. She'd been caught eavesdropping, though it had never been her intention.

He stopped ten feet away. "You heard everything?"

"I heard enough."

He shuddered. "That young woman scares me."

Beatrice tucked the knowledge into her heart, though she failed to acknowledge why it should please her. "She's very beautiful."

"I fear her looks are only skin-deep. She practically threw herself at me."

Beatrice grinned. "I didn't mean to spy but I couldn't help but see how you backed away from her."

"I would have run except I was penned in." He saw the empty slop bucket and picked it up. "Come. I'll walk you back to the house." He draped an arm about her shoulders and they walked with matched steps.

She understood he only did it to keep Emma at bay, but it nevertheless felt as if she fit right there. The thought had no business exposing itself. It did not belong in her world. She would continue with her plans...

She couldn't quite remember what the plans were.

Levi could not say what possessed him to put his arm around Beatrice. Yes, he hoped Emma would see them and realize he wasn't interested in her. But it wasn't Emma that had his heart thudding against his ribs. It was Beatrice. He hadn't realized she hovered nearby when he spoke to Emma, but it pleased him that she had overheard. He wanted her to know Emma held no interest for him. Never would he have the urge to pull her close like he did as he walked across the yard with Beatrice.

He tried to remember all the reasons he knew he should be fleeing such thoughts.

Why Beatrice shouldn't stay on the ranch even after Maisie's leg healed.

They reached the house and he set the slop bucket down and stepped away from Beatrice. His side, where she had brushed against him as they walked, grew suddenly cold, but he would not pull her back to that spot.

He was getting far too used to having her around. Growing to enjoy her presence, her smile. Learning to look forward to her comments that made him chuckle. He'd like to see her reaction to the cathedral of the trees, to the birth of baby calves and foals, to—

She wasn't staying. She wouldn't want to even if he asked.

She had other plans and so did he. He reminded himself what they were—guard his heart. He quietly, firmly closed the wobbling doors of his heart.

"Ma, Pa." The youngest Bagley boy trotted by the house toward the Bagley wagon. "Lookee what I found."

Mr. Bagley plucked something from the boy's hands and held it aloft.

"It's the kitten." Beatrice picked up her skirts and headed for the wagon.

Levi followed on her heels.

"It's too little to be any good to anyone." Mr. Bagley made to toss it aside just as Beatrice reached him and grabbed the kitten.

"It's mine." The boy lunged at Beatrice but she stepped aside.

"How can it be yours when it's on this property?" Beatrice demanded, cupping her hands over the yowling kitten so no one could take it from her.

The Bagley family gathered together in a tight group.

"It weren't in your barn or nothing, were it?" Morgan asked.

"Nah," young Ray said. "It was out there all alone and lost."

Beatrice took another step back right into Levi and then eased forward so they didn't touch. He didn't move and remained right there to back her up. He didn't care for the ugly expressions on every one of the Bagleys.

"That kitten belongs to Dolly. She must be out there somewhere."

"I didn't see no Dolly girl. You ought to thank me for rescuing it if it means so much to ya. Instead, sounds like yer accusing me of stealing."

Mr. Bagley's stance widened and his fists went to his hips. "My boys ain't thieves."

"'Sides," Morgan added. "That little cat ain't big enough for anything. It'll die, sure."

"It will not." Beatrice hurried toward the house with the kitten.

Levi looked from one Bagley to another. Emma scowled at him as fiercely as the others. Having no wish to antagonize any of them further, he followed Beatrice.

She went around the house. "Where's Dolly? Did that boy frighten her into hiding?"

She didn't wait for an answer, which was a good thing because Levi had none she would like.

"Dolly, Dolly," she called. "Listen."

He listened. Heard nothing.

"That boy scared her." She rubbed her cheek against the kitten, tears filling her eyes.

He trailed a finger along the kitten's back. His knuckles brushed Beatrice's cheek. He pulled his hand aside and rubbed it against his leg, which did nothing to slow the tingling that swept up his arm.

"We have to find her." Beatrice turned away, the kitten held close to her heart. "Dolly. Dolly. We have Smokey. She's safe and sound. Where are you?"

He grabbed her hand as they searched for the child. After several futile minutes he pulled her to a halt. "We'll never hear her. I wonder if Smokey knows where she is. Put her down and let's see."

Beatrice looked dubious. "What if she disappears, too? How would we explain that to Dolly?"

He could not guarantee the kitten wouldn't run off. "I have another idea."

"I hope it's better than the last."

He chuckled. "Me, too. Why don't we make Dolly come to us?"

She stared at him like he had two heads. "How do you suggest we do that?"

"Watch and listen." He turned toward the trees. "Dolly, Smokey is here looking for you. Can you hear her meow?"

Beatrice raised her eyebrows, definitely doubtful this would work.

He grinned. He'd heard a faint rustle and guessed— hoped—it might be Dolly. "Meow, meow. Smokey wonders where Dolly is."

Beatrice rolled her eyes. "If you think she'll believe that's really Smokey—"

He nudged her and pointed to a spot a few feet away. "What do you see?" he whispered.

"Dolly." She rushed forward and pulled the child into her arms. Poor Smokey would be crushed. But she didn't seem to mind and licked Dolly's teary face.

Levi knelt down beside them and wrapped them all in his arms. Never mind that he meant to keep a healthy distance from Beatrice.

She turned glistening eyes to him. "I didn't think you knew what you were doing. Thank you." She tipped her head up and kissed his cheek then withdrew. Her eyes conveyed surprise and something more…a feeling that echoed in his heart. As if this was where he belonged.

The earth stood still.

And then Dolly pulled Smokey into her arms. "That bad boy took him from me. Said he would hurt her."

Levi tried to bank back the anger that rushed up his throat. He pulled Dolly into his arms. "That boy won't hurt your kitten again." Or poor defenseless Dolly. He got to his feet and drew Beatrice up after him. "Let's get you all back to the house."

And then he had something to do so he could keep his promise to Dolly. He would tell the Bagleys they had until morning to leave. Pa and Maisie would stand by him once they heard the truth.

The truth. What was he going to do with his own truth?

He lengthened his strides, forcing Beatrice to trot after him.

The truth of what his heart wanted warred with the truth of what his experience told him.

Which was he to believe?

Chapter Fifteen

Beatrice fled to her room and closed the door behind her. Thankfully, no one witnessed her hurry and Dolly seemed as anxious to reach the safety of the bedroom as she. She leaned against the door and pressed her fingers to her lips. What had she been thinking to kiss Levi's cheek? Only that she was relieved Dolly was safe. But gratitude did not begin to describe her reaction. Never before had she felt such a jolt in her heart. A bolt of happiness that made her insides dance. Yes, he'd kissed her once before, but her initial reaction had been surprise. This time was different. This time she'd made the first move, been deliberate, but she had not been prepared for the response that raced through her.

Somehow she must get her reactions under control before she saw him again.

Telling herself he would never let himself care for her didn't help as much as she'd like.

She helped Dolly prepare for bed. Dolly insisted on story time, as usual.

Beatrice usually told her a Bible story. This time she

told about Ruth. She simplified the story for Dolly but she couldn't help thinking her life was like Ruth's in that she had gone to an unfamiliar land. From there, their stories went in opposite directions. Ruth was accepted and honored. Ruth became a wife and mother. Beatrice would continue her journey alone.

Dolly's eyes drifted shut. Beatrice put her into bed and tucked the covers around her.

Restless for answers to her longings, she opened her Bible. Reading from the Book of Matthew where her bookmark held her place only caused her disquiet to increase. *Oh, God, speak to my hungry, restless heart.* She flipped the pages of her Bible seeking an answer. The pages fell open at *Psalms* 138. She read it. Then read it again and again. "The Lord will perfect that which concerneth me: thy mercy, O Lord, endureth forever."

She pressed her fingers to the verse. "Lord, You know what concerns me." She tried to think specifics but her mind rattled with so many things. And her thoughts circled again and again back to Levi. His black hair, his all-seeing dark eyes, the way he lounged against a fence as he watched an animal, the feel on his fingers against her thumb, the roughness of his skin as she kissed him.

"Lord, do not forsake me." That wasn't what she meant. "Make me strong to do that which I must do." She closed her Bible, put it on the table next to her bed and prepared for the night.

She did not belong in this world. Wasn't even sure she was welcomed in it, though Maisie appeared to appreciate her help. She'd found being independent more of a challenge than she imagined possible and she didn't mean solely the tasks she felt totally inept to manage. Her heart had proved to be even less manageable.

She woke the next morning to the rattle of a wagon in the yard and leaped from bed to glance out the window. The Bagleys were leaving. She couldn't say she was sorry to see them go. Sounds of activity came from the kitchen. She groaned. It had taken hours to fall asleep last night and now she'd overslept. From the voices reaching her, she knew everyone else was already there. She wakened Dolly and helped her dress, then slipped into her own dress, brushed her hair hurriedly and wrapped it in a careless bun. No time for fussing this morning. She dashed to the kitchen. Maisie sat in her chair. Big Sam handed her a cup of coffee. Levi stood at the stove.

His gaze slipped to her hair. Already she could feel strands falling from the bun, but she resisted an urge to reach up and tidy it.

"Sorry I overslept. I see the Bagleys are leaving." She should not have mentioned the fact.

Levi and Big Sam exchanged looks.

"They're in a hurry to get to Idaho." Big Sam sounded amused. "Especially after I suggested they should be." He chuckled. His gaze dropped to Dolly, who headed for the door with her kitten. He waited until the door closed behind her. "I won't tolerate that kind of behavior here."

Maisie reached for his hand. "The child had endured far too much without being tormented by a bully."

Beatrice smiled at Levi. He'd spoken up on the child's behalf. Not that she was surprised. She'd come to expect high ideals from him. Would he defend her, come to her rescue if the need arose?

Telling herself not to let her thoughts get sidetracked, she turned her attention to preparing breakfast.

Levi remained near the stove, making her movements feel awkward and clumsy. She was bound to make a mistake and ruin breakfast if he didn't move.

"Someone is going to town today if you have a note ready to go to your aunt."

"Oh, good. Thank you. I do." She'd written the note after much pondering and finally just came out with the news that Maisie was soon ready to take over her own work and Beatrice hoped her aunt had heard of a job for Beatrice. "I'll get it right away."

"It can wait until after breakfast."

Beatrice's nerves strummed like a violin during the meal. The tune grew more brisk when Maisie announced she felt better and intended to get up and move around more today.

Big Sam sputtered a protest but Maisie smiled sweetly at him. "Don't you think I know what I can do better than anyone?"

Levi chuckled. "Pa, you know you'll give in to her, so why put up a fuss?"

Big Sam held his hands up in a defensive gesture. "At least let me think I'm the boss in my own house."

"But you are," Maisie said with such sweetness that Beatrice joined the others in laughing.

Her thoughts grew serious as they finished the meal. She brought her note from the bedroom and handed it to Levi, then turned her attention to washing the dishes. Maisie got to her feet and began measuring out ingredients for bread.

Beatrice laughed. "You couldn't wait to get on your feet and tackle that job."

"I don't know what you mean." Maisie gave her such an innocent look Beatrice almost believed her, until Maisie chuckled. "You'll learn to make bread if you want to. I think you can do almost anything you set your mind to."

"Thank you." The words strengthened Beatrice's resolve. She would miss the ranch and the Harding family when she left, but like Maisie said, she could do whatever she set her mind to and she had set her mind on proving she could—

Her hands grew idle. What did she want to prove? That she could be independent? Or that she belonged? Or was it that someone valued her enough to put her above their own plans?

Maybe all of those.

She had only glimpses of Levi throughout the morning. He and Big Sam came in for dinner, but ate hurriedly without taking time for conversation. Big Sam said they had to begin work with the horses. Beatrice had no idea what that meant except it appeared to be urgent.

Someone rode in late in the afternoon, just as she was putting the finishing touches on supper. The rider went directly to where Levi and his father had a horse inside the corral Levi had built and handed them a handful of papers.

It was the cowboy returning from town. Would Aunt Opal have sent a reply?

Likely not, she reasoned. It would take time to find someone willing to take on a woman as inexperienced as she.

The men strode toward the house and she hurriedly served up the meal.

Levi entered first, his face shining from washing up at the outside wash basin. "Your aunt sent a reply."

"Really? Already?" Her heart stalled. "I wonder what it means."

Levi's eyebrows rose. "Perhaps read it and you'll find out."

"Of course." She opened the envelope and removed the piece of paper. Unfolding it, she read her aunt's words.

She must have looked as stunned as she felt for Maisie asked, "Is it bad news?"

"No, it's good news." Wasn't it? It was what she wanted. What she'd hoped for. "My aunt says there is a widower in town who needs someone to care for his three children. He's willing to hire me for the job."

The words hung in the air.

She focused her gaze on Maisie, afraid if she looked at Levi she would see relief. "He indicates he will wait until you don't need me any longer." She didn't read the part that said he hoped it would be soon.

Maisie's surprise disappeared into a kind smile. "I'll be able to manage on my own in a few more days."

Dolly grabbed Beatrice's hand. "What about me?"

Beatrice hugged the child. "You can stay with me

until your aunt comes." No one raised any objection, so she assumed they found the arrangement satisfactory.

Dolly clung to Beatrice as she served the meal, and edged her chair as close as possible when they sat to eat.

Only after Big Sam had said grace did Beatrice allow herself to look at Levi. He watched her, a thoughtful look on his face. But she could not say if he felt relief or regret at her announcement.

She might ask him if he wanted to go for a walk later and she might drum up enough courage to ask what he thought.

But Big Sam said they had more work to do and they left right after supper and had not returned when it was time to put Dolly to bed. There wasn't a hope that the child would go on her own. Since Beatrice had revealed the contents of the note, Dolly had stuck to Beatrice like she'd been sewn to her skirts.

She wished she could offer the child more assurances, but they were still waiting to hear from the aunt.

As she lay in bed, next to Dolly and Smokey, she allowed herself to dream of a future here shared with Levi, surrounded by his loving family, with Dolly part of that plan.

It was an impossible dream and she turned on her side, brushing away the tears that seeped from her eyes. *God, You are my strength. Please help me through this change. It's going to be harder to say goodbye than I could have ever imagined possible.*

Unless Your plan is for Levi to ask me to stay.

I'd be quite fine with that arrangement.

But of course that was impossible and she knew it.

But if he did?

She dare not allow herself to consider the possibility.

Levi stayed outside until the last minute the next morning before he went to the house for breakfast. All night he had fought a mental war with himself. The note from Beatrice's aunt was exactly what Beatrice wanted from the beginning. A chance to be independent, to prove to herself, and perhaps her father, that she was more than a high-priced prize for some enterprising young man. *A suitable young man.* And that left him out of the picture.

But hadn't she fit into ranch life rather well?

That didn't change any of the facts, any more than it changed the color of his skin.

He washed up, then entered the kitchen, allowing himself one quick glance at Beatrice before he sat down. She appeared happy. Of course she was. Her plans had fallen into place.

His one concern—okay, his *other* concern—was how Dolly was handling this. He smiled at the child and she smiled back. Her eyes said as much as any words would. She felt secure with Beatrice. He was grateful Beatrice had assured the child she would go with her. His lungs caught at the knowledge Dolly would soon leave. He'd grown so fond of her.

After that he forced his attention on his food and on Maisie and Big Sam as they talked, though he would be hard-pressed to tell anyone what they talked about.

He fled the house as soon as he'd downed his cup of coffee.

Pa followed more slowly. "I want to keep working with that mare."

Pa didn't need him to help. "I think I'll ride out and see if I can find any clues that will lead me to those troublemakers." There was something about that cold campfire that bothered him and he'd like to have another look.

"Go see what you can find." Pa was already in the pen with the horse.

Levi's bedroll was still tied to his saddle and he left it there rather than take the time to remove it and put it away. He saddled Scout and swung to his back. Turning toward the house, he stared at it a moment. Would Beatrice stay if he asked her?

Of course she wouldn't. She was a fine city woman who should be in a fine home in town, perhaps with a girl to do the heavy chores for her. She was not a country girl.

She had proved otherwise, his wayward mind pointed out.

It didn't change a thing. He was still a half-breed and associating with the likes of him would make people judge her harshly. She was prepared to care for three motherless children. They would benefit from her presence.

He reined about and galloped away. At the cold campsite, he dismounted and bent over to examine the ground. There was a fresh hoof print. Someone had been here since his last visit. He stood and looked around. He took Scout and followed the trail. It wasn't easy and took complete concentration to find, but it was there. No rain had washed away the signs and the tracks didn't veer toward the river.

He reached a rocky spot and lost the trail. Slowly, methodically, he circled the wide expanse of the area, determined to pick up the trail again. Two hours later he found the sign he searched for and again set out after the rider. The trail climbed higher into the trees. It crossed a deep valley. Levi pressed onward. He would find this man, and the others. He would demand an explanation and put a stop to the harassment.

Daylight faded. He could not track after dark. He was too far from the ranch to go back and wasn't willing to give up following the trail. Like his brothers said, it felt personal on the troublemaker's behalf and had grown personal on Levi's part. He would find these men.

He unsaddled Scout and left him to graze while he spread his bedroll, drank from his canteen and ate beef jerky.

Stretched out in his bedroll, his thoughts returned to Beatrice. How long before she left the ranch?

He grabbed at his chest as a knife-sharp pain pierced his heart. How could he let her go?

But what did he have to offer her?

Not a fancy house, not a life of ease, not prestige or even acceptance into every home in town.

He stared up into the starry sky as a truth grew clear.

It was acceptance she sought and it was the one thing he couldn't offer her. With him she would find intolerance from many.

He closed his eyes and breathed against the pain consuming his insides.

* * *

Beatrice woodenly went through the work of the next two days. She'd hoped Levi would give her a reason to stay, but instead he had ridden away without so much as a goodbye. This was his answer. But she hadn't expected it to hurt so much.

Her lungs had developed a permanent pain that would not ease.

She hoped she hid it from Maisie.

"Are you not feeling well?" Maisie asked.

Beatrice kept her attention on the cake batter she mixed up. It seemed she had not succeeded in hiding her feelings. Dolly was outside with Smokey so she answered as honestly as she could. "I feel fine. I suppose I'm a bit nervous about meeting this man and his children."

"You'll do just fine if it's what you want to do." Maisie kneaded dough for dinner rolls. She was doing more and more each day. Soon Beatrice wouldn't be needed and she'd go back to Granite Creek and her future.

"It is, isn't it?" Maisie asked.

At Maisie's gentle inquiry, Beatrice looked at the woman. Her kind eyes were almost more than Beatrice could handle. She sniffed to keep her tears at bay.

It took a moment before she could trust herself to answer. "I want to do something that will allow me independence." Only *independence* wasn't the word that came to mind. *Value* was. She wanted to be valued by someone.

But not just anyone.

She wanted someone to care enough for her to take risks, to defend her, to protect her.

Maisie spoke again, interrupting Beatrice's thoughts. "Independence can be very lonely."

Beatrice nodded. She already felt the loneliness of her choice but Levi had offered no alternative. She glanced out the window. Would he stay away until she'd left? Big Sam had said he'd gone in search of the men who had been causing trouble around the place. But why now? Was it simply to avoid her? Maybe he thought she would expect something from him.

Did he fear she would kiss him and beg for him to care?

"I can't imagine why Levi is away so long." Maisie sounded worried. "I hope he hasn't encountered problems." She gave a mirthless chuckle. "Here I am fretting even though I know he can take care of himself."

Take care of himself. The words hammered inside Beatrice's head. Obviously Levi wanted nothing more.

The next day was Sunday. Maisie said she expected the rest of the family to join them as they had previously. Beatrice half-heartedly prepared food.

That night she told Dolly the story of Noah and the ark. God had protected him through a flood. Beatrice knew He was strong enough to carry her through the challenges ahead of her.

Levi had followed the trail for two days, always climbing, always going deeper into the mountains. He came upon another campsite where the three men had joined up. Several times he wondered that after all these weeks, they had left a trail he could follow. Had they grown overconfident and careless?

Or was he riding into a trap?

Either way he had no intention of stopping until he got to the bottom of this.

Two hours later, he pulled Scout to a halt. The back of his neck prickled like someone watched him.

He waited, every nerve humming with tension, every sense in high alert to his surroundings. He didn't have to wait long before he heard a rustle to his right and shifted his gaze in that direction. Another rustle to his left and he knew they had him surrounded.

"I hear ya," he called, hoping to eliminate their hope of surprising him.

A man stepped out in front of him, a pistol leveled at Levi. Another man stepped out from either side. He knew these men. Brothers of Fern Dafoe. But what did they want with him? He and Fern had parted ways months ago.

He didn't bother to raise his arms and kept silent, waiting for them to make the first move.

George, the oldest, signaled him down.

Levi took his time about dismounting.

The two other brothers, Manny and Crow, went to stand by George.

Levi crossed his arms over his chest.

"Come along." George waved his pistol in an arc, indicating Levi should follow.

Levi didn't move. He knew this trio well enough to know they were troublemakers. They and their father lived on the thin edge of the law. They moved around a lot, mostly because they got run out of towns such as Granite Creek. Fern had wanted Levi to join them when they left, but he had no desire to be part of their way of life.

When he didn't move, Crow grabbed his arm and jerked him forward. Crow—whether that was a name his Indian mother had chosen or a nickname because of his black hair and sharp nose, Levi didn't know and wasn't about to ask. He knew the man had a mean streak as wide as the ocean.

Levi followed, slowly, deliberately taking his time. Scout followed of his own accord. The horse wouldn't go far without Levi. Nor was he likely going to let one of these men catch him.

They reached a campsite that could do with some cleaning up and Crow released Levi's arm.

"I suppose you're wondering why we brung you here." George seemed to be the spokesman.

It was on the tip of Levi's tongue to say Scout had brought him, but he didn't care to instigate anger in any of them.

Manny chuckled. "Guess you aren't so high and mighty now, are ya, Harding?"

The way Manny drawled out the Harding name, Levi suspected this had something to do with his heritage. But he couldn't imagine what. These men were half-breeds like him.

Not like him, though, he corrected. He never wanted to be like them.

"You think you're too good for our sister, huh?" Manny spoke but the other two had matching scowls.

"I have no idea what you mean."

"Sure you don't." The three of them proceeded to

spout off their opinions in a mishmash of words, making it difficult for Levi to make sense of what they said.

"You told Fern you didn't want to go with her."

"You said you belonged on the ranch."

"You was a Harding and proud of it."

"You think youse too good for us."

He broke in to the tirade. "I am a Harding and proud of it. I do belong on the ranch."

"You're a half-breed just like us. You ain't no better." Manny lurched toward him, but the other two held him back.

He could have honestly said he was not like them, whether or not they shared a similar heritage.

"That ain't what we planned, 'member?" George said.

Levi figured he'd know all too soon what they had planned.

He guessed he wasn't going to like it. And it might keep him away from home for some time. He figured he could handle the Dafoes, but would they delay his return to the ranch. Perhaps so long that Beatrice would be gone.

If only he'd told her that he had feelings for her. Maybe he'd never get the chance now.

Chapter Sixteen

Sunday morning arrived. Beatrice smiled as she helped Dolly dress and brushed and braided her hair. She kept the smile there as she made breakfast, even though Levi had still not returned. The smile grew stiff as she greeted Johnny and Willow and their children, then Tanner and Susanne and their family. Inside, her heart was hollow and empty.

Levi couldn't have made his opinion any plainer if he'd written it in black, bold letters on the side of the barn.

They again sat on a hillside, but despite the clustered family and Dolly pressed to her side, Beatrice felt so alone tears stung her eyes.

She joined in the singing with a sad lack of enthusiasm and barely heard what Big Sam said. After the service, the meal was eaten and then the children went to play and the men wandered off toward the barn.

Shouldn't they be concerned about Levi's absence? Shouldn't they launch a search party? What if he was lying injured somewhere, waiting to be rescued?

But it appeared she was the only one who had such thoughts.

An agonizing thought explained why.

They all knew the truth. Levi was avoiding her.

It was time she moved on.

She waited until the next morning to make her announcement. "Maisie, if you can manage without me—" She knew Maisie could. "I'd like to return to Granite Creek today."

Silence greeted her words, then Maisie spoke. "Of course. I understand. Big Sam will bring your buggy to the house after breakfast."

Dolly caught at Beatrice's sleeve and Beatrice turned to the child. "I go with you?"

Beatrice hugged Dolly. "Yes, you will be with me." Until the aunt made arrangements. Perhaps even now, the woman was in town. Or had sent word. By being in Granite Creek, they'd be where the aunt could easily find them.

Dolly clung to Beatrice, who found herself unable to look directly at either Maisie or Big Sam.

Maisie waved away her offer to help do dishes. "You've done enough and I can't tell you how much I appreciate it." She glanced out the window and back to Beatrice. "I wish you could stay but…" Her voice trailed off.

It was obvious that Maisie thought Levi was waiting for Beatrice to leave before he returned. Knowing she couldn't disguise the pain this knowledge brought, Beatrice hurried to her room to finish packing up both her belongings and Dolly's.

"Can I keep my cat?" Dolly asked.

"Of course you can. She's your best friend."

Dolly nodded, her eyes wide with uncertainty and Smokey clutched to her chest.

Beatrice stopped packing, sat on the edge of the bed and pulled Dolly to her lap. "We will be okay, you and I. We will go to a place where we belong."

"But why can't we stay here?"

"We can't, that's all."

"Why isn't Levi here? I thought he liked me."

I thought the same. "Sweetheart, he does like you. I don't suppose he knew we would be leaving so soon." She hoped Dolly would accept her explanation and the words would provide some comfort to her. They fell vastly short of offering any to Beatrice.

Levi had left as soon as she got the note from Aunt Opal. Indeed, it was likely the reason he left. He had made his opinion very clear and there was nothing Beatrice could do but get on with her life.

A few minutes later she and Dolly were in the buggy headed back to town.

She had no idea of where the future would take her, only that she must face it alone, and as they traveled back to town, she said a mental goodbye to everything around her.

As she crossed the river, she recalled how Levi had rescued her.

If only he would ride up now and rescue her.

The thought twisted and turned inside her head. Why did she think she needed rescuing? She was free to follow her own plans. Only she wasn't free to follow her heart. If she was, she would stay at the ranch, learn how to do all the things a country woman did and hope someday Levi would—

Would what? Learn to love her? Or did she mean learn to believe he could be loved?

She lifted one shoulder in resignation. It made no difference either way.

They arrived back in town and the first stop she made was at the sheriff's office.

"You wait here," she told Dolly. "I'll only be a few minutes."

Dolly's lips were pinched tight, her eyes wide.

Beatrice paused to hug the child. "I won't leave you. I promise." She went into the office and introduced herself. "I have Dorothy Knott with me. Have you heard from her aunt yet?"

"No, ma'am, not a word. Is the child staying with you?"

"Yes, I'll be at the Gage house."

"Good enough. I'll bring you word as soon as I get it."

"Thank you." She returned to the wagon and proceeded to Aunt Opal and Uncle Elwood's house.

Uncle Elwood greeted her at the door. "I'm glad to see you. Your aunt has been under the weather for a few days. And who is this little girl?"

She again introduced Dolly. "I'll explain later. Does Aunt Opal have the influenza?"

"She's just exhausted. Thanks be to the good Lord that the epidemic is over."

"Let me get my things in and I'll take care of Aunt." She put her belongings and Dolly's in the room she had previously occupied. She paused at the doorway to look around at the simple room with a very pretty quilt in an intriguing pattern on the bed. Aunt Opal said she'd made it with the help of several ladies in the community. A few weeks ago she had been amazed at the idea of women working together to do something so practical and so welcoming. But now she understood the value Aunt Opal had in this community and how people worked together.

And to think this woman was her mother's sister. Their lives were so different.

She took Dolly with her to Aunt Opal's bedroom and introduced them. "You rest, Auntie. I will take care of the house. I can manage now. I learned a lot at the Sundown Ranch." She would not tell her of the most valuable lesson she'd learned—to stay true to her goals and set her mind to being independent. For a little time she'd let herself believe life could be more. She could be more. It wasn't a lesson she intended to repeat.

"Thank you." Aunt Opal squeezed her hands in appreciation. "By the way, there's a letter from your father on the hall table."

She went down the hall and found the letter. She breathed in courage as she opened the envelope. A few minutes later she shoved the letter into her pocket and went to prepare tea for Aunt Opal.

Father was still certain she would return home and fulfill his plans for her.

She wouldn't. He wanted her for his reasons. Would anyone ever value her for being her? Where did she belong?

Why had she let herself grow so fond of Levi? *Fond* was far too weak a word. She loved him and would follow him anywhere—town or country or even into a nomadic way of life. But he had not invited her along.

She had to find her own way. Alone. Perhaps she'd find satisfaction enough for her heart in caring for three motherless children.

Levi sat with his back to a tree, his wrists bound behind him, his ankles tied tightly. The Dafoe brothers seemed to think it fun to mock him.

"Let's see how smart you are now, Mr. Harding."

"Ain't so big now, are ya?"

"Fern sees you like this and she won't be wanting you anymore."

After a bit they grew weary of the sport. "Let's go see about those horses at the ranch." They rode off.

Levi guessed they meant Pa's breeding horses. He had to get free and warn Pa. He whistled for Scout. The Dafoe men had tried to catch the horse but he had eluded them. He came immediately to Levi's call.

He wished he had taught his horse to untie ropes, but it had never before crossed his mind. But Manny had been careless, in a hurry, and after a bit of squirming, Levi slipped his wrists free and quickly untied his ankles. The Dafoes had ridden in an easterly direction. If he veered slightly to the south he could hope to get to the ranch before they did.

He swung to Scout's back, bent over his neck and rode for all he was worth.

Pa looked up at Levi's thundering approach.

Levi reined in. "Pa, I know who has been causing all the problems." He explained about the Dafoes though he didn't say why they were so troublesome. "Maybe just their nature," he said in response to Pa's question. "They're set on doing something with the horses." Twice before he'd found evidence that they'd tried to let the horses loose. Again, he could not understand why they would be intent on such vandalism, but then he'd never been able to understand why old man Dafoe participated in his ways and encouraged his boys to do the same. Seemed to Levi they could have made a good, honest living with less effort expended.

"Get Charlie. He came back this morning."

Levi jogged over to the bunkhouse. "Charlie, we got trouble coming." He explained the situation as Charlie trotted by his side.

Pa met them at the barn and handed them each a rifle. "Wait until they are at their mischief." Pa stayed at the barn. Charlie hunkered down out of sight behind the cookhouse and Levi parked himself on top of a nearby feed shack.

"Here they come," he called.

He tensed as he waited. Pa would give the signal when it was time for them to step into the open.

The Dafoes paused at the crest of the hill and studied the ranch. Seeing no evidence of men being around, they slowly rode closer. They were cautious, Levi would give them that. And wily, too. How many times had they slipped in and out leaving almost no evidence? He ground his back teeth together. They had skills taught to them by their Indian mother just like Levi and his brother did. But there the similarity ended. At least in Levi's mind. Perhaps not in everyone else's.

They reached the pen, where the horses grazed

placidly. They edged along until they reached the gate. George leaned over to undo it. Before his hands touched the wire, Pa stepped out.

"Hold it right there. Put your hands in the air."

The three jerked about. George reached for his pistol.

Levi stood. "I wouldn't do that if I were you."

"Best think again," Charlie said, stepping from the shadows.

"Hands in the air," Pa repeated and the Dafoes jerked their arms upward. "Boys, tie them up."

Levi jumped from the roof and jogged forward. He yanked Manny from his saddle and tied his hands behind his back. He made sure the rope was tight enough the man wouldn't be getting free any time soon.

Charlie grabbed George.

Pa held his rifle on Crow as he dismounted.

"Aw, we was just funning you," Manny whined.

"We'll let the sheriff decide that." Pa tied Crow. "You boys want to take them to town?"

Levi looked toward the house. "I got something else to take care of."

"If you're thinking of Beatrice, you're too late. She left already."

The ground beneath Levi's feet seemed to shift. "Left?"

"Gone back to town." Pa shoved the men back on their horses and tied their ankles.

Charlie gave Levi a look of disgust. "You let her go? What's wrong with you? You still hung up on Helen? Couldn't you see she was only pretend?"

"Huh? What kind of assessment is that?"

"An honest one if you care to hear the truth."

Levi wasn't sure he did or that it mattered. But Charlie didn't give him a chance to say so.

"She pretended to be nice to you only because she wanted to be amused. When you weren't around she didn't mind bad-mouthing you. I heard her myself. You deserve someone who sees you for who you are."

"What we both are," Levi said with some disgust, "is half-breeds who don't belong in either world."

"Yeah, that's what some think. Can't argue that. But like my pa says, when you get to thinking everyone thinks that and you're worthless, you need to stop and think of those who accept you and love you. Beatrice was one of those. But I guess you never figured it out."

Pa called from the barn. "Let's go to town."

Levi whistled for Scout and swung to his back. "You go with Pa. I got things to do." And he rode north, away from town.

He had to figure out who he was…not only in the sight of others, but also in his own mind.

Not until then was he fit to go after Beatrice.

Two days later, Aunt Opal declared herself fit as a fiddle. "Have you decided to accept the widower's offer?" she asked Beatrice.

"It seems the best choice." They sat on the porch watching Dolly play with Smokey in the yard. "But I don't want to make any changes in Dolly's life. Will the man mind waiting until we hear from her aunt?"

"Why don't you meet him and tell him the situation? You could meet his children and you'd be able to tell if this job would suit you."

Beatrice agreed and Uncle Elwood took a message to the man.

That afternoon, Ralph Simpson came to call. Beatrice greeted the man cordially. He was tall and blond with an angular chin. Nothing in his looks to make her think she couldn't accept this job. Nothing except a long aching wish for something different.

She met the children. Two boys, ages eight and ten, and a little girl of four. All of them seemed sturdy and boisterous in comparison to Dolly, though in truth they did little but say hello.

Aunt Opal offered to watch the children while Beatrice and Ralph went to the parlor to talk.

"I am on my way to Oregon," Ralph began. "I need to cross the mountains before the snow comes."

"What will you do in Oregon?"

"Farm. I hear the land is rich and bountiful."

Beatrice nodded. Oregon was so far away. She'd cherished a hope that they would live in town. Perhaps Levi would find a faint regard for her and come calling. But Oregon? She swallowed hard.

"Is that a problem for you?"

She shook her head. "But I can't leave until Dolly's aunt comes." She explained Dolly's situation.

Ralph got to his feet and went to look out the window. He clasped his hands behind his back—the picture of a man in deep study. After a moment, he turned to face her. "Can you not leave her in your aunt's care?"

She could but she would not. "I promised her she would stay with me until her aunt—"

"Yes, yes. But time is of prime importance. I don't

want to be caught in a winter storm. My wife's illness and death has delayed us enough."

"Might I suggest you spend the winter here and leave in the spring when travel is safer?"

He let out a weary sigh. "I must get there as soon as possible. If I spend the winter, I'll have to wait for the passes to open. It will be late to start plowing."

"I see."

"One more thing. It wouldn't be appropriate for us to travel together unless we're married."

Married! "But I don't know you. We've just met." A dozen more protests rushed forward but she closed her mouth. "I'm afraid I'm not interested in such an arrangement."

"You aunt gave me to think you were open to accepting the position of my children's nanny. A marriage between us would be in name only. I love…loved…my wife and have no need of another." He looked past her, around her, anywhere but directly at her. Not that she had any desire to meet his gaze, either.

A marriage of convenience might suit him but it did not suit her. She clung to the faint hope that Levi would come calling. "I'm sorry," she repeated.

"My offer is open for two days." He hurried from the room, called his children and left.

Beatrice remained in the parlor in a state of shock. Ralph's offer was no better than the arrangement her father planned.

Was that all she could expect? A loveless marriage?

Aunt Opal came to the door. "Did you come to an agreement?"

Beatrice opened her mouth to answer but choked

and couldn't speak. She rushed to her bedroom and threw herself on the bed.

A few minutes later Aunt Opal tapped on the door. "May I come in?"

"Yes." Beatrice's voice was muffled against the pillow, hiding the tears that threatened.

"I take it you didn't care for the man."

Anger mingled with disappointment and sadness. She turned to face her aunt. "He wants me to marry him."

At least her aunt looked shocked at the idea, giving Beatrice some comfort.

She explained Ralph's circumstances. "My father wanted me to marry a man who would become the son I never was. Now this man wants to marry me simply to provide a mother for his children. Am I of no value to anyone?" She ended on a wail.

"Come here." Aunt Opal opened her arms and Beatrice went gladly into her embrace. Her aunt patted Beatrice's back a moment and made comforting noises then she began to speak. "I'm sorry your father has treated you so poorly and my sister, too. How could they fail to see what a treasure you are?"

Beatrice let the words soak into her soul.

Aunt Opal leaned back to look in Beatrice's face. "What is even sadder is that you fail to see it."

"Me? How can I see otherwise? I am nothing. Of no value."

"Child, what you are saying is that God made a mistake in making you. Do you think God makes mistakes?"

Beatrice began to shake her head and then stopped. "Maybe this once?" she said with an attempt at humor.

Aunt Opal's smile was tender. "Not even this once. You are fearfully and wonderfully made."

Beatrice jerked upright. "That's what I told Levi. Where is it in the Bible?"

"It's Psalm 136, verses fourteen and fifteen." Aunt Opal handed her a Bible. "Look it up and read it. Believe it." She left the room.

Beatrice found the verses and read them over and over. *Marvelous are thy works. My soul knoweth right well.*

Only her soul didn't know it.

But God said it. She must believe it. Her gaze went again to the fourteenth verse. *I will praise thee.* Could she praise God for who she was?

With her heart humbled, she fell to her knees and thanked God for who she was, for who He had made her to be.

A few minutes later, she returned to the kitchen.

Aunt Opal smiled. "You have chosen to believe it. I can tell."

She hugged her aunt. "Thank you." She went to the porch to watch Dolly playing. God had made them all and had a wonderful plan. She hugged her arms about her, certain that Levi was part of that plan.

Lord, she prayed, *help him see he is fearfully and wonderfully made.*

If he believed it would he see her as belonging in his life as she ached to do? She had no choice but to trust God to make it so.

Until then she would wait.

She was still watching Dolly and thinking about Levi when the sheriff rode up.

He swung down and joined her on the porch. "I have news."

Her heart dipped at the tone of his voice.

"Come inside so we can talk." She asked Aunt Opal to keep an eye on Dolly and for the second time that day she led a man to the parlor and took a seat while he spoke.

"I'm afraid it's bad news. We received news from the solicitor that the aunt has passed away. As far as we can tell, there are no other relatives."

Beatrice stared at the man as the news sank in. "What will become of her?"

"She is now a ward of the state. Unless someone adopts her, she will be placed in an orphanage."

An orphanage? Dolly? "No. I will adopt her."

The sheriff shook his head. "I don't know if single women are allowed to adopt."

"Then just leave her with me. I'll give her a home."

He looked about the room. "Are you planning to live with your aunt and uncle?"

"No. Yes. I don't know." She had to think this through and come up with a plan that would allow her to keep Dolly. "Can't you leave her with me for a few days? Allow me time to work out something?"

"I don't suppose a few days will make any difference." He got to his feet. "Now if you were to tell me you were about to be married, that would change everything."

She couldn't honestly tell him that.

Or could she?

Chapter Seventeen

Levi had ridden far up the mountains to a favorite spot where he and his brothers had often camped. And where they had talked about their Indian mother. He spent hours sitting by a campfire, lost in thought.

Who was he? Where did he belong? He sifted through his memories, trying to find answers in his past.

Tanner had found connection between the past and the present by going to the cathedral of the trees, where their mother, Seena, had felt close to God. But Levi could barely remember his ma there.

Johnny had found belonging in the affection of a baby boy. Levi couldn't understand that, though little Adam was cute as a button.

What did he remember of Seena? He remembered her singing in words he did not understand. But her voice comforted him nevertheless.

Mostly he remembered how he had gone to bed one night thinking all was right with his world and woke up the next and nothing was right. His ma was gone.

Later, he realized she'd been sick many days, but at the time he only thought the night had stolen her away.

Pa must have realized Levi was having trouble sleeping and brought home a pup. Shep became his best friend. He slept on Levi's bed and Levi felt safe.

He smiled. One night Shep had gotten all muddy and Pa wouldn't let him in the house. As soon as everyone was asleep, Levi had slipped outside and found Shep in the barn and had curled up beside him.

He had been a frightened little boy. But he wasn't that any longer.

But who was he?

He ached for the answer.

A deer with two fawns at her side tiptoed from the trees to drink at the little stream nearby. Levi could sit motionless for hours, something his ma had taught him though he barely remembered her. He could track man or beast most anywhere. So much about him had been inherited from his mother's side. But he also knew how to break a horse and take care of a cow, and he had a love of the ranch that came from his father's side.

But he was neither white nor native.

Who was he?

Beatrice filled his thoughts over and over. He heard her voice in song, heard her comments about the world around them, saw her swinging skirts as she carried laundry to the line, and he remembered things she said.

You are fearfully and wonderfully made.

She'd challenged him to believe it. He'd challenged her right back.

Could he believe it? And if he did, would that give

him the right to go after Beatrice and tell her what was in his heart?

Believing it was as simple as choosing to do so.

He let the truth seep deep into his being. Yes, he was a half-breed and there would always be those who saw that as an ugly thing. But he didn't need to let the opinion of others influence how he saw himself.

He jumped to his feet and let out a whoop. "I am fearfully and wonderfully made." He lifted his face to heaven. "Thank You, God."

Did believing it give him the right to go after Beatrice?

Maybe the question was, did he have the courage to go after her and confess his feelings, knowing she might reject him?

Did Tanner and Johnny have these same struggles? Had Big Sam found it hard to admit his love to Seena and then to Maisie?

Perhaps part of loving was the risk involved in opening up one's heart.

But without that risk, a person could go through life safe but very lonely.

He wasn't ready to do that.

It took him ten minutes to break camp and head home. He'd take time to bathe and change his clothes and then go to Granite Creek. He'd find Beatrice and confess his love.

He whooped as he rode home.

If he hadn't misunderstood Beatrice's smiles and her kiss—he'd pressed his hand to his cheek—she entertained a degree of fondness toward him. He'd pretended it wasn't so, clinging to his belief that she was a city girl and he a half-breed, and that made love between them impossible.

How could he have been so blind and stubborn?

What if she'd given up on him? Maybe even gone back to Chicago to do as her father demanded? He urged Scout to a faster pace.

He must get to town as soon as possible.

Beatrice stood before her uncle, who had reluctantly agreed to perform the marriage ceremony between herself and Ralph Simpson. She'd agreed to his offer of marriage on the condition they adopt Dolly.

At first he had objected. "I already have three children."

Beatrice had persisted. "I won't leave her."

"Will you favor her above my children?"

The question forced her to examine her heart. She'd met his children three more times and had found it difficult to warm up to them. And truthfully, the way they shunned Dolly made her want to scold them. But she knew she must treat them all the same. "I will not favor her in any way, though I will protect her."

He had studied her face then turned to study his children where they chased each other around the yard while Dolly clutched Smokey to her chest and watched.

Deep lines in Ralph's face indicated how difficult life had been for him.

She should touch his arm, assure him they could make this work, but she couldn't bring herself to reach out to him. Her heart tightened. She simply didn't feel anything toward the man, apart from determination to do what she must to keep Dolly.

If only Levi had shown some interest in pursuing their friendship. But she must accept the truth. He didn't care. But she could face a loveless future. She was strong enough and sure enough of herself. She would enter a marriage of convenience for the sake of the child she loved.

She faced Uncle Elwood. She was about to be married. As soon as they said their vows, Ralph insisted they should begin the journey to Oregon.

Beatrice would not think of all that entailed. She'd only just learned to cook over a stove and would now have to cook over a campfire. There would be four children to tend, plus a milk cow. Ralph had given her to understand the cow would be Beatrice's responsibility. All she could say was she would do her best and learn as quickly as possible.

Ralph had said he couldn't expect more.

Both her bags and Dolly's stood packed and ready to add to the contents of the very crowded wagon.

Ralph had said he and the boys would sleep under the wagon. Beatrice and the girls could sleep in the wagon.

Explaining her decision to Dolly had been the hardest thing about the whole situation. She'd taken the child for the promised visit to her parents' graves. After letting the reality of their passing settle in, she'd told Dolly that she meant to keep her, but the only way she could was to get married so she would marry Mr. Simpson and he would become Dolly's new father.

Tears had trickled down the little girl's cheeks. "Why don't you marry Levi?" she'd whispered. "I want him to be my papa."

Beatrice had held the child close, her tears mingling with Dolly's. If only Levi hadn't ridden out of their lives.

She'd spent the last few days praying he would come to town and pay her a visit. If he expressed the slightest interest in continuing their friendship she would not marry Ralph. She'd persuade the sheriff to give her more time.

But he hadn't come.

She'd waited a week hoping and praying.

Finally, she'd accepted the inevitable and sent a message to the Sundown Ranch informing them she was marrying Ralph Simpson and extending an invitation for any who wanted to attend to please do so.

There had been no reply, a fact that hurt more than she expected.

She'd also sent a letter to Father and Mother, informing them of her upcoming marriage. She knew Father would be angry, but she'd be on her way over the mountains before he could do anything about it.

Uncle Elwood cleared his throat. "Beatrice, are you sure of this?"

Her heart hammered a harsh tattoo. She looked at Dolly, who was wearing a new pink dress she'd purchased at the local store. Ralph's children stood by his side.

Dolly slipped her hand into Beatrice's.

"I'm sure," Beatrice said, her voice strong and clear. Perhaps in time she would grow to love Ralph, though Levi would always own a large portion of her heart and mind.

"Very well. Then shall we proceed?" Uncle Elwood

opened a black book and began to read. "Marriage is an honorable estate and not to be entered into lightly or unadvisedly." He paused and studied each of them.

Beatrice caught her breath. Would Ralph change his mind? After all, he was not getting a bargain—a woman who would probably fail at any number of things and a child who wasn't his own.

But he stared straight ahead and Uncle Elwood continued.

"I therefore charge both of you that if you know any reason why you should not be joined in marriage you make it known at this time." He waited, again studying them as if he hoped one of them would offer a reason.

Behind Beatrice, Aunt Opal sniffled.

Uncle Elwood cleared his throat. "I hoped…never mind. Do you, Ralph Simpson, take Beatrice Doyle to be your—"

The church door banged open, interrupting Uncle Elwood's question as they all turned to see what caused the commotion.

Levi stood in the opening, backlit by the morning sunshine so she couldn't make out his expression.

"Levi Harding," Uncle Elwood said in his most sonorous voice. "May I ask the cause of this intrusion?"

Levi strode up the aisle. As he neared, his gaze bored into hers. He looked neither to the right nor the left. Nor did he give any attention to Uncle Elwood. He stopped six feet from Beatrice. "You cannot marry this man."

Her hackles rose. "I don't see why not. You've certainly never given me any reason to do otherwise."

He closed the distance until only a few inches separated them.

She could see the bottomlessness of his eyes, the tiny fan lines about them, the handsome color of his skin and so much more. She drank in every detail, searing it permanently on her brain.

"Why have you come?"

"To save you from the biggest mistake of your life." He caught her hands. "You can't marry a man you don't love."

"This marriage is not about love."

"Beatrice Doyle, stop being so blind and stubborn. You can't marry him because I love you and I want to marry you."

"You do?"

"Yahoo!" The loud sound of approval came from Dolly and they both stared at her.

Together they leaned over the child, hugging and kissing her.

Levi cupped his hand about Beatrice's neck. "Will you call off this wedding and marry me?"

Her eyes stung with happy tears.

"I love you," he said.

"Yes, I'll marry you. I love you." She swallowed back tears. "I thought you decided I wasn't a suitable woman for your way of life."

"You are most suitable." He leaned closer and kissed her quickly.

"Come on, children." Ralph shepherded his children down the aisle.

"I'm sorry," Beatrice called. "I hope you find someone else."

Aunt Opal continued to sniffle.

Uncle Elwood closed the black book with a thud.

Ralph and the children jostled past another man in the doorway.

"Now what?" Uncle Elwood murmured.

Beatrice stared. "Father, what are you doing here?" It hadn't been that long since she sent the letter. He must have decided earlier that she needed to fulfill his plans for her.

Father strode up the aisle without answering, without greeting Aunt Opal and Uncle Elwood. He grabbed her elbow and jerked her away from Levi. "You are coming home with me."

She pulled from his grasp. "No, I'm not."

"You have your duty."

She swallowed hard. All her life it had been about duty and disappointment. Disappointment in being a girl, duty to make up for it. But she was more than that. She'd learned her own worth while working on the ranch. She stuck out her chin and faced her father.

"If you want a son, adopt one. I won't marry to give you one." She quivered a bit at the look on his face, but Levi put his arm around her, giving her the courage to go on. "I have found people who value me for who I am."

Levi's arm tightened about her.

"I belong here."

Father's face darkened with anger. "You will never get another penny from me. I disown you as my daughter." He marched from the church without so much as a backward look and without even saying hello to his sister-in-law and her husband.

He hadn't even acknowledged Levi.

Beatrice began to shake. Tears flowed unchecked down her cheeks. Levi pulled her to his chest and rubbed her back. Dolly pressed close. Aunt Opal and Uncle Elwood put their arms about her.

"You will always have a home with us," her aunt said. "Though I expect you'll soon have your own home." Her aunt and uncle took Dolly and slipped away, closing the door behind them.

Her tears spent, Beatrice turned her face up to Levi. "Thank you for coming."

He chuckled though his eyes remained serious. "I would have been here days ago but I ran into trouble." He told her about tracking the men who were responsible for the vandalism at the ranch. "Then I had to spend a few days talking to myself until I could believe I am fearfully and wonderfully made. As soon as I believed it, I rode home intending to come to town and tell you. And I find a note saying you are about to marry someone by the name of Ralph Simpson. I rode here hoping and praying to arrive before you hitched yourself to that man. Why would you do that?" The hurt blared from his eyes.

"To keep Dolly." She then provided the explanation.

"Dolly will always have a home with us." He let out a long breath. "I have never been so scared in all my life as when I saw you standing here with that man. I didn't know if I was too late or not."

"All the time as I prepared for this day and as I stood before my uncle, I prayed you would come. When you didn't, I believed I wasn't a suitable woman. Just a city girl who didn't fit in."

His gaze trailed over her face. His finger followed the same path, sending delicious tremors along her nerves. His fingertip came to rest at the corner of her mouth.

"Turns out a city girl is just what this half-breed needs." His voice was husky. He lowered his head, intent on claiming a kiss, but she delayed. There was one thing she had to make certain he understood.

"Turns out this city girl has found exactly what she needs—a noble man with strengths from both his parents. A man to be proud of."

His smile lit his face. "You make me proud of my heritage."

"And so you should be." She lifted her face to him to receive his kiss and return it with her whole heart.

Epilogue

"Dolly needs time to adjust to so many changes," Beatrice said, content in the circle of Levi's arms as they sat on the hillside near the ranch, watching geese flying south.

"I need time to finish a cabin for us."

Every day he and Big Sam and a handful of cowboys worked on the cabin where they would live. It stood behind them, on the hill that would be covered with flowers when spring came again. Less than half a mile from the ranch house, they would have privacy yet be close enough to enjoy visiting Maisie and Big Sam often and for Levi to help on the ranch.

Dolly was with Maisie. They watched now as she left the house, looked in their direction and waved.

"How do you think she is doing?" Beatrice asked.

"I think she's doing very well all things considered. It's nice to hear her sweet little voice."

Beatrice chuckled. Dolly had started talking aloud after the scene at the church. "Maybe she's afraid if she doesn't speak up I'll do something she doesn't like."

Levi tightened his arms. "She has some very strong opinions on things."

They laughed together. How often they had enjoyed moments with the child. Although she had a mind of her own, she also exhibited a sweet, gentle nature. "She will keep us on our toes."

"Good thing she has Smokey to boss about. Some little brothers and sisters will give her something else to direct her energies to."

Beatrice snuggled against Levi's chest. They had talked about children and both wanted lots. They'd talked about so many things. Discussing hurts from their childhoods had brought healing for Beatrice and Levi said the same. They had talked about their faith, their hopes. They shared stories of their growing-up years.

Day by day, Beatrice fell more and more in love with this strong, kind, handsome man.

Only once had he mentioned his half-breed status and she had silenced him with a kiss.

Six weeks later the cabin was finished and the three of them toured it.

"Is this my room?" Dolly looked at the bed and bookshelves in one of the two small bedrooms.

"It's all yours."

"The other is yours?"

"Yes." They would be close enough to provide her with a sense of security.

There was a loft for a growing family. "And we can build on more rooms," Levi assured her.

The kitchen was bright with a big table near the

door with a window over it. The living area was cozy with a big armchair, two rocking chairs and a settee.

Maisie had helped Beatrice sew curtains and fashion quilts for both beds.

"It's time," Levi said at the sound of wagons entering the yard.

Maisie had said they could get married at the ranch house, but both Levi and Beatrice preferred to marry in their own backyard.

"You better go so I can get ready."

He kissed her gently then left to prepare.

Susanne and Willow entered the house. "We'll help Dolly."

Beatrice went to the bedroom she would soon share with Levi. Her heart could barely contain her joy. She donned the ivory brocade dress she had brought with her from Chicago, thinking it would be suitable for fancy social occasions. Little did she know at the time that the only social occasion it would be suitable for was her own wedding.

Susanne knocked and indicated Beatrice should sit on the stool so she could do her hair. "I'm so glad you are going to be my sister-in-law," Susanne said.

"Me, too." Willow stood in the doorway with Dolly, whose eyes were wide with wonder and excitement.

Beatrice reached for all of them. "It's wonderful to go from an only child to being part of a big loving family." They would never know how starved for love she'd been. She hadn't even known that was what she ached for until Levi came into her life.

"Are we ready?"

Susanne and Willow went out first, then Dolly.

Beatrice followed. All Levi's family was there along with her aunt Opal and uncle Elwood. All the people that mattered except her parents, and she knew she wouldn't likely hear from them again. It was a pain that was eased by the love that surrounded her in this place. Levi's brothers stood at his side.

She let her gaze go to him last, knowing that once she saw him she wouldn't be able to look away.

Her heart flooded with love and gratitude as she went to his side.

He took her hand and they listened to Uncle Elwood's words.

"I now pronounce you man and wife. You may kiss your bride."

Levi's kiss was gentle, full of the promise of his never-ending love.

Her heart beat steadily, sure of who she was and were she belonged.

But superseding that wonderful knowledge was the security of knowing she was loved by a man who would always be faithful and true.

* * * * *

Dear Reader,

How would you react if you found out you were a disappointment to your parents? How would you deal with being thrust into an unfamiliar situation where you were out of your depth? That's Beatrice's story.

But don't we all face similar situations? When we feel rejected, disappointed, or find ourselves in unfamiliar territory? I know I do. Sometimes the disappointment is with myself. Why did I do or say that? What will people think of me in this setting? How can I fit in?

Writing this story helped me see that with God's help, I am enough for any situation. I trust you will enjoy reading about Beatrice and Levi but will also be encouraged in your daily walk.

You can learn more about my upcoming books and how to contact me at *www.lindaford.org*. I love to hear from my readers.

Blessings,

Linda Ford

REQUEST YOUR FREE BOOKS!

2 FREE INSPIRATIONAL NOVELS
PLUS 2 *FREE* MYSTERY GIFTS

Love Inspired HISTORICAL

YES! Please send me 2 FREE Love Inspired® Historical novels and my 2 FREE mystery gifts (gifts are worth about $10). After receiving them, if I don't wish to receive any more books, I can return the shipping statement marked "cancel." If I don't cancel, I will receive 4 brand-new novels every month and be billed just $4.99 per book in the U.S. or $5.49 per book in Canada. That's a saving of at least 17% off the cover price. It's quite a bargain! Shipping and handling is just 50¢ per book in the U.S. and 75¢ per book in Canada.* I understand that accepting the 2 free books and gifts places me under no obligation to buy anything. I can always return a shipment and cancel at any time. Even if I never buy another book, the two free books and gifts are mine to keep forever.

102/302 IDN GH6Z

Name	(PLEASE PRINT)	
Address		Apt. #
City	State/Prov.	Zip/Postal Code

Signature (if under 18, a parent or guardian must sign)

Mail to the **Reader Service:**
IN U.S.A.: P.O. Box 1867, Buffalo, NY 14240-1867
IN CANADA: P.O. Box 609, Fort Erie, Ontario L2A 5X3

Want to try two free books from another series?
Call 1-800-873-8635 or visit www.ReaderService.com.

* Terms and prices subject to change without notice. Prices do not include applicable taxes. Sales tax applicable in N.Y. Canadian residents will be charged applicable taxes. Offer not valid in Quebec. This offer is limited to one order per household. Not valid for current subscribers to Love Inspired Historical books. All orders subject to credit approval. Credit or debit balances in a customer's account(s) may be offset by any other outstanding balance owed by or to the customer. Please allow 4 to 6 weeks for delivery. Offer available while quantities last.

Your Privacy—The Reader Service is committed to protecting your privacy. Our Privacy Policy is available online at www.ReaderService.com or upon request from the Reader Service.

We make a portion of our mailing list available to reputable third parties that offer products we believe may interest you. If you prefer that we not exchange your name with third parties, or if you wish to clarify or modify your communication preferences, please visit us at www.ReaderService.com/consumerschoice or write to us at Reader Service Preference Service, P.O. Box 9062, Buffalo, NY 14240-9062. Include your complete name and address.

LIH15

"Make another move, and I'll shoot you where you
stand…" He trailed off, jaw sagging. Had he entered the
wrong house?

"Don't shoot! I can explain! I—I have a letter. From
Will Canfield." A petite dark-haired woman standing on the
other side of his table lifted an envelope in silent entreaty.

At the mention of his friend's name, he slowly lowered
his weapon. But his defensive instincts still surged
through him. When he didn't speak, she gestured limply
to the ornate leather trunks stacked on either side of his
bedroom door. "Mr. Canfield was supposed to meet us at
the station. His porter arrived in his stead… Simon was
his name. He said something about a posse and outlaws."
A delicate shudder shook her frame. "He said you
wouldn't mind if we brought these inside. I do apologize
for invading your home like this, but I had no idea when
you would return, and it is June out there."

Her gaze roamed his face, her light brown eyes
widening ever so slightly as they encountered his scars.
It was like this every time. He braced himself for the

inevitable disgust. Pity. Revulsion. Told himself again it didn't matter.

When her expression reflected nothing more than curiosity, irrational anger flooded him.

"What are you doing in my home?" he snapped. "How do you know Will?"

"I'm Constance Miller. I'm the bride Mr. Canfield sent for."

"Will's already got a wife."

Pink kissed her cheekbones. "Not for him. For you."

His throat closed. He wouldn't have.

"I was summoned to Cowboy Creek to be your bride. Your friend didn't tell you." A sharp crease brought her brows together.

"I'm afraid not." Slipping off his worn Stetson, Noah hooked it on the chair and dipped his head toward the crumpled parchment. "May I?"

Miss Miller didn't appear inclined to approach him, so he laid his gun on the mantel and crossed to the square table. He took the envelope she extended across to him and slipped the letter free. The handwriting was unmistakable. Heat climbed up his neck as he read the description of himself. He stuffed it back inside and tossed it onto the tabletop. "I'm afraid you've come all the way out here for nothing. The trip was a waste, Miss Miller. I am not, nor will I ever be, in the market for a bride."

Don't miss
BRIDE BY ARRANGEMENT
by Karen Kirst, available June 2016 wherever
Love Inspired® Historical books and ebooks are sold.

www.LoveInspired.com